M000309519

The

LINE

By

Keith Farrell

The Line is a work of fiction. Names, characters, places, and incidents are either the product of the author's imagination or are used fictitiously. Any resemblance to actual persons, living or dead, events, or locations is entirely coincidental.

2018 Ravenel Independent Hardcover Edition

Copyright © 2018 by Keith Farrell

Published by Keith Farrell independently
and Ravenel Book, LLC

ISBN 978-0-692-04156-7

Cover Design: Katie Biondo

Dedicated to all those I have known who have lost their struggle with addiction or substance abuse, and those that loved them.

VT, SS, JM, DL, DJ, RR, ER, DA, BM, JA, RM

And to every individual I know still fighting for their life.

U.S. Addiction Treatment Helpline: 1(877) 987-0561

Author's Notes and Acknowledgements

More than 72,000 Americans died from drug overdoses in 2017; more than three times the number who died from that same cause in 2000. It's an alarming epidemic that receives little social or political attention. It doesn't fit neatly into today's moral outrage politics, and social programs and local efforts to help addicts are merely treating the symptom.

The truth is, our country doesn't want to ask the critical questions about drug use and drug policy. It doesn't want to consider what having a 40 trillion dollar illicit drug market in the United States means; the corruption and complicity required for such a massive industry to exist. We would rather lock up addicts than shut down banks that launder drug money. We want to treat users as the problem, rather than acknowledging that they are the victims of an institutionalized system of corruption that preys on the poor, the mentally ill, and the vulnerable.

More than 1,000 people died from drug overdoses in the state of Connecticut in 2017, a three-fold increase in just six years. Like other states, urban population centers see the most deaths. However, the impact on smaller communities is in some ways more profound. These are places where the loss of one individual is felt by a larger proportion of residents.

The week before my writing this, six people died from heroin overdoses in my hometown. That's a place with a population of only 30,000. These kind of loses reverberate through smaller communities with greater resonance, and yet nobody seems to notice.

These are the communities long used to being excluded from the national conversation. I now live in Charleston, South Carolina, a city of tremendous economic growth and development. So it's easy for me to see it when the news says the economy is strong. However, America is not one entity. While we are experiencing growth overall, there are communities where stagnation and even decline are the reality. Former factory towns and post-industrial cities where, despite what any politician may say, the jobs simply aren't coming back. Ghettoized urban centers where black Americans struggle to survive because even if they can find work, it often pays far too little to live. My book focuses on the former because that is where I lived and grew up.

This book comes from a place of grief and a place of anger. Grief for those I saw struggling and suffering, and anger for those who preyed on the weak, for a system too corrupt to care, and for a community collapsing before my eyes.

Through my battles with substance abuse and drinking, I have delved into the underworld where markets are black and morality gray. I spent years of my life living there, feeding my demons and running away from my problems. I met people who would turn on me for a cigarette and friends who would die for me. I've run with people with rap sheets longer than I care to admit—people who lived their lives outside of the law. There was a time when I did not feel like I fit anywhere in this world, and a counter-culture, outlaw lifestyle was very appealing. It was self-indulgence, sure, but it was also a feeling of freedom. I was living life by my terms.

The thing I learned from those days that sticks with me the most today is that it is impossible to judge people accurately. It's easy to judge a heroin addict or even somebody who smokes weed all day. It's easy to put people in categories and assume we know their stories; that we know why they do the things they do. The truth is, people are complex, and plenty of good people make bad decisions.

I'm not going to dissect the title of the book in its entirety here before you have even read it, but I will say that one of the themes it lends itself to is a refutation of this fantasy that there is a clear line between good and evil. People want to believe that morality is black and white, that actions are inherently right or wrong, but often the truth is far more nuanced. One intention I had through telling this story is to illustrate how blurry that line can be.

I love crime fiction because it allows for the exploration of social issues that demand our attention yet are often ignored. Crime as a genre, for me, isn't about thrilling heists or shoot-outs. It's about exploring victims, causes, and effects. What drives people to violence? What makes us hate? What role does society play? Though the subject matter may be grim, I hope that stories like this one might help people relate to and understand each other.

Writing this book was a cathartic process for me because it required processing and sorting through a lot of emotions. Completing it and sharing it with others has been far more rewarding than I had imagined. Thank you for taking the time to read it.

I want to thank my amazing, intelligent, and beautiful wife, Cassandra. Not only for providing me with the support and encouragement I needed to finish the book, and her skills as a talented writer and editor to help make it better, but for being the love of my life and a continuing source of inspiration, affection, and joy.

Of course, if there is one person I should thank for every achievement I ever make, it's my mother, Nina Farrell. My mother's tireless devotion to providing for me and raising me as a single mother deserves accolades. Hard work, perseverance, kindness, and respect are the words that come to mind when I think about what she taught me. Her support of me continues to this day. She is my biggest fan, and I would not be the man I am today without all of her effort.

I also want to thank my friend and screenwriting partner, Eland Mann, for helping to keep the artist in me alive. Additional thanks to his wife, Khaliuna, for letting me steal her husband's time.

A very special thank you to Sandy Barbieri, for editing the earliest, roughest drafts of this story—*may no one ever see the mess that you first saw!*

To Cody Ciazza, my brother from another mother; thanks for giving me insights as a former law enforcement officer and veteran.

And, of course, Jeremy Pollevoy and Robert Amoroso: my best, and at times, my only friends. Thanks for the support, the laughs, the companionship, and the rides.

Jason Terry could tell the interrogation room at the Canaan State Police barracks was seldom used. There he sat with his head hanging low, his right hand cuffed to the steel table, examining a stack of janitorial supplies left in the corner. Florescent lights flickered and hummed above him, revealing peeling blue paint on porous concrete walls.

He was making some effort to retrace the past two days in his head when the door made a loud *clank*, breaking his daze. It opened as the two detectives who had been questioning him returned. The fat one, a man named McAuliffe, seemed to take charge while his partner, Carlyle, seemed unsure how to proceed.

"Alright, kid," McAuliffe said. "We're going to need to start from the beginning. Everything you told us and more, as thoroughly as you can recall."

"Cigarettes?" Jason asked.

"There's no smoking in here," Carlyle informed him.

"You want me to go over all this—everything that happened... what I did... then I need a fucking smoke," Jason insisted. "This shit is kind of stressful."

McAuliffe motioned for his partner to pick up a pack of cigarettes.

"Nearest place is ten minutes away," Carlyle protested.

"I've got plenty of time. I'm not going anywhere," Jason remarked, yanking the chain cuffed to his wrist.

McAuliffe snorted in agreement, and Carlyle begrudgingly left on his assignment. Once he was gone, the fat detective stared at Jason intently.

Jason was a mess—unshaven, disheveled, and unwashed. He wore a t-shirt that at one time had been white, but was now yellowed with sweat. After a few moments, McAuliffe broke the silence.

"So, all I got from all that blubbing and ranting was: you killed some fella for stealing your girlfriend. Is that the long and short of it?" he asked.

"Not just because he stole her. He used her addiction. Got her back on drugs. Everything that happened to her is his fault."

McAuliffe smirked and shook his head knowingly.

"Now, now, son," he said condescendingly. "Nobody 'got' her back on drugs except herself. You know that's the truth of the matter, don't you? A man like yourself—you know all about that. Don't go blaming him for that," McAuliffe argued.

"You don't understand. Guys like this are different. They're predators. He preyed on her. He preyed on my cousin…"

"Tim?"

The detective's tone infuriated Jason.

"Yes. *That's what people like Trivoty do!* You people don't do shit about it, either," he charged. "Predators like him operate right in the open. Outstanding job you guys do here."

"You mean people like you. Drug dealers," McAuliffe stated. The words seemed to hang like a noose around Jason's neck.

"I just sell weed, man—people don't get killed over weed."

"Oh? Is that right? Seems a lot of people around you gettin' killed recently."

Jason looked away as if trying to avoid the conclusion McAuliffe had drawn.

"That's all a huge mess tied to *these guys*. Everyone knows it," Jason explained. "They sell dope, pills—they're tied to international gangs. It's organized crime. They're responsible for the violence."

"The Trivotys? Well, I guess there's just one, now that you killed Michael."

"Somebody had to. Before he hurt anyone else." Jason shook his head and tried to choke back tears. "They're all cancer…"

"Nobody's handing out awards; tone down the dramatics," McAuliffe chuckled.

A knock on the interrogation room door surprised the detective. He got up to see who it was, took a look back at Jason, then exited the room without explanation. Minutes later the door opened, and Connecticut State Trooper Dwight Evans walked in.

"I've got nothing to say to you," Jason snapped. He turned his head to ignore his visitor.

"Goddammit," Dwight said softly. "What are you doing here, Jason?"

"Confessing to my crimes. You should be thrilled," Jason replied with bitterness in his voice.

"And what is it that you did?" he asked.

"I killed Michael Trivoty. He's responsible for Maegan, and I made sure he paid for it."

"You're such a goddamn fool," Dwight said, scoffing in disbelief. "What's your game, Jason? What's going on here?"

"No games. He deserved to die. I don't feel bad about it at all."

"And George Calloway? Did you kill him too?"

"What?! Come on! No, George was into—well who knows what George was into. It doesn't matter. I killed Trivoty because of Maegan. It has nothing to do with anything else."

"And these bodies up in Sheffield? The dead cops and the boy?"

"I have no idea…" Jason laughed anxiously.

"Cut the shit!" Dwight snapped, slamming his fists down on the table. "Sandusfield's place—I know that's where you get your weed from. Don't play stupid with me."

"Look man! I don't know what the hell is going on with that, but this thing between Michael and I was about Maegan. That's it!"

Jason's tone was confident, but his eyes seemed to plead with Dwight to be believed.

"You think I'm an idiot or something? I know this is all connected. You coverin' for somebody? Is it Dickey?"

"Look, man, I am here to confess to shooting a man in cold blood. I shot Michael Trivoty in the head. I killed him because he was a disease."

"Right, of course," said Dwight. "One question, Jason, then I will leave you to lie in this bed you've made. What caliber did you use to shoot him with?"

Jason stared blankly at the floor and refused to answer.

"What caliber, Jason? You're going to have to tell them in your statement."

"Forty-caliber," Jason answered defiantly. "Made a nice fucking hole, too."

Dwight shook his head and sighed.

"I'm going to find out the truth, Jason. I know you don't want me to, but there is too much at stake here."

"If all of you had been doing your jobs then none of this would have happened," Jason spat.

"That may be the most truthful thing you've said yet," Dwight replied. "I'm going to set things right, either way."

"Too late for that. I already did it."

"Alright. Well, I'm heading out to have a nice talk with Dickey."

Jason's face became angry and fearful.

"You leave him alone! He's got enough shit going on. He's a veteran... and a widower."

"I know – it's a real shame," Dwight said before leaving.

Jason forced back tears. Moments later, Carlyle and McAuliffe returned with a pack of Marlboros, a lighter, and an ashtray. Jason opened the smokes and lit one up.

"We've all got it," he said, exhaling smoke as he contemplated the nature of what had brought him there. "That demon, calling us to those things we know are so bad for us... smokes... drugs... women..." He caught a glimpse of empathy in Carlyle's eyes. "You know what I mean, detective, don't you?" he laughed. "Yours is women, huh?"

"Why don't we get started?" McAuliffe said, placing a digital recorder on the table.

"I've always enjoyed killing myself with multiple vices," Jason continued, ignoring the detective.

"But then you killed a man for those same vices," Carlyle replied.

"I killed a man for spreading those vices like cancer and for hurting two people I cared about. People I love."

"Alright, why don't you start from the very beginning," Carlyle suggested, switching on the recorder. "Take us back to how you met Mary Ann."

"Maegan," Jason corrected him, irritated.

"Right, why don't you tell us about you and Maegan..."

Chapter One

BAGGAGE

3 Months Earlier

Jason Terry's mornings generally began on his porch with a large joint and a cup of coffee, black with a dash of sugar. There he would watch the cars pass down the road, and wave hello to his neighbor, Mrs. Williams when she would come out to get the paper.

"Smells good!" the seventy-eight-year-old often teased. She was a smoker herself, acquiring the weed she needed from Jason to help her with her many ailments. "Please stop over later," she said. "I am running low."

"Will do, Mrs. Williams!" Jason said with a smile.

His apartment was a loft above the garage of her Colebrook home. Her husband David had rented it to him three years ago before he died. Once Jason discovered Mrs. Williams's affinity for marijuana, the two became close. After she received her bone cancer diagnosis, Jason stopped charging her money. "I insist you take some money," she would always say, to which he would customarily refuse.

Mrs. Williams was like family, which was valuable to him, having never been close to his own. Jason's mother had raised him as a single parent until walking out on him when he was eight years old. He wound up staying with his aunt and uncle in nearby Torrington, which was fine until they had a son of their own. Jason had tried to be a big brother to Tim, but the family seemed to push him away as the boys grew older. By sixteen, Jason was spending most of his days and nights at his best friend Dickey's.

Jason finished his joint and checked his phone. He had three messages; one from Dickey, one from a customer who wanted some weed, and one from a girl he hoped to see later. He went inside, grabbed the keys to his 2000 Subaru Outback, a plaid button-up shirt, and set off.

The sale was for a quarter-ounce to a guy named Norm, a clerk down at the Winsted Grocer. Winsted, as small as it was, served as neighboring Colebrook's go-to destination for supplies. The small urban center which ran along Connecticut's Madd River was the remnant of an industrial city done in first by the great flood of '55, then by decades of unfavorable economic conditions. Main Street was a cluttered mess of businesses, apartments, and government buildings surrounded by blighted industrial properties looming overhead. If not for the people in the surrounding rural towns of Barkhamsted, Colebrook, and Winchester, Winsted's economy would have been in even worse condition. And there was plenty Winsted didn't have; locals had to travel fifteen minutes south to Torrington to find a clothing or department store.

As was the routine, Jason sent Norm a message when he was in the grocer's parking lot. A few minutes later, Norm stepped out for a smoke and quickly exchanged a hundred dollars for the bag. Jason nodded satisfactorily before nonchalantly pulling away into traffic.

He stopped off for gas, then headed back to town to see Dickey.

Dickey was a widower with two beautiful little girls who adored Jason. The feeling was mutual; Jason had never been so in love. The way they looked at him somehow filled a void in Jason's life.

Six-year-old Marie Calloway ran out to greet Jason in the driveway, shrieking with joy as he lifted her into the air. Her five-year-old sister,

Stacey, yanked at his pant leg. He secured Marie with his right arm and swooped Stacey up with his left. "Hello, my angels!"

He carried them up the walkway from the driveway to the porch where their father, Dickey stood stoutly, his massive arms folded. A large smile with big, white teeth greeted Jason from below a John Deer hat. "What's good, brother?" he asked welcomingly.

"Just popping in to see my girls," he said, giving Marie and Stacey a kiss before setting them down.

"Uncle Jay," Marie pleaded. "Can you play guitar for us?"

"Oh, not today, darling. I've got a date later and I have to get ready."

"Is she pretty?" Marie asked. Dickey and Jason chuckled.

"Why yes, she is," Jason replied.

"My mommy was pretty," Marie said with pride. Ellen, Marie's mother and Dickey's one and only love, had passed away nearly two years ago.

"Yes," Jason replied, caught off guard. He looked to Dickey, who winced. "Yes, she certainly was, darling – and you know what?"

"What?" Marie asked.

"You and your sister look just like her! Except for that nose," he said, grabbing at her nose playfully. "That funny looking nose came from your daddy."

The girls giggled.

"Poor girls," Dickey said with a chuckle, self-consciously grabbing his own nose. "Marie, Stacey, c'mon baby girls, it's time to watch a movie."

That meant it was time to get the girls situated with something on the television long enough for Dickey and Jason to smoke a joint out back.

Jason exhaled a large puff of smoke out his nose as he lit the joint.

"Another blaze session behind the old woodshed," he said, passing the joint to Dickey.

"Yup." Dickey hit the joint a couple of times and passed it back, coughing slightly. "Amazing we can even get back here. Remember all the brush and shit growing back here?"

"Oh yeah. You've done a lot of work to the place since last year. It looks great."

"Well, it isn't mine…" Dickey said with a laugh. "But I have to live here, so I don't want it to look like shit."

Had Richard Sr. known that Dickey and his girls would have ever needed a home, he likely wouldn't have left it to Dickey's brother. Nobody had ever thought Dickey would need anything from anyone.

"Might as well be yours. He ain't here; he doesn't live here — fuck him."

"No, he's not. Never has been. You probably see him more than I do."

"That's because I sell him weed."

"I still feel bad about all this. Like you're paying for me to live here," Dickey confessed.

"It all works out for me," he reassured Dickey. It wasn't entirely true, but Jason didn't mind sacrificing a little profit to help Dickey and his girls.

"Working with him is a fucking tragedy waiting to happen, Jay. How long till he fucks you over or screws up so bad he can't repay you?"

He knew Dickey was right, it was only a matter of time before George screwed him over.

"I know. I don't care. I expect him to fuck up and end up owing me money," Jason said.

"You know, the girls and I… we're grateful," Dickey replied.

"I love you, brother. More importantly, I love those girls. You're all they have, remember that," Jason said. The April breeze lightly whipped his hair with a warmth that promised spring. "Get some hunting done this year?"

16

"Shit... Been a while since I even shot a gun."

It had been since Fallujah. The truth was he avoided shooting or anything else that reminded him of his service. He had had some trouble reacclimating. Ellen's death had only made it worse.

"Sounds fun." He laughed a little and passed the joint.

"Well, shit, we will have to get our licenses..." Jason looked at Dickey and tried to hold a straight face. Dickey laughed.

"Licenses? Shit, man, we will walk right up into these woods and shoot whatever we damn-well-please. I'm a veteran; I'm not getting Uncle Sam's permission to hunt in my woods. Fuck no," he laughed.

"These your woods now? Because last I checked the property line was..." Jason teased.

"Hey, I played in these woods. We bled in these woods. State property means open to all who live in the state, right?"

"That's one way of looking at it, I suppose," Jason answered with a laugh. "You sleeping any better, man?"

"Yeah, thanks to the weed," Dickey said, deeply inhaling a long pull off the joint before handing it to Jason. "You brought me more, right?"

"Of course," said Jason. "You seeing that doc anymore?"

"The head shrink at the VA? Fuck him." Dickey noticeably tensed up; he didn't care for Jason's concern. He had finally gone to be evaluated at the VA and they'd referred him to a psychiatric specialist. However, he had stopped going after just one appointment.

"Yeah, I know...." Jason was holding back. He was concerned, but wary of intruding.

"Assholes wouldn't work with my schedule," Dickey said. "Don't worry about me; I'm fine. That's all I need, to get put on some government list that says I'm fucked in the head... they could take my guns... maybe even my daughters."

"Stop it. That's just paranoid internet talk there. You're a veteran. People respect that."

"Yeah? Maybe, maybe not. You've seen the news lately. Being a vet doesn't get you much, not even respect these days. Either way, it doesn't matter because I'm fine," he said. "What are you gettin' into tonight?" he asked as he tossed the joint roach and lit a cigarette. He handed the smoke to Jason then lit another.

"Maegan Riley, hopefully," Jason laughed.

"You'd be the millionth guy to get into that, son," Dickey joked, the two making their way back to his porch.

"Whatever, I'll wrap it up," Jason said. He brushed it off, but Dickey's remarks stung. Despite his reserves, he liked this girl even though he knew she had a bad reputation. He didn't want to hear about that. He was hoping she'd changed.

"You better wrap that shit up. She was dating Michael Trivoty, Andrew's little brother."

"Andrew Trivoty? That gang banger who stabbed Danny Steppler?" It was an infamous story in Winsted.

"Yup. And raped his girl… You know that crew that has the house down on Reckon Ave in Winsted?" Dickey asked.

"Yeah, of course. Junkies and thieves. They sling blow and heroin mostly, some prescription painkillers. Had to go there when I had that tooth problem to score some percoset. Bunch of winners in that group."

"That's Andrew's crib. Low life scum, brother. And she was all wrapped up in it. She's an addict, too," Dickey warned.

"She's had a tough life," Jason said. He knew what Dickey was saying was true, but something about her smile made him hesitant to believe anything bad about her. He'd always held a fondness for her.

"A life she makes tougher," Dickey retorted. "Girls like that always do."

"I've been chatting with her for a little while, texting and what not — I don't know. I know she has a history, but she says she's changed. Maybe she has, you know? People change. Either way, I have wanted to tap that ass

18

since I was in high school," he said as if to deflect Dickey's concerns by asserting his manliness.

"Well then," Dickey said through laughter, "Wrap it up, brother. Wrap it up. And don't fall for her. She's broken inside, bro. Trust."

"How would you know?"

"Before Trivoty, she dated my buddy, Craig. Cheated on him, was on dope…. Crazy girl, man."

"She's been clean for a while."

"Heroin addiction doesn't just go away. It's like a hungry animal scratching at the door. Not many succeed at keeping it out."

"We've all got beasts we battle with."

"Ain't that the fucking truth," Dickey said, patting his friend on the back. "Just be careful, bro."

The two then headed back inside for coffee. From the kitchen, they could see the girls, still enthralled in the animated movie Dickey had put on for them.

"You headed back to work Monday?" Jason asked, sipping from his mug.

"You know… I don't think so," said Dickey, chuckling.

"Coming up on a month, bro. Silvers doesn't mind?"

"I have the vacation time saved up. Besides, he's still pissed off at me. Probably doesn't mind me keeping some distance," said Dickey.

Dickey did not care for the way Jason had started regularly expressing concern for him — *he* had always been the older brother in their relationship. He was not only four years Jason's senior, but he had always been the stronger of the two. He had gone to war while Jason had stayed home and smoked pot. Somehow, though, losing Ellen had changed everything, including their dynamic.

"Well, you made him look bad in front of his daddy," Jason teased.

"Damned if I was going to take the heat for that shit. He forgot to secure the boom on the truck, not me."

"Still can't believe that damn thing took out an entire block of street signs and a fucking telephone pole before he noticed!" Jason laughed every time he recalled the story.

"Cost the company about ninety-k," Dickey added.

"Ninety thousand dollars because your boss is a moron."

"Morons cost this world more than you could imagine, brother. What do you think, we didn't have Dave Silvers-types in Iraq? Only there, they got people killed."

Dickey worked for Silvers and Sons Tree Service, primarily trimming and taking down trees. His supervisor, the only 'son' left at Silvers and Sons, was a pompous prick. He and Dickey never got along well, despite Dickey's attempts. Jason knew it was only a matter of time before Dickey left the job altogether.

Jason worried about his best friend a lot. He had never acclimated himself to civilian life after the Marine Corps, having been home for less than a year before Ellen died. That loss piled on top of whatever he was struggling with from the war. Dickey was the strongest man Jason had ever known, and he continually proved as much by putting on a smile and going through his days with his head held high, if only for the sake of his girls. But Jason worried that inside he was breaking.

MAEGAN RILEY SAT IMPATIENTLY through the counselor's personal story of addiction and how finding Christ had saved his life. It wasn't that she didn't find it inspiring, it was just considerably less so after hearing it so many times. His name was Chris, and she did owe him for spending so many hours listening to her problems. But she couldn't bear to hear his story anymore. Maybe it wasn't the content, she thought, but the way in which he told it. He was too scripted; it felt less sincere each time she heard it.

"…through the power Christ I was saved, and I know he can save you, too," Chris said.

They would meet there once a week in the recreation center next to St. Mary's Church in Torrington. There would be cookies and coffee laid out when they arrived, and then they would all sit in a circle while Chris led them in their discussion. Some were there desperately trying to get better, others simply because they had been court ordered to attend.

"Now we will hand out chips for sobriety. Now, I always say this, if you can't claim a chip today, it's okay. You're here now, and that's such an important step."

This is what she was waiting for — the reason she had come at all. She had not touched dope for six months, and she wanted that damn chip. Sure, she had openly mocked the chips to her family, but at least it was *something.* It was something she could physically hold that represented the battles she had won.

Chris would always start by calling for anyone who wanted that day to be their first day of sobriety to come up and receive a chip. They looked like poker chips—blue little plastic coins with "1 Day" printed on them. Maegan watched a young girl with bleached-blonde and pink hair hesitantly make her way to claim a chip. The group applauded, and the young girl smiled. Maegan did not applaud; she felt incredibly sad for the girl.

Chris would then call for the "10 Day", "1 Month", and "2 Month" people to claim their chips. Usually, they never got past two months. People stopped coming. Maegan was sure *some* of them had gotten better and no longer needed the group — at least, she hoped.

"Today we have a special chip to hand out," Chris said, smiling as he held it high for the group to see. It was gold with a triangle inside. The words 'Unity, Service, Recovery' were embossed on the face. Inside the triangle read '6 months.'

"When I met Maegan she had tears in her eyes. She had just ended a toxic relationship, and wanted to seek help. She turned to us here at St. Mary's, and she poured herself into the healing process. Through her faith and her strength, Maegan has been clean for six whole months. Please come get your chip, Maegan."

Chris smiled, and Maegan could not help but blush. She stood up and crossed the circle to Chris, who hugged her. "I am so proud of you!" he said to her.

"Thank you," she said. "I don't think I could have done it alone."

After the meeting ended, she stayed to talk with Chris while she waited for her ride.

"Is your mother using again?" he asked her.

"Probably," Maegan said with a sigh. "I can't really tell. She hides it."

The two walked along the back edge of the church's parking lot, which rested beside a small brook. Maegan smoked; Chris tried not to mind.

"Have you thought about what we talked about last time?" Chris asked.

"Going to live with my uncle?"

"I think it would be a much more stable environment for you," he said.

"Yeah, I know… I have thought about it. I guess I kind of even want to…"

"But…?"

"But I feel like she needs me there. The house is going to shit as is."

"Your brother still not going to school? Partying all the time?"

"More or less. Kaleb is never around anymore, but Danny has his friends over all the time, and they trash the place."

"And she doesn't care?"

"Nah, she never did. She's too cool… She always wants to be the cool mom," Maegan answered after a moment.

"And how are you doing?"

"I'm good. Six months." She held up the chip and laughed.

22

"Are you still taking the Suboxone?"

"Not very often," she said. "Hardly ever, actually." That wasn't true, but she wanted to impress him and allay his concerns.

"Good. I think it is a valuable tool, but I have seen too many grow dependent on it. You never truly break the addiction if you have to continue Suboxone or Methadone. I know a lot of people would disagree with me, but…"

"No, I know," Maegan assured him. "You're right."

An old tan Ford pickup truck pulled into the parking lot; Maegan's Uncle Dwight arriving to take her home.

"Thank you again, Chris," Maegan said. They hugged one last time.

"You coming back?" Chris asked as she was about to climb into the truck.

"I don't think so," she said with a smile.

"We're always here if you need us," he replied with a nod.

JASON TERRY STARTED SELLING weed at a young age. At first, it was merely the lure of free weed which encouraged him. He'd buy a half ounce at a time, selling what he didn't need to his friends to break even. It wasn't long until he started buying whole ounces and making a profit. Dickey knew a grower from the VFW, Randy Sandusfield. He introduced the two, providing Jason with an unlimited supply for little cost.

Soon he was moving four ounces a week, then eight. Then he started finding friends who wanted to sell and make a little cash. Altogether Jason sold or distributed about a pound of medical grade marijuana every week — which was a rather large amount for such a small area. People who didn't even know him were getting high off his supply.

He had quite the setup. He personally only had to sell to a handful of people, and he not only made enough money to pay his bills and keep his car running, but he had all the free weed he could smoke. It wasn't a grand life, but it was comfortable, and that was all he wanted, aside for maybe a companion.

"Is that Orange Kush again?" Tim Madison asked, sliding a bag of weed into his pocket and placing sixty dollars on Jason's center console. Every strain of high-quality weed had a name, some considerably more inventive than others.

"Nah bro, this shit is Black Diesel," Jason answered, taking the money and putting it in his back pocket. "And again, you didn't get it from me. If your parents ever found out…"

Tim was only sixteen years old, and while his parents had helped raise Jason, there was a lot of tension between them already.

"Last shit was fire, yo," Travis, Tim's best friend, chimed in from the backseat.

He had met the boys near a mini golf and arcade center in downtown Winsted. It was a popular hangout for kids and an innocuous place to meet for a drug deal.

"All my shit is fire," Jason countered sharply. "And I mean it, man. Don't let your parents find out you're smoking. They'll blame me for sure."

"Yeah, I know. Don't worry," Tim said.

He was a short kid with curly brown hair and carried a general look of confusion with him. He was an airhead. A natural burnout.

"Can you drive us to my place?" Travis asked from the back. He wore baggy, obtrusive looking clothing and a loud, flashy baseball cap embroidered with the logo of some urban-styled clothing company Jason didn't recognize. "By the lake?"

"Yeah I guess," Jason said with a sigh. He turned on his radio; *Black Rebel Motorcycle Club* came blasting through the speakers. "Put your seatbelts on," he said to the boys.

"Seriously?" Travis laughed.

"I don't care about your safety, sweetheart; I don't want to get pulled over," Jason said snidely.

Tim laughed and Travis grumbled under his breath as they both buckled up.

"WHAT THE FUCK?!?!" April Riley shrieked from the kitchen "You fucking fucks drank my fucking beer?!?" She emerged from the fridge, cigarette hanging from her lip, a wine cooler in her hand, and slammed the door.

"Don't look at me!" her son Danny, yelled back from the living room where he was playing video games. Then he muttered to himself, "I didn't touch your shit. You probably got drunk and drank them all yourself. Crazy bitch."

"What was that?!" she yelled.

"Nothing!" he answered, lighting a cigarette.

April ran her long fingernails through her bleached blonde, frazzled hair and cursed under her breath.

"Would you two shut the hell up?" Maegan said, emerging from the hallway. "Jesus Christ, just calm down."

"Did you drink my beer?" April asked, fire in her eyes.

"No, mom, I didn't drink your beer."

"Somebody drank my fucking beer," she insisted.

"Would you put some clothes on, mom? Seriously?" Maegan asked.

April was wearing a thin white tank top and a tiny pair of shorts. For a fifty-year-old woman who had lived a rough life, April didn't look bad—a fact she flaunted.

"Oh relax! Nobody is around. And besides, I look good!" She playfully smacked herself on the ass and laughed.

"Jason is coming here in a little while, and I would like for him not to see this," said Maegan, gesturing to her mother. "Or this," she added, sweeping her arm toward the piles of unwashed dishes and clutter littering the counters and tabletop.

25

"Jason?"

"Yes, mother. Jason. I told you about him."

"Ohh! Yes, that's right," her mother answered with a smile. "Jason, the *nice* boy."

"Yes, the nice boy," Maegan said, grabbing April's cigarettes off the counter and lighting one.

"What's that mean?" Danny asked, passing by to get a soda from the fridge. "Nice boy?"

"It means he isn't a dirtbag," said Maegan.

"Does he have a criminal record?" Danny asked.

"No!" Maegan snapped with certainty and then paused. "Well, I don't think so." They all laughed at her response. "He's just a respectful guy, you can tell."

"In other words, he isn't your type," Danny teased.

"You're right, honey," April said. "You don't want him to see all this; you better get ready and go outside when he gets here."

JASON HAD SMOKED a large joint in preparation for his date, but he was still nervous. Maegan was a beautiful girl. He'd had a thing for her since he first saw her way back in high school, but four years was too large a gap at that time. To his delight, they had bumped into each other at a gas station a few days earlier, and Jason had mustered up the nerve to get her number.

He'd had girlfriends before, but they never lasted long. He wasn't good at dating; he found himself lost just talking to most girls. They made him feel nervous and unsure of himself. Somehow, even when a girl was into him, he felt inadequate.

He pulled up to Maegan's house on Washington Ave in Winsted and beeped his horn, as she'd requested. A couple of minutes later she came out and hopped into his car. She beamed at him and invited him to hug her. "Hello! It's good to see you," she said.

"You too!" he replied, his heart leaping as they embraced. He was in awe; she was breathtaking. She had the loveliest smile, one which revealed an adorable set of dimples. Everyone had always remarked on it, a smile that could light up a room.

They drove to a nearby Mexican restaurant and had tacos. When they finished, Maegan proposed they go out to get some drinks.

"Not a bad idea," Jason said. "I wasn't sure if you drank."

"I'm a drug addict. I never had a problem with alcohol," she said with a smile.

"Alright then. How about we get out of town?"

He knew she had lived a party lifestyle and had been around. He didn't want to go to a bar where she might see some guy from her past.

"Where are you thinking?" she asked, intrigued.

"Let's head out to New Hartford," he suggested.

"Tell me you're going to share some of that weed I smell in your car with me," she said with a giggle as they left the restaurant. Jason smiled, finding himself able to relax with her in ways he hadn't experienced before.

They smoked pot the entire way to New Hartford, music blasting. Maegan laughed with joy. "It feels so good to be out and having a good time!" she exclaimed.

By the time they hit the Swinging Parrot in New Hartford, Jason felt quite relaxed. He gently placed his hand on the small of her back as they walked up the steps to the bar. Inside, he politely pulled her stool out for her.

The bar was packed. There was a RedSox game on all eight big screen televisions.

"Do you watch baseball?" Jason asked her.

"Not at all," she laughed.

"Me neither, not in the slightest," he chuckled.

The waitress came, and they ordered drinks: two whiskey and gingers. When the drinks came, they were drunk quickly and seconds were ordered. By this time they were very much buzzed, and Maegan could not stop smiling. She stared off into the crowd, as if she were intently focused on something.

"Whatcha looking at?" Jason asked, leaning in closer to share her angle.

"I'm people watching," she said.

"Oh, I always do that," he replied.

"Those two, they're on their first date, and that one is not into it," she said, nodding her head to two gentlemen sitting near the bar.

Jason was very happy to see the waitress come back with more drinks and his order of sweet potato fries. "Thank you," he told her.

"See the guy with the sweater—the one with the white hair?" Maegan continued. "Look how he's acting. He's nervous, fidgety, yet smiling. He's insecure."

"Oh? I can relate," Jason teased.

Maegan laughed.

"The other guy is obviously here to watch the game. He doesn't much care about this guy at all, actually," Maegan said, turning her head sideways in contemplation. The other man, who was noticeably younger than the gentleman in the sweater, was indeed more focused on the television than the man beaming at him from across the table.

"Interesting…"

"And, see," she pointed at the younger man as he rose from the table. "This is like the fourth time he's left the table since they've been here. He keeps going to answer his phone and smoke cigarettes."

"You're a good people watcher," Jason observed.

"Damn right." She smiled. "Looks like he's just using the bathroom this time, though," she reported, continuing to watch the drama unfold.

He noticed how close he was sitting to her and nearly pulled back out of instinct. Then he looked into her soft, brown eyes and felt moved to kiss her, so he did. He was unsure of himself and full of doubt, but he went for it, and she kissed him back. The bar exploded in applause, people hooting and hollering in excitement; the RedSox had hit a home run. For a moment, though, they both thought the celebration was for them.

"I have to pee," she said, laughing off the moment.

Moments after she had left for the bathroom the younger man they'd been watching returned to his date with the older gentleman. While he waited for her to return, Jason ordered them another round.

She came back with a look of disbelief and amusement. "Someone was smoking crack in the bathroom." She laughed, shaking her head.

"What?" Jason asked incredulously.

"Crack-cocaine. Somebody down there was smoking it," she affirmed. "I think it was the disinterested guy."

"Get out of here," Jason said, laughing in disbelief. "Don't be silly."

"I swear to God, I smelled crack, and he was down there looking high as hell." She shook her head, laughed, and sipped her drink.

"You know, I don't believe I know what crack smells like," Jason said after a moment.

"Oh…" she was taken off guard. After a short but awkward silence, she simply replied: "I do."

"Okay…" Jason answered hesitantly. He didn't know what to say. He knew she had had a rough life, but the details were hard to reconcile with the feelings he felt for her.

"I've had a crazy life, Jay, but I don't want that anymore. I've lost too much because of it already. I wouldn't be here with someone like you if I still wanted any of that."

Her eyes connected with his and pled for him to see her as he so wanted to — as a *good* person. He wanted to believe that she could put all that behind her and that maybe somebody like him could help her do it.

"I hope you mean it. You're better than any of that shit," he said.

"Thank you." She smiled, batted her eyes, put her arms around his neck, and kissed him.

They talked some about their lives, how Jason's mother had left and how Maegan's was an addict living off the state. Jason stared contently at her face as they talked; she was radiant and beautiful, but there was an emptiness in her eyes. Was it sadness?

After some time, Maegan finished her drink and stood up, signaling her desire to leave.

"So, you gonna take me home?" Maegan asked, kissing him softly and running her fingers down the back of his neck.

"I was certainly hoping to," said Jason, running his hand softly up and down her leg.

HE WOKE UP IN A COLD SWEAT, his heart beating loudly, gasping for breath. He patted himself down to assure himself he was unharmed and then rose from his bed. His body had two distinguishing features: a United States Marine Corps tattoo over his left breast and a jagged scar down his left side where the shrapnel had torn into him.

The night terrors were the worst part. During the day, Dickey could keep the thoughts at bay. He could focus on his girls and when all else failed, drink beer or smoke pot. But when he slept, the memories would haunt him.

He looked at his phone; it was 1:20 AM. The visions from his dream haunted him. Fire. Blood. The screams of children. The faces of men he had killed. Faces that were vague and indistinguishable, except for one: an American face.

Heading down to the porch, he stopped to check on his girls. Both little angels were fast asleep. Stacey reminded him of her mother when she slept. That was the hardest part, he thought —missing her whenever he looked at them.

Dickey took his joint down to the front porch, opting to sit on the steps rather than his chair. He took deep drags and tried to relax. Hopefully, if he got high enough, he could get back to sleep. He would have to be up in just over three hours to get the girls ready for school.

The wind blew, causing one of the two big pines in his front yard to emit a loud crack. Dickey looked up at the tree suspiciously.

"Don't you start giving me shit," he said to the tree. "You've got to be strong. No time to deal with you right now."

The trees were massive; planted as twins long ago. Dickey was quite fond of them, but knew someday he would have to take them down. One good storm could fall one of them and send it crashing into his house.

Dickey smoked and tried again to relax. The screams of Iraqi children echoed somewhere in the back of his mind. He wanted nothing more than to feel Ellen's touch again.

He had only been home for eight months when she was diagnosed. Things progressed quickly from there. She'd refused to undergo chemotherapy, terrified of what it might do to her. She tried holistic treatments, but all the vitamins and herbs did nothing, and Dickey and the girls watched as she deteriorated. Finally, after months of pleading, she agreed to seek aggressive treatment. By then, it was too late.

If he was honest, he resented her for it. He felt abandoned by the person he most trusted in the time he most needed her. He had fought through hell three times to get back to her and the girls. When her time came to do the same, when it was her turn to fight for them, she didn't have the will to do so.

BACK AT HIS APARTMENT, Jason and Maegan laid naked on his bed. He slowly ran his fingers through her hair as she drifted toward sleep with her head upon his chest. He couldn't believe a woman of such beauty was in bed with him.

At the same time, their relationship was giving him anxiety and apprehension. Every woman in his life had hurt him, and considering Maegan's past, he wasn't sure he could trust her not to do the same. Despite

31

his hesitance, he felt compelled to continue seeing her. He was already attached to her, whether he liked it or not. The realization of how vulnerable he was caused him further panic. For now, he tried to ignore his concerns.

He traced his fingers along the lines of her tattoos. On her right hip there was a rose, the thorns tinged red as if they were digging into her flesh. On the back of her shoulder, there was a little devil with angel wings and a halo.

"I really like you," she said to him suddenly, lifting her head to kiss him.

"I told myself not to like you," he said with a laugh between kisses.

"Oh yeah?" she said indignantly. "Didn't want to fall for the slut?"

"No, it's just that…"

"It's fine, Jason, don't lie to me — everyone else does that enough," she said.

There was something refreshing about her honesty. Once again she somehow managed to make him feel comfortable in ways no other woman ever had.

"Fair enough," he said. "But don't lie to me. Are you ready to have a better life?"

"Yes," she said. "Oh my God, yes!"

He felt like a hero and she looked at him like he was.

"Okay then," he said with a smile.

"Do you have plans tomorrow?" she asked, sitting up and pushing him down flat against the bed.

"Nope. I'm kind of self-employed," he joked.

"Good, because you're not sleeping tonight," she said as she straddled him.

DWIGHT EVANS AWOKE AT 5 AM, as he did every morning, to go for his daily run with his German shepherd, Max. Dwight would leave his house located in the center of Colebrook and run down route 183 for about a mile or so before crossing through the cemetery and heading back. On most days, Max would follow him right out the door, but on this morning, the old boy just looked up at him from his bed and refused to move.

"You gettin' lazy on me, Max?" Dwight asked, as he affectionately rubbed his dog behind the ears.

Max rose to the challenge; stretching, shaking, and then following Dwight out the door. Dwight had owned Max for seven years. Although he wasn't the police force's dog, but he did accompany Dwight on nearly every call. As such, Dwight affectionately referred to him as "partner." Being the sole officer of a backwoods town in the northwest hills was lonely at times. Max made the long, boring shifts a little easier.

Dwight was painfully aware that as a purebred German shepherd, Max only had a couple more years left in him at most. Max's age was starting to show already: his eyes were dull, his fur worn, and his snout was graying. He was often tired by the end of a run.

When they returned, Dwight filled Max's water bowl from the faucet, and then went to shower, shave, and dress. He walked up the stairs wincing with his fingers pressed against his temple; the pain was back. He had recently begun experiencing a high-pitched whining noise that accompanied his headaches. It was an incessant ringing that would permeate his every thought.

He popped a handful of aspirin before showering.

His police-issued uniform was brown with blue and gold trim, worn with regulation boots and a trooper's hat. He took time to put it on with care each day. To him, this ritual was a matter of respect. He may have held a lowly post, but he represented the law with the dignity he felt it deserved.

By 7 AM he was on the job patrolling Colebrook with Max beside him inside his gray, police-issued Crown Victoria. Nearly the whole town was under his purview – the reservoir and dam were the jurisdictions of the state's Department of Environmental Protection officers.

After patrolling for an hour, he stopped at Rachel's—the only place in town you could get a breakfast sandwich and a cup of coffee. He left Max to guard the car and went inside to a warm welcome.

"Mornin', Dwight!" Rachel called from behind the counter as she made rounds with the pot of coffee.

"Good morning, Rachel," he replied.

"The usual for ya, today?" she asked.

"Please and thank you," Dwight said, sitting down at the counter to read the paper while he waited.

She placed a cup of coffee down in front of him, which he splashed a little cream and sugar into before drinking. Moments later his radio came alive. "Unit seventeen, ten-fifty-five, code eighty-seven, twelve-twenty-two Fairmont Ave."

"Unit seventeen responding," Dwight answered into the radio receiver attached to his shoulder.

"Going to need your sandwich to go, hon?" Rachel asked him.

"Yes, Rachel. Thank you."

Dwight pulled up to the residence at 1222 Fairmont Ave about twenty minutes later. The coroner and the volunteer ambulance had already arrived from Winsted.

"Mother found the body," the medics told him. "She called 911 for an ambulance, said her son wasn't breathing. He was D.O.A., but we deduced it was an overdose, so we called you."

"Heroin?" Dwight asked.

"Looks like," the medic sighed. "Track marks all over both arms."

"Another one," Dwight said, shaking his head. "How old?"

"Nineteen years old," the medic said.

They both looked down and shook their heads some more.

"Dope and what-not upstairs?" Dwight asked.

34

"Nope. Not a sign of it other than the fresh track marks. Ask the mother," the medic said before leaving.

Dwight nodded.

The coroners were bringing the boy's body down the front stoop when Dwight entered the house. The boy's face was blue and yellow. In most heroin overdose fatalities, the drug causes the lungs to slow to such a rate that the user essentially suffocates under the weight of their own chest.

He gave his condolences to the grieving mother and tried to get some basic information about her son and his habits from her.

"Ma'am," he said candidly. "We know it was an overdose; we need the evidence. Now, you turn it over to me and I won't charge you with tampering with evidence."

She looked at the floor and didn't respond.

"Or we get State's drug task force down here," he continued. "They can rip apart your house, find the evidence, and then throw you in jail, either way. Because we know you got rid of the drugs and the needle."

"Is this how you treat a grieving mother?"

Her mascara had run down her cheeks. She clutched a snotty, wet handkerchief with both hands.

"No, ma'am. This is how we prevent more grieving mothers. State needs the dope that killed your son so we can determine if it was a bad batch or if your son just took too much. Helps us track the sources and keep tabs on any potentially bad batches."

That was the policy, at least, and what his superiors told him to say. He wasn't sure how much of it was true. All he ever saw was more heroin, more addiction, and more suffering.

"And what then?" she asked. "What then? Arrest someone? So they can spend five years in security with room and board, clothes and food paid? My son was a good man. I flushed the damn drugs because I didn't want people knowing him as a drug addict!"

Dwight looked at her, sympathetic for her loss, and nodded.

35

"And the syringe?" he asked.

"In the garbage container on the side of the porch," she said through sobs. "Are you going to arrest me?"

"No."

He went out to his car and retrieved a pair of latex gloves and an evidence bag. He carefully removed the syringe from the trash and secured it in an evidence locker in his trunk. Before leaving, he left his number with the mother and told her to call if she needed anything. Then he drove toward his sister's house while eating his breakfast sandwich, which he shared with Max.

APRIL RILEY STILL CARRIED the name of her dirtbag ex-husband. He was an abusive, asshole biker who had fathered two of her three kids. The house she lived in was run down and littered. Danny, the son who still lived at home, liked to throw parties— the evidence of which was all over the lawn. Neighbors were never surprised to see Dwight's car there, but were surprised to learn he was family.

"Hello, Brother Officer," April said through wafts of smoke as he entered the house. She smoked heavily, even more heavily than she drank. "Here to lecture me again about my parenting? To check my arms for marks? To harass me about the noise my son makes? What is it? I'm sure you're not here to say hello…"

"Actually, I'm here to check on Maegan," Dwight said, scanning the mess.

"How sweet. She ain't here," April scoffed. She made her way to the sink, which was overflowing with dishes. "Damn kids sure do make a mess." She turned on the faucet to fill the coffee pot. "Some coffee, dear brother?" When she wasn't rude to him she opted to be patronizing.

"Just had a cup, thanks. Where is Maegan?"

"Don't know, she didn't come home last night. Probably turning tricks somewhere," she said. A thin attempt at humor.

"What do you mean she didn't come home?"

"She's twenty-seven years old. I don't have to keep tabs on her."

"Yeah, April, you're supposed to. She's been out of rehab barely five months. You just let her run around?"

"She went out with some boy—a *nice* boy, for Christ's sake. Relax a little."

"Who?"

"Jason Terry. Seems very nice. His shirt even had a collar when he picked her up."

"Jason Terry?" Dwight laughed. "Typical… Really, April?" He knew the name. Colebrook was a small town. "You think he's a nice boy? He's no good for her; he's a goddamn drug dealer."

"It's just a little pot, lighten up! She smokes a little weed. It's not a drug."

"Is she going to her meeting next week? The support group?"

He picked up a dusty framed photo off the living room hutch. It was Maegan's fourth-grade class photo. He loved the photo; he had the same one in better shape. Her unmistakable smile and adorable dimples seemed almost unchanged. She was the daughter he never had.

"I'm not sure. You'd have to ask her," April replied.

"I know you're busy sitting on your ass drinking and collecting welfare, but you should realize that being involved in your daughter's life might be the last chance you have to do something meaningful with yours." He put the picture down, angry at his inability to influence his niece's life, angrier at her mother for flouting the very responsibility. "It's your fault she fell through the cracks, and it's your fault she was addicted to the same drugs you were by the time she was twenty. You're a terrible mother, April, and a terrible sister." He stopped himself for a moment, but saw his words had seemed to rattle her. At the chance of something he had to say sinking in, he continued. "You're just looking to use whoever you can to get by. Your oldest won't talk to you. Danny is on his way, too. And Maegan? Well, she seems to think you need her here, or she'd be living with me. Of course, maybe she wouldn't like that seeing as she wouldn't be dating drug dealers."

"Why do you even talk to me, then? If I am such a fuck-up, why come around here at all?"

"Honestly, the idea of you walking around here every day, living for free and burdening your son and daughter with every financial need Uncle Sam doesn't provide, using drugs, drinking like a fish, and thinking you're high and mighty and righteous on top of it just gets under my skin. I guess I like to drop by and remind you of reality."

He hadn't come there for this, but it was how nearly every visit with her ended.

"Some brotherly love right there," she scoffed, lighting a smoke and waiting for her coffee to brew. She looked permanently hung over. She had large dark circles surrounding her eyes and her teeth were rotting.

"I love you, sis. I stuck by you time and time again when you made bad decisions. But mom and dad and I had to let you go when you chose heroin over your family every time. And that's exactly what you did. You don't get to put that on me."

"And what did you ever do for me except judge me and my life? Look, you even went and made a career out of it. Judging others by your code. How many dopers you bust wishing it was me?"

"You got me wrong there, sis. I don't want to bust you or make you pay. I think of whoever sold you that first bag… Whoever first tied you off and pushed death into your veins. That person took my sister from me."

His heart aching and scorn in his eyes, he left. As he walked out to his car, the high-pitched ringing in his head grew louder, like a train approaching in the distance.

Chapter Two

DOMINOES

Mark Sandusfield peeked inside from the back porch, anxiously checking to make sure his father was still asleep. Satisfied the lights inside the house were still off, he lit his joint. He smoked for a while, muffling his coughs with his arm when needed, listening to the sounds of the woods. High-pitched yelps filled the air followed by distinctive howls. Mark held his breath and listened intently.

"Mark! Goddamn it, boy," his father barked from behind, startling him.

"Damn it! Don't sneak up on me like that!" Mark said, hitting the joint — he was already caught.

"Boy, what did I tell you?" Randy sternly asked his son as he snatched the joint away.

"No more smoking…" Mark grumbled, shaking his head.

"Until…"

"Until my grades come up."

"Have they?" Randy asked. He put the joint up to his lips and drew a hit from it.

"No, they haven't," Mark admitted begrudgingly.

"What is this, Maple Kush? Where'd you get this from?" Randy asked as he exhaled slowly through his nose, discerning the flavor of the smoke.

"Where do you think I got it from?" Mark replied sarcastically.

"Well, did you mark it in the book?" Randy asked.

He knew Mark took weed from the finished batches, but he hated the dishonesty.

"It's just a joint, dad. It isn't going to throw our totals off," Mark insisted.

He was sixteen and snarky. To Randy, their totals were not the point.

"Coyotes are out tonight," Randy said, looking off into the trees.

"Yeah, I thought that's what that was," Mark said, listening to the noise.

"They're celebrating a kill," Randy told him.

"C'mon, don't be an asshole," said Mark, nudging his father with his forearm and motioning for the joint.

"Get your damn grades up, and you can smoke all the pot you want," Randy countered.

"But I still have to water the plants, and hang them, and dry it, and trim it, and cure it…"

"That," Randy said, pointing to the large wooden garage that looked like a small white barn. "That is what pays our bills — that's what will give you a college education if you want it."

"I hate school, just buy me a Corvette," Mark joked, motioning again for the joint.

Randy took another hit then relinquished it.

"Get to bed soon," Randy said as he walked away.

"Yeah, yeah," Mark mumbled. He hit the joint and listened to coyotes howl.

Randy went inside the house, grabbed his pack of filterless Camels off the kitchen table from beside his .357 revolver and headed back to bed. He worried he had failed Mark by providing for him with a life of black market income and off the grid living. He knew none of it was ideal for the boy, but damned if he didn't try to give him some boundaries, discipline, and guidance despite the circumstances.

He'd justified it for years; weed wasn't *that* bad. It wasn't addictive. There was no violence involved in what he did, but he knew it was not a good example for his son. After he left the Army, he had tried to find honest work—even working as a police officer in Winsted for a short time. That's what sealed his decision; the department was corrupt, and the officers were total dickheads. None of them played by the rules, so why should he?

In his years serving in the Special Forces, Randy had made a lot of connections in a lot of places. It was easy for him to get set up once he decided to make the move. He found the perfect property. It had no official address, no mail service, and no trash pickup. It was one of three houses built of a bankrupt development and one of only two houses located on the road. The other house he convinced his only friend, Albert, to buy. Because they were off the grid, the homes were a steal—less than half the market value they would have been anywhere else.

Randy's connection, Louis, had set him up with a network that ran weed and money up and down the east coast. His weed went south and west, usually towards New Jersey or New York. Soon after he started, the people who ran the operation had asked him to take weed from California and distribute it to their key people from Massachusetts, Vermont, New Hampshire, and Maine. He was allowed to do so at a considerable markup because the product from out west was so cheap. He didn't quite understand it, but they told him it was part of an arrangement to keep peace with another group. He didn't ask many questions; that was the nature of this business.

Everything was going well, but Mark had never been part of the plan. Randy was probably too old to start a family when he accidentally knocked

41

up Mark's mother. That was back in 1997, shortly after he had become a cop. She thought if she were pregnant, Randy would have no choice but to marry her. To her surprise, he ended the relationship as soon as he found out.

The first few years were rough. Randy refused to see his son, but eventually curiosity got the better of him. He would pick the boy up and take him to the movies or for ice cream. It was easy; noncommittal. Then in 2007, everything changed. Mark's mother was killed by a drunk driver headed the wrong way down route 8 near Waterbury.

Faced with fatherhood, Randy had initially tried to quit the weed business, but Louis pleaded with him not to. "These aren't the kind of people I want to make mad... I did this for you... I put my neck out for you... You can't just stop... You're too important... Maybe in time, not now... He wouldn't be the first kid to grow up around a couple pot plants."

The truth was, Randy had never really wanted to quit. What was we he going to do? Work at the local market for twelve dollars an hour? How was he going to provide for his son on that? His military retiree pay was only enough for him to live off. Weed, as unconventional and perhaps unsavory as it could be, was a way he could provide Mark with everything he needed including healthcare, dental, and hopefully college tuition. All the things a father with a real job could provide.

"WE LOST THAT LOVING FEELING! Now it's gone, gone, gone, goo—one!" George Calloway sang along joyously with the Righteous Brothers as he sped down the road in his blue 1978 Pontiac Bonneville. He made his way around Highland Lake in Winsted, an open beer between his legs, puffing on a fat joint — just a typical afternoon for George. It was a gorgeous day out, and he was determined to enjoy it.

He finished his Bud Light and chucked the can out the window into the woods. Then he took one last pull from his joint and tossed that out the window as well before hastily veering his car into the parking area by the boat launch. After parking, he fiddled with the radio till he settled on a station playing 'White Room' by Cream. Satisfied with the tunes, he dug his pills out of his pocket.

42

He had been prescribed OxyContin for his back following a car accident a year earlier. The script had long expired, but his habit had not. He crushed a pill on his dash with his lighter and then snorted it with a straw.

"AHHHHH YEAAH!" he said, snorting again. He rubbed his nose with his hand and sniffed hard as he reached into the back for a new beer. He felt better than he had in some time; winter had been a real drag.

A friend of his had been letting him stay with him at his lake house. It provided George with a stable place to live, which kept Dickey happy. His older brother had told him he wasn't welcome anymore. Not until he was sober. He said he couldn't allow his girls to see him like this.

He wasn't fit to be a part of his own nieces' lives.

That was fine. If Jason was willing to bribe him to let Dickey and the girls live in his house, then so be it. George never cared for the house anyway; too many memories. This situation was preferable. The weed Jason supplied him was the best around, and cheap enough that George could live off of it. Although, as his habits increased, his money was becoming much tighter.

That's why he was feeling good today; his money situation would soon change. George had a meeting with Gary Augustine, a local supplier with major connections. Gary could get *anything,* and at a respectable price too. That's why George had come to him about getting into the Oxy game. If he could give him enough at a decent cost, then George could make some serious money and not have to worry about finding pills every day.

Until then, he was killing time. The sun was dancing on the lake, the birds were singing, and he was ready to enjoy the day. He lit another joint, inhaled deeply, and immediately began coughing until he was red in the face.

"Woo, goddamn!" he exclaimed, chugging some beer to soothe his throat.

His phone buzzed in his pocket — another of his friends looking for weed. He was all out, aside from his personal stash. He had been eagerly waiting for Jason to return his calls. Annoyed and impatient, he text-messaged Jason again, asking where he was. A few minutes later he finally got a response. Jason wanted to meet at the Barkhamsted reservoir.

He threw the Bonneville into drive and punched the gas. The tires squealed as he haphazardly tore out of the boat launch and down the road, past two young girls riding their bicycles.

THE BARKHAMSTED RESEVOIR was a beautiful feat of engineering and architecture. Ornate stone walls wrapped around the embankment and met at a single tower, which stood like a castle against the water.

"About time you answered me, I got people blowing up my phone," George griped as he climbed into Jason's car.

"I've got a girlfriend now, I'm not available at the drop of a whim," Jason informed him, drawing on a cigarette. "I've only got two for you. I'm short at the moment," he said, cutting right to business.

"Two?" George asked. *Was he joking?*

"Yeah, you can have more tomorrow," Jason said.

"I need a kwopper to give to one guy now, Jay. C'mon," George protested. If he didn't have at least four ounces to sell that day, he would not have the cash he needed to put down on the Oxy deal with Augustine later.

"Fine," Jason sighed. "We'll have to go to the farm, then."

"Oh yeah?" George's demeanor changed immediately. "I finally get to see the farm!"

"Don't expect a tour," Jason advised as he dialed his phone. "Hey, Randy. It's Jason. Wondering if you wanted to have lunch? Okay, great. See you soon."

"We good?" George asked, concerned.

"Yeah, of course," Jason answered. He flicked his cigarette butt out the window and dropped the gear shift into drive. "Guy has more weed than we could probably fit in the car."

44

George's eyes widened at such a thought.

The farm was at the end of a series of dirt roads near the border of North Canaan, Connecticut and Sheffield, Massachusetts, which were absent from any map.

"What is this? It's down here?" George asked, perplexed as they drove deep into the woods.

"This was going to be a suburban community. When the housing market burst back in 2006, the plans were abandoned, leaving those who had bought ahead with the option of either making a home in no-man's land or selling for a severe loss," Jason answered as he navigated his car down the narrow, uneven, dirt roads.

"So does he have neighbors?"

"Yeah, some former Army sniper the dude pays for security."

George was enthralled.

"I should have brought a beer," he thought out loud.

Randy heard Jason's Subaru approaching from down the road and told Mark to fetch him a pound of Mother of Berry from the garage. As the car pulled up, Mark returned with a brown grocery bag stuffed full of vacuum-sealed bags of cannabis.

"Wait in the car," Jason instructed George.

"Seriously? I want to see the farm, man," George whined.

"Not a chance. Shut up and wait here," Jason chided him.

"I can fucking smell it from here!"

"Shut up and wait here," Jason reiterated before exiting the car.

George watched him walk up the back steps of the house to the porch and shake the hand of the man he knew must be Randy Sandusfield. He watched them chat for a few minutes, then Jason pulled an envelope stuffed full of cash and left it on the table next to Randy. They chatted some more before Jason got up, grabbed a brown grocery bag from under the table, nodded farewell to Randy, and headed back to the car.

"Easy as that," said Jason upon getting back into the car. He secured the goods under a blanket on the back seat and then backed out of Randy's driveway.

"What is this road even called?" George asked, bemused by the isolated location.

"It's not called anything. It doesn't have a name," Jason replied.

"Oh.".

"You know you can never tell anyone about this place, right?" Jason asked, suddenly concerned by George's interest.

"Yeah, no shit, dude," George scoffed. "What do you think I am, retarded?"

Jason said nothing. He found himself second-guessing his decision to bring George there but dismissed his doubts. Surely, George was smarter than that.

MICHAEL TRIVOTY SLAMMED his phone down on the kitchen table in frustration. Maegan had refused to answer his calls or return his messages.

"That fucking puta, bro?" his older brother Andrew asked from across the table.

"She's with that Terry boy," Michael scowled.

"Jay Terry, that boy with all the good smoke?" Eddie asked.

Eddie was Andrew's longest friend and his number one soldier. Solid and built like a rock, Eddie stood at 6'6" and weighed just over 275lbs.

"Yeah, that's the little bitch," said Michael.

"Fuck that Terry bitch and fuck her, too," Andrew said, swigging his beer.

"What's up, playas!?" a stocky man entering the kitchen through the back door with a thirty-pack of beer yelled.

The man with the refreshments was Caesar, Andrew's other closest friend. He had an intimidating appearance: a shaved head with a dragon tattoo covering his skull.

"What's up, Caesar?" Andrew said, rising to greet him with a fist bump, handshake, and a quick hug.

Eddie nodded to him accordingly.

"What's the matter, kid, you seem down?" Caesar asked, nudging Michael.

"Just some dumb bitch," Michael muttered.

"Ah, well." Caesar cracked a beer and pulled a bag of brown powder from this jacket. He sprinkled some on the back of his hand and snorted it. "Fuck all that, let's have some fun."

He took Michael's hand and dabbed a small pile of powder onto it.

"Yeah, yeah," Michael said, still disheartened. He snorted the heroin and felt a wave of relaxation wash over him.

The house that Andrew owned on Reckon Avenue was a friendly place to drop by and score and party for his friends and associates, but friendly people knew to come to the back door. That's why when Andrew's dog began barking out in the front yard, they were all concerned.

Andrew's dog was a smelly, angry pit bull named Dexter. He was a fighting dog from Bridgeport, which Andrew had claimed as payment for a debt. The dog and a beating were all Andrew could extract from a man who had long ago broken himself. Often left tied to the front porch, the mangy bull had long since killed off any grass in the front yard and now trotted along a muddy, shit-covered terrain that anyone hoping to enter the Trivoty house first had to pass. If either Michael or Andrew were there, Dexter would behave; only barking and bearing his teeth to visitors. Anyone who dared to pass without a Trivoty nearby would find Dexter's jaw locked onto an appendage.

That was the predicament Andrew found two boys in from the nearby high school. One of them seemed to think that if he slowly approached the beast – eighty-five pounds of lean muscle and teeth – from a crouched position with his hand out that it would yield. The other boy stood back, wincing in fear every time Dexter would lunge.

"Going to lose a hand that way," Andrew called down.

Andrew shared their father's bronze Salvadoran skin. He had a tattoo of a dragon running down his right arm, and another of a tiger down his left. For half the year, Andrew wouldn't wear a shirt. He'd sculpted his body through multiple short-term stays at Cheshire Prison, and he loved to show it off.

"Dexter! Heel!" The dog stopped barking and was sitting by Andrew's feet in seconds. Andrew laughed at the boys' timidity. "Come on inside; he won't hurt you… now."

The house had been fairly nice at one point, but that was years ago. In its current state of squalor, it housed Andrew, his brother Michael, and at any time, a handful of other members of their crew. As the two boys followed Andrew through the house, they passed two men nodding out on the couch, the needle they'd shared on the table beside a bag of dope, a lighter, and a burnt, bent spoon.

"Tim, right?" Andrew asked. The kid nodded. "Whatcha need? A bundle?"

"Nah, just a couple dubs," Tim answered.

"Why spend twenty, when you can spend seventy, sell a few bags and get yours for free?" Andrew suggested, handing a bundle of little baggies to the kid.

"I guess that makes sense," Tim said. His friend Travis disagreed.

"I just wanted to try the shit, not go selling it," Travis protested.

"Don't worry about it, it's easy," Andrew assured them.

Still, Travis seemed uncomfortable, and Tim backed off to settle his nerves.

"Just a couple bags this time," he said, handing the bundle back to Andrew.

"Alright, but you come back whenever. If you need to get right, I always got work, if ya know what I'm sayin'."

After the two had left, Andrew opened his top drawer and used a key to open his lock box. He pulled out a stack of small bills and began counting. His brother Michael came into the room and greeted him with a light jab on the shoulder. "What's good, bro?" he asked.

"Counting scratch, gotta see Augustine tomorrow, get more D."

On the street, heroin was often called 'D', short for 'dope.'

"How's it looking?"

"Maybe about eight-nine hundred profit, here."

"That's it?"

"Not so bad for a week's work, little brother. How's your weed business doing?"

"Shitty."

"What do you mean? Slinging eights and dubs, you should be making more money than the D."

"Shit ain't sellin'. It's shitty mid-grade brick weed. Nobody wants it."

"Why not?"

"Town's flush with good greens. Medical grade shit. Everybody's buying from that Terry bitch."

"Poor-ass, broke mother fuckers don't want that shit. What is it fifty, sixty bucks an eighth? Sell your shit to street kids, man. Thirty bucks a slice."

"No one wants it. Too many seeds, bro."

There was a time when cheap weed was king, but thanks to growing legal medical and commercial markets, everybody had acquired a taste for quality.

"So how do we get us some of that *good-good?*" Andrew asked.

49

"Terry kid, he's the only one with a good hook-up."

"So talk to him, see if he wants to expand a little."

"Fuck that! Little bitch's got my girl."

"Man, forget that bitch! You need to focus on your shit," Andrew warned, before changing subjects. "Whatchu got goin' on today, hermano?"

"I've got some business to take care of," Michael said, grabbing his nose and snorting.

"You need some backup?" Andrew placed his hand on his brother's shoulder. Business typically required muscle.

"Was going to see if I could take Eddie," Michael replied. "Just in case."

"Eddie!" Andrew called as the two made their way back to the kitchen.

"What's going on?" Eddie answered.

"Take a ride with my brother. He has some business to take care of, and I don't want him alone," said Andrew.

He spoke softly, as if he were asking a favor, but Eddie knew it was an order.

"Alright, I got this girl to pick up after we're done, anyway," Eddie said.

"You got a date, Eddie?" Andrew teased.

"Big, bald, and beautiful," Eddie said, rubbing his head.

Everyone laughed. Shortly after, Michael and Eddie left together.

MAEGAN GASPED AS HER HANDS crashed down onto Jason's kitchen counter, attempting to brace herself. Jason pressed up behind her, pulling her hair back to expose her neck, then passionately kissing it, his left hand running up her shirt. She moaned as he worked his way up her neck

50

with his lips and tongue while taking firm grasp of her breast. She turned, short of breath, and kissed him feverishly.

She grabbed him by the waste of his pants and pulled him closer, undoing his belt and sliding his pants down. He dropped to the floor and lifted her skirt, kissing her softly on her hips, down to her thighs. He ran his hands softly up the back of her legs, softly kissing between her legs.

She moaned as he went to work, her legs quivering as she tried to hold herself upright, her knees buckling when he would hit the right spot. After a few minutes, he stood up, grabbed her ass with both hands and lifted her up onto the counter. He dropped his boxer shorts as she pulled off his shirt. Taking a moment to look into her eyes affectionately, running his fingers through her hair, he kissed her with all the passion he held for her. Passion he had suppressed for too long. She pulled him close and gently bit his neck as he entered her.

After, they sat naked, cuddled-up together on Jason's couch smoking a joint. They talked for a while about Maegan's mother. Jason knew much of the story. He had been friends with her brother Kaleb in high school when Maegan was still only in middle school.

"I remember seeing you when you were just fifteen years old," Jason said. "God, that sounds so creepy!" he laughed.

"You were just a kid, yourself!" she said in his defense.

"I remember thinking you were going to be a beautiful woman when you grew up." He kissed her forehead. "I was right."

She passed him the joint and exhaled slowly, coughing a little. He handed her some water and continued to smoke.

"So, we talk about my fucked up life a lot," Maegan said. "How about yours? How did you end up living away from any family before you even graduated high school?"

Jason sighed, dabbing the joint out in the ashtray on the coffee table.

"My father was never around. I don't even know who he is. My mother—she split on me when I was eight years old. Took off with some guy she'd met. Left me three boxes of cupcakes, a six-pack of juice cups,

51

and a number for my aunt and uncle. She left a note telling me she had to leave and that I could call my aunt and uncle, but not to call until the next day. I guess she wanted to get as far away as she could before anyone knew."

"Jesus Christ," Maegan shook her head in disbelief.

"Yeah. So, I stayed with my aunt and uncle for a bit, but they ended up having their kid, my cousin Tim, about a year later. Things were just never the same. I don't know what it was. Financial stress, maybe? Resentment because of what my mom had done? Or maybe they just couldn't pretend to love me the way they loved their son."

Maegan ran her fingernails up and down his arm as he talked.

"I'm sorry, babe," she said, kissing him softly on his cheek.

"Dickey saved me, really. Getting his parents to allow me to live there."

He had never talked to anyone about these things.

"What was that like?" she asked, lighting a cigarette.

"Fun, mostly. Except George grew to resent me and Dickey's friendship," Jason confessed. "So that caused issues at times."

"Is that why you put up with him?" she asked, rising to her feet and retrieving her purse.

She had been putting this moment off for a while, but she couldn't for a second longer. She found the packet of Suboxone at the bottom of her purse, opened it, and slipped the dissolvable tablet into her mouth.

"What's that?" Jason asked with concern from across the room.

"Suboxone," she told him, puffing her cigarette and reclaiming her seat beside him.

"What's Suboxone?"

"It's something they prescribe to addicts, Jason." Maegan looked down in shame.

"It's like methadone? It gives you a dope high?" he asked.

"No, it's not like that. It just curbs the part of the brain that still wants heroin."

She was partly telling the truth, partly lying. It was a painkiller and users did get a high from it, although not a strong one. The idea was to flood the receptors in the brain that craved heroin with Suboxone.

"You still get cravings?" Jason asked, surprised.

"Yes. Sometimes." She didn't know what else to say. "I may for quite some time. Maybe forever, I don't know," she muttered.

Her biggest fears concerning Jason were coming to bear before her eyes. She could see the look on his face. She knew that look. He didn't want to be with an addict, let alone have a life with an addict, marry an addict, or have children with an addict. Who would? Who would want to love her now?

"Well," Jason said after a few moments. "I hope you don't ever go back to that."

"I don't want to, believe me," she said, standing up and beginning to dress. "I have to go," she added. "My uncle is taking me to dinner," she told him.

"Yeah, I told the girls I would stop over and eat with them and Dickey tonight," he replied. Both were happy to have somewhere else to go.

He wanted to pretend that her addiction didn't concern him, but the truth was he had not considered the implications of being with someone with a dependency issue. He looked at her as she dressed. She was so beautiful, and he felt comfortable with her. Maybe he could be a positive force, he thought. Maybe he could help her get past all that once and for all. He wanted to try. She was worth it. But the more he came to care for her, the greater his anxiety became.

"PLEASE! PLEASE!" ERIC SCHULTZ pleaded with Michael Trivoty from his knees. His lip was fat, his nose bloody, and his face already swollen from repeated blows. Eddie had knocked him around a little then dragged him back into the woods behind a closed down department store that was once the local A-Mart.

He tried to get up, but Eddie powerfully shoved him back into the dirt.

Michael stared blankly down the barrel of his .9mm Beretta at Schultz's face. He was a thirty-year-old manager at the nearby McDonald's. His uniform was tattered and torn, dirt and piss stained.

"I'm getting tired of having to come after you, man," Michael said, watching with hidden delight as Schultz squirmed and shook with fear. "All for a few hundred dollars, too. Bitch-ass can't even cut me three hundred out of your fancy management paycheck?"

"I have bills! They automatically deduct… I have direct deposit! I don't even see my checks, they just go into the bank! I'm trying to take care of my son…"

"Shut the fuck up!" Michael yelled, kicking him in the gut.

Eric groaned and keeled over.

"You want to take care of your son?! Then stop shooting dope! But don't blame me for this shit, or *direct deposit*!" Michael spat.

"I'm sorry! I'll pay you!" Schultz shouted.

"Whatcha got now?" Michael asked, nudging him with the gun.

"Nothing, maybe twenty bucks, that's it!" Schultz cried.

"Your car is a piece of shit, too," Michael said, shaking his head. "I should just fucking kill you because it's honestly less trouble than this bullshit every week, and your broke ass ain't got nothing I want…"

"Please don't! I'll pay! I will!" Schultz promised.

"When?"

"Friday!"

"And if not?"

54

"I will; I will…" Schultz insisted.

Michael knelt down and stuck the muzzle of the gun against the temple of Schultz's head. "I want to hear you tell me what will happen if you don't."

"You'll…" he stammered and gasped for air — a thirty-year-old man brought to tears in the dirt with soiled, piss soaked pants. "You'll kill me," he said after catching his breath.

"You're such a pathetic piece of shit, I would probably be doing your son a favor," Michael said.

He got up and let out a good heartfelt laugh. Eddie smiled and chuckled as well.

"I'll tell you what," Michael added before leaving. "If you go ahead and kill yourself before then, I won't hold the kid responsible for the debt."

The two chuckled as they walked down the path toward their cars, leaving Eric Schultz in a puddle of blood, snot, piss, shit, and mud, sobbing uncontrollably.

"UNCLE JAY IS HERE!" Stacey excitedly informed her father, pulling lightly on his pant leg.

"Is he now?" Dickey replied. "Why don't you go let him in, sweetie?" he told her, knowing Jason would very well come in on his own. "Now," he said, turning his attention to Marie who was sitting on the kitchen counter. "We're going to chop up these here peppers and put them in the sauce."

"No onions, right?" Marie asked, concerned.

"No onions, darling," Dickey assured her. "I know you don't like it when I cut those up."

Jason came in carrying Stacey in his left arm and used his right to open the fridge and grab a beer.

"How's it going?" he said with a smile.

Dickey smiled back. He loved seeing Jason with his girls. "It's going, brother. It's going," he answered, grabbing the beer from Jason's hand and forcing him to retrieve another.

Jason lowered Stacey to the floor, and Dickey scooped Marie from the counter and set her down beside her sister.

"Go play with your sister for a bit, I'll call you when supper is ready," Dickey said, giving her a light pat on the bottom.

"Okay," Marie answered, grabbing Stacey's hand. "C'mon," she told her sister.

Stacey was always eager to follow her sister anywhere.

"Saw George, today," Jason informed Dickey, grabbing a piece of pepper from the cutting boarding and biting into it.

"Get your hands out of my dinner," Dickey said, pointing the chef's knife at him. "What was the low life doing?"

"Eh, just needed to score more weed, of course. I brought him up to the farm. Probably the most time I've spent with the guy in years," said Jason, popping the rest of the pepper slice into his mouth and sipping his beer.

"Old Randy Sandusfield," Dickey said with a slow shake of his head. "There's a guy even crazier than me. Poor son of a bitch."

"Real badass you told me," Jason said, intrigued.

"Randy was spec-ops, Delta Force. He saw action all over: Beirut, Grenada, Desert Storm in Iraq, Somalia. Who knows where else?"

"Delta Force, huh?

"Yeah, real ass-kickers. Anyways, Randy's never really talked much about it, but you can see it," said Dickey, cutting peppers into quarters and then dicing them with the blade.

"See what?" asked Jason.

"That look we all get when it stops working," Dickey said, grasping to explain how he knew Randy must feel. "All this," he said, motioning to

56

his home and belongings with the blade. "When none of this works anymore because you're just too fucked up. Look at him; special operator turned pot kingpin. You think that's what he wanted? He couldn't acclimate... He couldn't find a niche—not for the person he'd become over there. Not here in west bumble-fuck, Connecticut."

Jason was a bit stunned; he had never considered the circumstances that bring a war hero to live off the grid growing marijuana. He supposed he had always assumed that was the life Randy wanted, but considering the man had served in the Army and as a police officer, Dickey's explanation was a better fit.

"Let's put that sauce on to simmer and go outback quick," Jason suggested, flashing a joint at Dickey.

"Read my damn mind," Dickey said, tossing a handful of chopped green peppers into the pot of tomato sauce on the stove.

DWIGHT TRIED TO SPEND TIME with Maegan as often as possible. He knew he was the only positive influence in her life. From what he could tell, she appreciated it.

"I just think it's for the best," Dwight said, looking at her sympathetically. "You need a better environment."

"It's really tempting... and I am flattered — I just don't know," she said, flashing her beautiful smile.

"Do it for me, too," he said. "Max and I, we get lonely up there. House could use a woman's touch."

"Trust me, I've noticed," she said with a laugh. She dabbed her straw around in her glass, mixing the ice cubes around in her orange soda.

"Yeah, I bet." He smiled. "Come live with me, Maegan."

"Okay," she said, turning slightly red. "It means a lot to me. Thank you."

"Come here," he said, motioning for a hug. They both rose from their booth and embraced. He kissed the top of her head affectionately. "I love you," he told her.

"I love you, too," she said.

"Am I interrupting?" the waitress carrying their pizza asked with a laugh.

"No, pizza is always welcome," Dwight joked.

He was happy knowing she would be leaving that place. He had never had kids, and Maegan was the closest thing he had to a daughter. Heaven knows he was the closest thing she had to a father. He'd struggled to fill the gap and to be there for her while her mother was in and out of hospitals and rehabs. His parents had helped as well, as best they could before they'd moved south.

"My mother probably isn't going to be happy about it," Maegan said with a grin.

"No," Dwight conceded. "She won't be."

"Oh well. She'll get over it," Maegan replied.

"What's wrong with you tonight?" Dwight asked, his eyes narrowing.

"What do you mean?" she asked.

"You look... off... distant," he said. "You okay?"

"Yeah, just tired I guess," Maegan said, looking down and biting into her pizza.

"Well try to get some sleep tonight," Dwight recommended.

"I will. I am going to see my boyfriend, though," she informed him with a smile.

"The Terry boy?" Dwight asked, shaking his head. "He's a drug dealer, Maegan."

"No, he isn't!" she exclaimed. "It's just a little weed. Relax, Uncle Dwight."

"Maegan, I don't want you seeing drug dealers."

"It's not the same," she insisted. "He's a good guy, believe me."

"He sells illegal substances for a living, sometimes to kids, Maegan."

"What are you talking about?"

"He's got a file a mile long!" Dwight said. He was getting angry, but tried to remain calm.

"Jason would never do anything to put me at risk. He would never do any of that shit I was into, trust me," she said emphatically.

Dwight could tell she was locking up. He didn't want to fight with her or push her away and he certainly didn't want her changing her mind about moving in.

"Fine, just be careful, please," he said with a sigh.

"Trust me, he's a good guy," she reiterated.

He had better be, or he would rue the day he started dating his niece.

A COUPLE OF RACCOONS HAD MANAGED to knock over a garbage can and were busy tearing into their trashy treasure when they heard Swamp stumbling near. They looked up as if to assess the danger and then returned to gnawing on garbage. Maybe they decided their bounty was too good to abandon, or maybe they had become too used to people to be scared by smelly old Swamp. The coons had become a regular fixture at the apartments above the Torrington bar, on account of the owner's dispute with the trash company, resulting in an overfilled dumpster and piles of trash around Swamp's back door. Swamp didn't mind; made it less likely the owner would bitch about his back rent.

Swamp was still fuzzy. He had shot up about two hours ago and then nodded out, only to wake up and discover he was out of cigarettes. He gathered up his last $7 and headed out to buy a bag of tobacco from the gas station down the road. He needed to have some cigarettes rolled before he got high again. In fact, he thought, he had better score some more dope while he was out.

That decision led him past the gas station, further down the road to Shop Stop.

When one wanted to score dope and had no cash, there was one solution: baby formula, which Swamp was able to purchase using his food stamps. Of course, buying baby formula required getting the store management to unlock a secured case, on account of how many junkies would steal the stuff. And, of course, buying baby formula with food stamps while looking like an addict, usually earned him some nasty looks. He didn't mind. Like most addicts, his sense of humility was long gone. He bought a package of tobacco with cash, as well, and headed out the door.

Baby formula was a hot commodity for junkies because using dope poisons a mother's milk. Addicts with babies, therefore, needed the formula and, being addicts, were usually short on cash. His connection, Liz, had two little ones and the newborn required formula. Liz, being crafty, slung dope so she could support her habit without any cost and get free baby formula. She was always happy to see Swamp because she knew he always had formula.

"I was actually going to have to go out soon and buy some if someone didn't bring some by," Liz said with relief.

Her apartment was a sty; crusty pans atop the stove, a sink full of nasty dishes, overflowing garbage, empty beer cans on every surface, and cigarette butts everywhere. The place smelled like cat piss and ashtrays.

"Glad to help," Swamp told her.

Not long after, he was on his way home, a bundle of heroin in his pocket. He lit up the smoke he'd rolled at Liz's and hurried home to shoot up. As far as Swamp's standards go, he had dope, he had cigarettes — this was as good as it got.

Just then, a black Camaro with tinted windows passed by and came to a quick stop at the corner in front of him.

"Oh, son of a bitch!" Swamp yelled, stomping his feet in protest. The car's reverse lights came on. "Mother fuckers won't leave me alone," Swamp muttered, recognizing the Camaro.

The car backed up and stopped beside him. The driver's window rolled down, revealing a large bald man glaring at him with eyes as cold as steel.

"Get in the car," the man said.

"Man, fuck you!" Swamp barked back.

"Swamp, you know I waited for you to score on purpose," the man told him. His tone was soft, but serious. "Now you can get in, or I can bust you for whatever you picked up at Liz's and bring you in."

"This is fucked up, you know that? This is entrapment!" Swamp argued.

Detective Mayhew had made a habit of squeezing information out of him.

"Entrapment? Did I sell you the dope?" Mayhew asked with a laugh.

"Huh?"

"Get the fuck in the car, Swamp."

Swamp huffed and groaned, but reluctantly went around to the passenger side and grabbed the handle.

"No cigarettes, Swamp!" Mayhew snapped.

"Jesus Christ! Killing me!" Swamp groaned, flicking his smoke onto the road as he climbed into the Camaro.

Mayhew drove around the block to the Shop Stop and took a parking space near the back of the lot.

"Give me something," Mayhew told him, his cold blue eyes inspecting Swamp's sorry state — he couldn't wait to get that smelly piece of shit out of his car.

"I ain't got nothing to give today, man," Swamp protested.

He was a straggly guy in his mid-forties, but he looked like he was pushing sixty.

"Swamp, I told you, I have been too patient with you. If you want to keep walking around with your head in dopeland every day, then you need to provide me with info."

"I told you everything I know!" Swamp protested.

"That's bullshit, Swamp!" Mayhew snapped. "You know the players in this town. You know what's what. Been around too long to pretend otherwise. Lab tells me more than 85% of the dope we seized in the past six months is coming from the same source. The volume is unfathomable. There's a vein, and I can't find it."

"I don't know nothing about that," Swamp said guardedly.

He looked out the window ignoring Mayhew's glare.

"There's another overdose death in this town every week now," Mayhew said, shaking his head. "You want that for your town?"

Swamp just stared away, refusing to speak.

"What's the name Andrew Trivoty mean to you?" Mayhew asked.

"Some player up in Winsted, that's all I know," Swamp said.

"He's a part of the chain, I know that for sure. I'm not sure who's moving it into town, though. That's what you're going to find out for me," Mayhew told him.

"How am I going to do that?" Swamp asked.

"Keep your ears open. There's a nice crisp fifty dollar bill in it for you if it pans out," Mayhew told him.

Swamp's eyebrows raised.

"Well, I can do some digging," said Swamp.

"I bet you can," Mayhew said with a laugh. "But that's for another day, it doesn't settle us, here and now." He leaned in closer and glared at the man cowering in his seat. "Give me a dope house," he commanded.

"Man, I can't give you all of them, I won't be able to score!" Swamp protested.

"I could always go bust Liz," Mayhew said. "Get SWAT to kick down her door."

"She's got kids, man!" Swamp exclaimed. "You're cold!"

"I don't give a shit. The state will take those kids away quicker than you go through a dime bag. Probably be the best thing for them, honestly," Mayhew said. "Yeah, I'm going to call it in," he added, grabbing his radio receiver from under his dash.

"Wait!" Swamp cried. He rubbed his face with both hands and swore. "Alright, alright. Hoffman Street! Right up here," Swamp told him, pointing up the hill across from the shopping center.

"Alright, let's take a drive by, and you can point it out. Then I'll bring you home," Mayhew said, throwing the car in gear.

Swamp promised the house on Hoffman would be a substantial bust. After dropping him at his ratty apartment, Mayhew returned to observe the activity there for a bit. He watched heavy volumes of traffic come and go from the house for a while, then dialed his partner on his cell phone.

"Guillermo, I think I got us a big one, buddy," Mayhew said, watching a young couple leave the house. He could spot an addict from a mile away, and there were a lot of addicts visiting this house.

"How big?" his partner asked.

"Maybe as big as Del Monica… maybe bigger…" Mayhew said. "Come meet me at Shop Stop and check it out; it's over on Hoffman," he added.

"I told you, Wyatt, I'm on diaper duty tonight. Sheryl is at her ladies night thing," Guillermo said.

"Come on, she'll be home soon. You always say she's in bed by ten," he urged.

There was a long pause.

63

"You think it's as big as Del Monica?" Guillermo asked, recalling the glory of their biggest bust.

"I think it's *bigger*," Mayhew said with a laugh.

"Alright. Ten-thirty. Shop Stop."

"Alright, big boy. See you then.".

He hung up and watched as a car full of teens pulled up to the house.

GARY AUGUSTINE LIVED in an apartment above a closed down auto repair shop and gas station on the outskirts of Riverton, a small town bordering Winsted and Colebrook. He spent most of his days there, partying and living life as he pleased. Although the building was an eyesore, his place was fully loaded with nice furniture, big screen televisions, and all the luxuries one would expect a man of means to have. He was by no measure rich, but selling dope afforded him a comfortable lifestyle.

Gary enjoyed drugs, but his real pleasure was pussy. The younger, the better. That night her name was Vivian. Gary was always telling her how much he loved her ass, insisting she wore nothing but a thong when they partied together. She loved the adoration and attention and would gladly strip for him, so long as it wasn't too cold.

"We can take some Ecstasy and just rub each other all night long," he said to her, waving a plastic baggy with blue pills at her like treats being lorded over a dog.

"Ooh, sounds fun!" she giggled.

"God, you are beautiful," Gary said. "I want to do a line off that sexy ass of yours. Come here," he said.

She was about to roll over and serve as a table for him when there was a knock at the door.

"Oh, that's Georgie boy, come by for his Oxy," Gary said, nudging Vivian. "Be a doll and go let him in for me," he added, reaching for the platter of cocaine on the coffee table.

64

Vivian got up and grabbed her clothes off the floor. She began to put her pants on when Gary stopped her.

"Ut-uh!" he said. "Did I ask you to get dressed?"

She paused for a moment to contemplate the request before dropping her clothes on the floor with a smile and heading for the door.

George was surprised to see a girl wearing barely anything answer the door.

"Oh, uh, hello," he said, his mind wiped clean from the sight. "I, uh, is Gary here?" he asked.

Vivian laughed and turned away. He watched her walk back to the couch, his mouth agape.

"What's up, Georgie!" Gary welcomed him.

"How old is she," George asked under his breath.

"Oh, I'm not even sure," Gary replied. "Babycakes, how old are you?" Gary asked her.

"Almost seventeen," Vivian said, striking a pose and proudly shaking her tits.

"Jesus Christ…" George said, looking around nervously as they all sat on the couch.

"What?!" Gary laughed. "Fifty years ago she would be old enough to be married. Lighten up, man."

"No, it's just, she's young and the law says…" George stammered, clearly uncomfortable.

"It's not like she's blowing you, dude," Gary said with a laugh. Vivian laughed too. "Unless you want her to," he added with a wink.

"No, no, thank you," George said uncomfortably. "So, I've got the money for the down payment." He was eager to leave.

"You know you like her, look at you!" Gary said with a laugh. "She's hot! Admit it!"

"She's just young is all…"

"Just numbers!" Gary said with a heartfelt laugh. "Look at that ass!"

Vivian stroke a pose. She was never very inhibited to begin with, but when she was high, she had no restraint.

"Can I just get the pills?" George asked uncomfortably.

"Sure you don't want to take E with us?" Vivian asked, inching closer to him. She gently brushed his arm with her fingers. "I get so crazy when I do," she said with a wink.

"Maybe next time," George said, standing up and pulling the cash from his pocket. "Can I get the pills and leave, please?"

"Sure thing, Georgie boy."

Gary returned with a manila envelope stuffed full of OxyContin pills and exchanged it for cash.

"Oxy 30s, one-thousand pills for twenty grand," Gary said, handing him the envelope.

"Excellent, and here's ten percent down, as agreed upon," George said, handing him $2k in assorted bills.

"You owe me eighteen thousand dollars, homie. You realize that, right?" Gary said. He lit a joint and took a few puffs before handing it to Vivian. "You understand the seriousness of that, right?"

"Absolutely!" George told him. "I can snort half this envelope and still make the money I need to pay you."

"That's right, that's why it works for everyone, man. Hit me up in a week and give whatever you can scrape up by then. Make sure it's at least a few grand."

"Thanks, Gary, I'll talk to you soon," George said.

"Bye now," Vivian giggled as George left.

ERIC SCHULTZ WAS VERY DRUNK that night when he came home to the four-room apartment he shared with his son. Dried, crusted blood was still on his face from the beating he had endured, though he had changed his clothes. For hours he had delayed coming home, to avoid his son seeing him in such a state.

He found the boy in the living room, playing video games in the dark. Sean had sandy brown hair like his father, only his was longer. It hung down shaggily in front of his eyes. At eleven years old he already knew he wanted to be nothing like his father. His hair was his silent revolt.

"What happened to you?" Sean asked, barely looking up from the screen.

"Some guy got rough at the restaurant," Eric said, taking his jacket off. "Your old man had to step in. You should see the other guy. He's worse," he said, trying to mask his shame with a laugh. Sean barely made a sound in acknowledgment.

Eric knew the boy didn't respect him. Why should he? He worked at McDonald's for a shit wage and struggled with addiction and substance abuse issues. If not for his mother's drunken drama, he would have probably chosen to live with her.

"You're spending too much time playing that damn thing," Eric said, lighting a cigarette and sitting beside the boy on the couch. In truth, he didn't much care, but he had run out of things to pawn.

"It's fun," Sean replied.

"Yeah, well, it's going to turn your brains to shit. I'm getting rid of it tomorrow," Eric informed him.

It was the only way to cover his debt to Trivoty.

"What?!" Sean asked in bewilderment. He slammed his controller into the couch. "You're joking."

"No, I'm not joking. You spend too much time on the damn thing. You need to do something more active, like sports, or… I don't fucking know. Go outside. Do things! You're young. Can't have you cooped up in here every damn day," Eric said.

"I have friends… I have a team of friends, and we play online, and they count on me to…"

"Get some real life friends, then. I can't keep paying for your internet access on that thing, either," Eric said.

He wasn't lying; all his bills had proven more difficult to manage in light of his relapse.

Sean's eyes welled up with tears. His face turned bright red.

"This isn't fair! You can't just take it from me!"

"I'm your father, and I'll do what I damn-well-please," Eric told him. "That's enough from you. Go to your room! Get ready for bed!"

Sean stormed away in tears. When Eric heard his son's bedroom door crash shut, he too began to cry.

THE TRIVOTY HOUSE WAS RAGING that night. Andrew's crew was up from Hartford. Most of them were members of Los Toros Furioso, or the Toros, as they were infamously known. The Toros were a transnational Salvadoran street gang as known for their loyalty as they were feared for their viciousness. Most wore bandanas, do-rags, saggy jeans, and tank tops. Many members had their faces heavily tattooed.

Andrew had never joined the Toros, but after his last stint in prison he had made some solid connections and became a *becerro,* a close associate eligible for membership. But Andrew didn't want to be a part of the gang; there were too many rules. It was a highly structured organization with a strict code of conduct. Breaking the rules made one subject to punishment. Andrew was never one for rules, but he found the alliance necessary to survive prison.

In exchange for their protection while in prison, Andrew had set the Toros up with Gary Augustine. Gary's cousin was a made-man with the Carrillo crime family down in Long Island. Gary and his cousin's people had been pushing Andrew to help them sell their heroin in Connecticut. The Toros were happy to oblige, and being a trusted friend, Andrew was their first choice to run things in the northwest corner.

While some competition would always exist, their plentiful supply of powerful heroin allowed them to dominate the market in the rural northwest.

It was easy money, unlike Hartford, where the gang had been involved in a couple of high-profile shootings over turf disputes.

The Toros and their crew took off early that night, leaving Andrew, Michael, and Caesar drinking beer and smoking pot around a game of dominoes on the kitchen table. Eddie had disappeared with the girl he'd brought to the party.

Dominoes was Andrew's game. In prison, he had earned the nickname *Bones* due to his penchant for the game. He would often tell Michael stories about winning packs of smokes while the entire yard watched and cheered.

Michael suspected his brother's tales of prison glory were exaggerations. It just wasn't *hood* to regard it in any other way. '*Prison? Shit! That ain't nothing, son!*' Andrew had serious street cred, and part of that was from the fact that he had already been to prison and openly talked about it like it was summer camp. He had done several stints, the last of which was his longest.

He'd stabbed a rival and then raped his girlfriend in front of him as retaliation for setting-up Michael to be beaten and ripped off. The state was unable to prove the rape, as the victim refused medical treatment, but they had him dead to rights on the stabbing. He pled guilty to aggravated assault and served five years.

For Michael, it was a defining moment. He had been beaten badly on the fake buy and spent two weeks in a hospital in Torrington. It was five days before he regained consciousness and by that point, his brother was already in processing. When Michael learned what Andrew had done, he felt proud. His brother had avenged him. In doing so, Andrew cemented his role as Michael's hero.

"So George told you this Terry guy won't even meet with you?" Caesar asked, placing a domino on the table.

"Fuck that Terry bitch! How's he going to just turn me down without a meeting?" Michael complained.

He had tried setting up a meeting with Jason so he could get some of the high-quality weed flooding the town. Jason wasn't interested.

"Probably doesn't help that he's nailing your girl," Andrew chuckled, sipping his beer. He motioned at the dominoes. "Your move, chump."

"Man, fuck this game! I'm tired of this bullshit. I can't sell this shit weed, and this pussy-ass chump is nailing my girl and hogging all the good stuff!"

The thought of someone else touching her caused his blood to rise.

Andrew laughed at his little brother's temper.

"So do something. Be a man, little boy. Solve your fucking problems."

"I oughta shoot the fuckin' kid," Michael replied. He immediately looked to his brother to gauge his reaction, but Andrew just stared at the dominoes and sipped his beer.

"You could, sure, but they'd lay it on you for sure. How is that goin' to get you his weed, bro? Be smart."

"We rob him?" Michael asked, now wholly unconcerned with the game.

"Now you're thinking." Andrew lit a joint and handed it to him. "It's good shit, too. I had that Tim kid grab me some. Apparently, he's Terry's cousin or some shit."

"How do we rob him? I don't know much about his operation," asked Michael.

"Then that's what we need to focus on; finding out more about his operation. Forget that beat-up skank," Andrew said.

The words hit Michael hard, causing a sudden tightness in his chest and shortness of breath. Andrew was his hero, and Maegan was the only girl he'd ever loved. He didn't know how to process hearing him speak badly of her. It made him angry.

"Yo, don't talk about her like that." He looked defiantly at Andrew, but his brother ignored him.

"Bitch is a cum guzzling tramp," Andrew said to Caesar with a nudge. Caesar laughed.

"Where's Eddie?" Caesar asked.

"In back with that Jenn girl we picked up," Michael said, making a dick sucking gesture with his fist and mouth.

All three laughed. Moments later they were alarmed to hear a screaming from the back of the house.

"Fucking whore!" Eddie's voice bellowed, followed by the desperate cry of a young woman.

The three exchanged baffled looks. The girl shrieked again, and then there was a loud *crash* and the sound of shattering glass.

"Eddie!" Andrew exclaimed as they rushed to the back bedroom.

They burst through the door and found Eddie naked on the floor, straddling a petite Hispanic girl who was also nude, pounding her face repeatedly with his giant fists. Bits of broken glass from the mirror above the dresser covered the floor, cutting into her back and his knees as he pummeled her.

Michael couldn't believe how hard he was punching her. Her little, delicate face was breaking before his eyes with each blow. They leaped to tackle him off of her. It took all three men to wrestle him away and pin him to the ground. Once he was finally subdued, Andrew checked the girl. He gave her a little shake, but she laid still and unresponsive. Her face was shattered; her nose flattened, her teeth broken. Her left eye was protruding from its socket, and the right was swollen shut. She was quickly turning purple, blood pouring from her nose and mouth onto the floor.

Seeing the damage he'd done, Eddie began to panic.

"Ahh God damn it!" he cursed.

"What happened?" Andrew asked emphatically.

"Holy shit," Caesar exclaimed, looking at the bloodied mess of a girl on the floor. "She agreed to fuck me for a dub bag. Then I fell asleep," he

71

explained. "I woke up and found her going through my dresser, helping herself to my cash, so I put her through the fucking mirror."

Michael knelt down next to her and placed his ear near her mouth to listen for breath.

"She's still alive," he proclaimed. "She's still breathing."

Andrew grabbed a pillow off of the bed and handed it to Eddie.

"Finish her off."

"What?" Eddie asked in disbelief. "No way, dude. I can't just kill her."

"Oh, but you'll beat her to a bloody fucking pulp," Andrew said, pushing the pillow into Eddie's arms.

A chilling silence followed while all four men contemplated the situation.

"What do you think happened here? This is *your* mess!" Andrew barked at Eddie. "Clean it the fuck up, or you'll become my problem to deal with."

"Shit bro…" Michael said. Even he felt bad for the girl.

"What, bro?" Andrew barked at Michael. "You want to call the cops? Is that what you both want to do here? Call the police? We'll all go to jail, and Eddie, you'll be put away for a long time. But hey, if that's what you want…" Andrew held his phone out for either of them to grab. No one did. "You sure? Tomorrow's taco night in Niantic, motherfuckers. I'll call the cops right now. I could go for tacos."

There it was again. He had been to prison, he wasn't afraid of it, and he knew they were.

Eddie took a deep breath and knelt down next to her. Caesar shook his head and left the room.

Eddie looked up at both brothers, his face heavy with regret and hesitation. Andrew nodded encouragingly.

Michael felt like he was going to be sick. He quickly left the room as Eddie suffocated the poor girl. She'd come there for a good time, only to die naked on the floor, surrounded by people she did not know.

She didn't put up a fight. The beating had nearly killed her already.

Chapter Three
THE BABYSITTER

"Girls, please!" Dickey called up the stairs. "Hurry up!"

He was returning to work that morning and couldn't drive the girls to school. As such, they had to be ready earlier so they could catch the bus.

"Be sure to walk your sister to her preschool class, okay sweetie?" he told Marie before the girls boarded the bus. "Stacey, baby, grandma is going to pick you up, okay?"

She nodded her head, and he hugged them both tightly.

"I love you girls. The babysitter will be here when grandma drops you off."

He kissed them both and sent them off. The bus pulled away, leaving a cloud of exhaust hanging in the moist morning air.

Dickey lit a cigarette and sat down on his porch, savoring every moment he could before going back to a job for which he felt increasing disdain. He pulled out his cell phone and tried his brother, but received no answer. Normally he couldn't be bothered to worry about what his brother was up to, but that day he was concerned. George's friend, Shane, whom he usually hung around with, had stopped by the day before looking for him. Even more concerning, George's Social Security check remained unclaimed on the kitchen table. Dickey had reason to believe his brother had once again gotten himself into trouble.

He tried to shrug off concern for George—something that had gotten easier with time—and dialed the girls' babysitter. When she didn't answer, he left a message asking her to call him if she needed a ride. "I can have Jason or somebody grab you and swing you over to the house if you need, I just need to know as soon as possible so I can arrange it. So, give me a call. Thank you."

The breeze came in, rustling the two giant white pines across his driveway. Dickey stared up at the stoic trees and shook his head.

"Grown too big for your own good now," he said to the trees, exhaling smoke through his nose. He related to them. "Yanked up by the sun yet fighting for light your entire life… And now the only place left to go is down."

THE DESKMAN AT THE Sheraton Hotel in Windsor had probably never seen such a motley crew of visitors like the one that came and went from George Calloway's room: straggly men with gaunt statures, vacant eyes, and ghostly complexions along with women who looked like workers from a slummy strip club.

Normally, such an endless parade of unwanted types would cause the hotel to intercede, but this guest was spending a lot of money. He had booked their nicest suite and was feeding all his guests from the hotel kitchen. The staff had begun to believe he must be some sort of grunge rocker or movie star.

Of course, George Calloway was no rock star. He was a man of many vices and little self-control; a man who was enjoying his newly earned revenue stream. Thanks to an envelope stuffed with pills, George was having the time of his life. Every day he sold pills, snorted pills, and handed out pills like candy to friends.

There's a term for when people who aren't used to money suddenly come into more than they're accustomed to and proceed to spend it like fools: *ghetto rich*. For those who become ghetto rich, living for even a short while like they're wealthy is too tempting. Considerations of fiscal responsibility are sacrificed in the pursuit of instant gratification. Everyone has spent money they shouldn't have in the heat of the moment, but not everyone blows through ten grand partying with their friends at an airport hotel. George hadn't realized it yet, but his money was dwindling, and so was his envelope.

"Nothing's happening!" Rachel Adams told George from the floor.

"Slow down and little and give it some time," George replied.

They had dated in high school and were on and off ever since. It never worked out; they were too alike. They both lived to party, and together they fed each other's demons.

"Nothing's happening!" she said again in frustration. She looked up and rested her arms on his legs. "You're too high." She tucked his flaccid penis back into his pants. "I tried," she said. "Give me another pill."

"You know where they are," George said, lighting a cigarette. "But you owe me a hummer."

"Well, let me know when little George wakes up," she said.

She staggered across the suite's master bedroom to the closet and dug into George's suitcase. At one time she was the prettiest girl in Colebrook, a fact anyone who met her today would be pressed to believe. Her blonde hair was thinning, her skin wrinkled and leathery, and all her teeth were rotten. She had always been skinny, now she was gaunt.

"Crush one up for me, too, baby," George requested.

She grabbed a mortar and pestle from the bedside table and began to crush up two Oxys. When she was done, she knocked the powder out onto a magazine and used a razor to chops the clumps up. She cut two lines and handed the magazine and a rolled-up hundred dollar bill to George. He snorted half his line up his left nostril, the rest up the right. His eyes watered and his face became flush. He rubbed his nose vigorously and sniffed, waiting for the burn to subside. Rachel followed suit.

76

There was a knock on the bedroom door. Rachel put a satin robe on and answered it. It was George's friend, Shane.

"We're out of pills, man," Shane said, looking past Rachel.

George, feeling the effects of the Oxy even more after his last line, slowly motioned for Shane to come in.

"Baby, give him ten pills for the group," George mumbled.

"I tell you, buddy, you had me scared when you just disappeared," Shane said as Rachel retrieved the pills.

"Living the dream," George laughed.

"Yeah, I even stopped by Dickey's looking for you."

"Why would you do that?" George asked, trying to sit up. "Stay the fuck away from that house," he said. He rubbed his eyes with his hands and shook his head. "Stay the fuck away from there," he repeated, waving his finger at Shane. "You got me?"

"Yeah, man, I — I thought you were dead or something," Shane stammered.

"Don't matter if I was. Why do you think I stay away? Best thing I can do for those girls is keep me and you and all of this away from them." George shook his head, upset, but close to nodding out. "I'll fucking kill you… Don't ever."

George's eyes shut as he drifted fast asleep while Shane watched. Rachel handed him the pills and shook her head.

"He's been partying really hard the past few days. Don't listen to him," she said, patting Shane on the back.

He nodded, put the pills in his pocket, and left the room.

JASON PULLED INTO MAEGAN'S mother's driveway and kissed her goodbye.

She smiled and blushed. He made her feel beautiful and deserving of love.

"You sure you don't want me to help you move?" Jason asked, bewildered.

"Listen," Maegan said with a sigh. "My uncle is kind of a state cop."

"So what?" Jason asked.

"He's Colebrook's resident trooper."

"Wait," Jason's eyes widened. "Evans?! *That's* your uncle?"

"Yeah, and he kind of knows all about you and isn't your biggest fan," she said, nervously tucking her hair behind her ear with her fingers.

"Yeah, he busted me once," Jason said in disbelief.

"He didn't tell me that," she said. "What happened?"

"Pulled me over for speeding, my car smelt like weed—I had *just* finished a huge joint. He pulled my car apart and found a couple pre-bagged eighths. Charged me with intent to sell. I argued in court that I had purchased them that way and it was for personal use. I got it thrown out after doing some community service and completing a drug class."

"Well, I guess I can't blame him for not liking you," she said.

"What?" Jason scoffed. "He's an overzealous jackboot who searched my car without a warrant."

"Well, he was just doing his job, and you were breaking the law."

She'd had her own issues with the law, but that didn't matter. She knew her uncle was a good man and a good cop.

"Yeah, I guess I was," Jason conceded. "So, how is this going to affect us?" he asked.

"It won't," she said, leaning over and kissing him again. "He knows I'm with you. It's fine. He doesn't like it, and you won't be invited for dinner, but it doesn't matter," she assured him.

"I suppose living with a cop is better than your environment here," he concluded. "I will see you later, right?"

"It's a date," she agreed.

They kissed, and she jumped out of his wagon and headed for the house.

Maegan's older brother, Kaleb, was waiting for her on the porch. His dark green eyes glared at her with contempt from under the brim of a beat up RedSox hat.

"What, did you come by to yell at me?" she asked, climbing the front steps.

"Figured someone has to try and talk sense into you," he told her. "You're running away, going to live with Uncle Dwight?" He lit a smoke a sighed.

"Sure as hell ain't my responsibility to deal with her shit," Maegan protested.

"What about Danny?" Kaleb asked, motioning inside. "He's fifteen years old, what about him?"

"What the fuck am I supposed to do?" Maegan barked. "You got out. You started a family. Don't you dare tell me I have to stay here and deal with this shit!"

"Listen, Meg, I don't want to fight. I got Marissa pregnant; I had to leave. And I didn't come here to yell at you. Mom asked me to come here." He sat down on a grungy porch chair and sighed. "She wanted me to take Danny. Pled with me. She's going to bury herself when you leave. Your not being here… She has no reason to keep up the façade."

"You're taking Danny?" she asked, guilt clutching her voice.

"No, I can't," he said. "No room and even less money."

They sat in silence for a few moments, each of them thinking about their responsibility to their family and their conflicting need to get as far away from it as possible.

"I'm an addict, Kaleb," she said. "I can't go through this. Uncle Dwight knows that."

"I know," he said, nodding his head slowly and staring at the floor. "You were young, you probably don't remember when dad and mom used to fight."

Maegan took a seat next to him, grabbed the pack of cigarettes from the breast pocket of his flannel, and lit one as he spoke. She had heard things growing up, but everyone had always kept the details from her.

"They screamed at each other daily, but that was nothing," he continued. "They would fight, Maegan — and I mean *fight.* It was always something, you know? There was this dread… Coming home from second grade on the bus, sick to my stomach about what I was about to walk into. I used to think they would kill each other."

"Jesus…" Maegan didn't know it had been that bad.

"You were just a baby — maybe two years old, at the most," Kaleb recalled. "Mom and dad started fighting about a fucking cake."

"A cake?"

"Yeah, a cake. He had bought one of those frozen chocolate cakes from the store and mom got pissed when he gave me some before dinner. Not a big deal. I'm sure in normal families it wouldn't have been the cause of violence, but in our family it was." He shook his head and sighed, tears building in his eyes. "So dad picks mom up and slams her against the wall and starts choking her—I mean he's squeezing her throat so hard her face is turning purple. And I started screaming '*Daddy! Daddy! Don't hurt mommy! Leave her alone!*'" Kaleb sobbed and took a deep breath. "And finally, it's like he hears me, he stops… Or, at least, he loosens his grip and then *bam!!* Mom punches him square in the nose, breaks his nose, then she knees him in the balls."

"Holy shit," was the only response Maegan could muster.

"So, mom takes me, grabs my hand and we run back to your room to grab you from your crib, and then we bolted for the door. We got in the car and sped away. It was absolutely terrifying."

"What happened?" asked Maegan.

"We went to stay at grandma's, and a couple of days later mom told me we were going home, she and daddy had worked it out. She said that daddy wasn't going to be around for a while, that he was going to stay with some friends. I remember being relieved he was gone, and hoping he wouldn't come back. Unfortunately, he did," Kaleb said, using the end of his lit cigarette to light another before tossing it onto the lawn. "We were eating dinner. Dad walked in calm as I'd ever seen him. He walked up to us at the table, said hello, and then he pulled out a gun and shot her four times."

"*What?!*" Maegan was shocked. She had never known her mother suffered abuse, let alone attempted murder.

"Then he pointed the gun at me, told me to keep my mouth shut. Then he just left. I called nine-one-one and waited beside mom in a pool of her blood for them to arrive."

"Holy shit! Where was I?"

"She had put you down for a nap not long before," he replied.

"*Four times?!*"

"She got lucky. First shot hit her right above her left collarbone, went clear through and knocked her to the ground. The three shots he fired to finish the job hit her in the ass, her leg, and the back of her right shoulder. Mom spent two weeks in the hospital."

"Holy shit," Maegan was stunned. "Why didn't anybody ever tell me this?"

"Mom didn't want you or Danny to know. I guess she figured we could spare you the pain of knowing your dad tried to kill your mom."

"Holy shit, Kaleb," she looked at him, tears pouring from her eyes. "Do you think your problems…?"

"That's when the bed wetting started, the nightmares, the anger issues. Yeah, I think it all connects somewhere, you know? I still wake up in the night screaming, at least three times a week. Marissa hates it."

"Screaming?"

"'Mommy,' I scream 'mommy' in my sleep. Wakes her up."

She grabbed him and hugged him, the first time she had done so in years. After a moment, he welcomed the embrace and hugged her back, both sobbing.

"What I'm trying to tell you," Kaleb said, wiping his face dry with his shirt sleeve, "is that mom has had a hard life."

"She shouldn't have married a scumbag from a biker gang," Maegan said condescendingly.

"But, if she hadn't, neither of us would be here," he countered.

"Maybe we'd be better off," she remarked. She could not explain it, but somehow this revelation had stirred up even more animosity toward her mother.

"We all have our struggles, Meg. It's the lot we've been cast. We have to do our best to fix what needs fixing in ourselves and move on. Get a job, get your own place, and take Danny with you," he suggested.

"He doesn't want to go anywhere. Maybe in time he will change his mind. Right now, I gotta get out here before she takes me downhill with her," she explained.

"Alright," Kaleb said, nodding slowly. "You need help moving?"

"Please!" she said with a faint laugh. "Dwight's bringing the truck down later, but if you want to use your truck and bring a load up there in the meantime."

"Alright, but only because I feel bad for yelling at you," Kaleb said with a grin.

"NO, IT ISN'T CANCEROUS... It's just a tumor. A fairly large one, Mom. That's just it; it's in a very tough spot in the brain.... It means it's risky.... Well, I don't know. Very risky. Yeah, I mean, I probably have at least a year or two if I don't, but if I do it and they make a mistake, or it doesn't work, that's it..."

Dwight spoke into the receiver of his phone as he sat by a glass of Scotch, alone at his kitchen table, in the dark. He broke down the details like he was explaining the facts of a case.

"I get headaches. Sometimes I hear things that aren't really there. It's hard to explain… I know…. Well, I appreciate your prayers. Tell Dad I love him. I love you, too. I'll come down to Kentucky soon and see you both…. Okay, Mom, love you." He hung up the phone and took his drink.

"Looks like neither of us is long for this world, partner," he said to Max.

The sounds had started a few years ago. Dwight would hear chirping or a high pitched whistle that sounded like a teapot. The headaches had started about a year later; blinding, piercing migraines which would leave him in bed for days. There seemed to be no rhyme or reason to their occurrence. Finally, after ignoring the matter for some time, a brain scan revealed *it*. The unwanted intruder — a tumor that was growing on his brain. It was a harbinger of mortal ends; an insult to his very being, which somehow magnified his every failure, regret, and wasted moment.

He had avoided speaking to his father about it at all. He tried to reason with himself as to why, but the truth was he was ashamed — ashamed of his fear. His father was a fighter. If his father had a tumor, the old man might have to been stopped from cutting it out himself. No hesitation would be given when it came to surgery, not in the face of a threat so grave. But Dwight had been putting off seeing the surgeon and scheduling an appointment for the operation.

There was a knock at his door. Max's ears perked as he sat up. Dwight peeked out the window then got up to open the door.

"Relax buddy, it's only Maegan and Kaleb."

Dwight helped them unload Kaleb's truck and offered to make coffee when they were finished.

"I have to get going," Kaleb explained. "But it was good to see you," he added before saying his goodbyes.

"I could sure use a cup," Maegan replied after Kaleb had left.

Dwight nodded, put his arm around her, and they walked to the kitchen. Max followed behind, eager for Maegan's attention.

His house was a small cape. The ground floor was comprised of the living, kitchen, and dining room. Upstairs were two bedrooms and a bathroom. Maegan would be taking the second bedroom, but until Dwight had time to move her bed, she would be sleeping on the couch.

"I'll get the bed tomorrow or the next day at the latest," Dwight assured her as he poured her a cup of coffee.

"Mom is definitely using again," Maegan told him. "I can tell by the way she acts."

"I was afraid that was the case," he replied. "Sugar?"

"Just a little cream, please," she said.

"I'm sorry, Maegan," he said, placing his hand on her shoulder. "I know how much you love her."

"No, really, it's fine. She'll be in detox before we know it and then I'll get that house cleaned up."

"You would go back?" he asked.

"Well, someone has to look after Danny," she said.

"Maegan, I asked Danny to come live here. He won't return my calls. I think he's angry at me, but I still want him to come."

"He won't," she insisted. "He doesn't like cops. Or accepting help."

"That house is not a healthy place for him to be, either," Dwight said.

"I know, I'll stop by and check in on him."

"Just don't put yourself around anything you shouldn't be around, Maegan. You can't. Whether it's your mother or anyone else. Don't put yourself in bad situations."

He wanted her to listen so badly, but he knew she was stubborn and didn't want to push her away, either. His head still hurt; the ringing was back and getting louder.

"I'm not," she said, petting Max. "I spend most of my time with Jason."

"He's a drug dealer, Meg,"

"It's just a little pot. Nothing big. Relax. Don't be such a cop with me," she said with a laugh. She gazed at his drink and the bottle of aspirin sitting on the counter. "Headaches still? You should see a doctor."

"Yeah…" he said as he spooned some sugar into his cup of coffee. He noticed the pack of cigarettes protruding from her back pocket. "Got a smoke?" he asked.

"Since when did you start again?" she asked, retrieving her pack from her pocket and handing him one.

"Some things you just miss, no matter how bad they are, I guess," he said.

"Isn't that right? Always the things we know are bad for us, too…"

"Drugs, booze…"

"Men…"

"Women…" he chuckled. He used her lighter to light the smoke.

"Still not dating?" she asked with a curious smile.

"I just don't have time, I guess."

"You seem pretty free right now," she replied coyly. "I mean, what do you do after work?" she asked with a chuckle.

"I guess after the divorce, I just never really got into the dating thing… Wouldn't know where to start."

"At least you got Maxie-boy," Maegan said, petting him affectionately.

"That's for sure. Wouldn't know what to do without him."

Maegan lit a smoke herself and sat down at the kitchen table with her coffee. "Kaleb told me what happened to mom when I was a baby," she told him, scanning him closely to gauge his reaction.

"You mean what your father did." He sat down beside her and placed his hand on her leg, "I wanted to tell you, but really, I didn't believe it was my place."

She understood, but it still hurt. She had always believed she could trust him; that he was the only person who was honest with her.

"It's okay," she said after a few moments. "What happened to my dad?" she asked.

"He served seven years in Niantic, then was paroled. A few years later he moved out to California. No idea where he is now or if he is even alive."

"And what about Danny's father? He just vanished one day, and we never heard from him again."

"Prison, for at least another five years," Dwight said, shaking his head. "He got caught bringing a large amount of cocaine into the state."

"Christ, mom picks winners, huh?" she asked with a cackle.

"Always has," he agreed. "I hated your father, threatened his life once," Dwight recalled.

"You didn't," Maegan said in disbelief.

"Oh, I did. Unfortunately, I didn't follow through."

"Wait—You actually threatened to kill my father?" Maegan asked. Her eyes were wide, her mouth slightly agape in awe. "For real?"

"I used to think about it quite often, to be honest. That's when he was using your mother as a punching bag," he confessed. "Sometimes I wish I had. Your mom nearly died, and she got worse afterward. She was a drunken fool before, and yeah there were drugs, but after the attack, that's when she really went downhill."

"Do you think you could ever do something like that?" she asked skeptically.

"Apparently not," Dwight answered.

"You can't blame yourself for that, or for what happened to mom," she told him.

He put out his cigarette.

"I really shouldn't smoke," he said with a sigh. He could not resign himself to his fate just yet.

"HI JENNIFER, THIS IS MISTER CALLOWAY calling again. Just checking because I have not heard from you and it is Monday, so it's one of your nights with the girls… Just call me back, because I need to know if you need a ride… Okay, thanks."

Dickey hung up his cell phone.

He grabbed his ham sandwich off the dash of his work truck and took a bite. As he ate, he watched a few members of his crew feed pieces of a downed tree limb into the chipper. After his sandwich, he tried to reach his brother on the phone with no luck.

There were only twenty minutes left of his lunch break, and Dickey had to figure out who was going to watch the girls that night. He dialed up Jason to see if he was free.

"What's up, bro?" Jason asked when he answered.

"Can you watch the girls tonight, feed them and hang out with them for a few hours till I get home?" Dickey asked.

"I was supposed to go see Iron-Man with Maegan, but we could do a later showing. Where's the babysitter?"

"I can't get ahold of her, which is weird because she usually needs a ride on Mondays."

"So, there is a chance she'll show up," Jason replied.

"I don't think so. She normally answers my calls. I don't know what's going."

"Did you call her parents?"

"No, you think I should?"

"I don't know, man. Kids will be kids; she's probably off with a boyfriend somewhere," Jason said with a laugh. "Listen, don't worry about it. I love spending time with my nieces," he added.

"Alright, be at the house for three. That's when their grandmother is dropping them off."

"Will do, buddy."

"Hey, you seen George?" Dickey asked before hanging up.

"Nope, but you're not the only one looking for him," Jason replied.

"How's that?"

"Lots of people asking, not sure what's going on. He's gone and pissed someone off."

"I figured as much," Dickey said with a sigh. "Alright, I'll see you later, brother."

THE GIRLS WERE ECSTATIC to see Jason sitting on the porch when their grandmother dropped them at home. He knew enough to enjoy their enthusiasm while it lasted. One day too soon, they would be teenagers and have no time for him. He hugged them affectionately and carried them inside.

"Where's Jennifer?" Marie asked him.

"I don't know, but your dad asked me to come hang out with you guys, so I thought that was pretty cool. Don't you?" he said, kissing her cheek.

She smiled and nodded.

"Because we're family and that's what families do," he added. "We take care of each other, and we're always there for each other," he said, kissing her and her sister again before letting them down.

At least, that's how Jason thought a family was supposed to work. He didn't know firsthand. Dickey and his girls were the only family he'd ever had. It was a family he had chosen. To him, that meant more than blood ever could.

WYATT MAYHEW'S APARTMENT was on the north end of Torrington, about a mile up the road from the police station. The second floor flat overlooked a busy street, a credit union, and a package store. It wasn't a particularly great view, but Wyatt still found respite in sitting on his porch while he smoked and drank.

The house his apartment was in was a large two-family built in the 19th century, which was common for the neighborhood. And, like most of the homes in his neighborhood, it was at one time a lovely house which now stood in need of repair. The paint was peeling and chipped, the wooden fencing; old and moldy, and the roof; worn and weathered. Such had become standard for Torrington. Nice homes slowly deteriorating while property taxes rose and businesses left, creating more blighted properties and, of course, leaving less revenue for the city.

He remembered when this place had seemed immune to the problems that plagued it today. There was a time when he was young that Torrington had industry; when taxes were affordable and families wanted to plant roots there. Now empty factories blighted every view, and empty businesses stood out like ghosts—a haunting reminder of their economic reality. Everything was dying around them, and most were unaware of the true fate they faced, like frogs being slowly cooked to death.

Death, ironically enough, was the only business that seemed to be doing well. Wyatt often joked that the nicest buildings in Torrington were funeral parlors. The business of death was one immune to economic recessions. There was a time not long ago when Wyatt had believed his job was also immune — "people will always need cops," he used to say. It turns out, despite how imperative their jobs were, police officers were generally not appreciated. When the government runs short on money, cops can indeed get laid off. So far, TPD had avoided any job cuts, but state's budget projections didn't bode well. More cuts were bound to come, which would impact the city's budget. Less money could mean fewer cops on the streets, and that was the last thing the town needed.

If anything, Torrington needed more cops but they weren't going to get them. Crime rates were up, from petty theft and drug possession to armed robbery and murder. The town was awash with heroin, with addiction feeding much of the crime. Homelessness was a huge problem. Twenty years ago, you could count the number of homeless on one hand. Now a tent city had been established not far from Wyatt's apartment. The shantytown had sprung up in the woods behind to the old A-Mart, a clothing and department store chain that had shut its doors years ago.

Wyatt held his beer high in the air to salute a passing black and blue. The officer driving flashed his lights quickly to acknowledge him. *Torrington's finest*, Wyatt thought with a smile. Most of them were good cops, even if many were young and naïve. He finished his beer and crushed the can in his fist before tossing it into a bucket full of crushed cans. He hated his days off—nothing to do but get drunk and think.

He lit a smoke and wandered back inside. The apartment was nice, though bigger than he needed for one person and mostly empty. Hardwood floors and solid Maple trim gave the place a cozy feel. There was a time when Wyatt had expected to share the place, but that had never come to be. Things hadn't worked out with her. She had never liked that he was a cop and he didn't know what else to be.

Being a detective was the only thing he was ever really good at. He didn't do it for the pay, or for the pursuit of glory. He did it because it burned inside him. The desire to protect and the willingness to fight against what was wrong in the world blinded him to anything else. His obsession and stubbornness proved to be valuable tools and set him apart from the pack as a detective. *Maybe that was also what drove her away.*

He grabbed a can of soup from the cupboard, poured it into a bowl, and popped it in the microwave for two minutes. *Another thrilling dinner in terrific company.* While he waited for the soup, he grabbed another beer from the fridge and cracked the top. Then, being a man of habit, Wyatt sat down to eat his dinner and watch the five o'clock news.

90

The lead story was about the mayor signing a resolution that allocated funding for a drug called Narcan, designed to block opioid censors and save a person's life during a heroin overdose. The city was going to pay to have this drug available to all emergency personnel.

"We need to take proactive steps to ensure we save lives," Mayor Delvalle said. "This puts us in a position to address the problem," he continued.

The statement was enough for Wyatt to swear out loud and turn off the TV. How was saving people already addicted to poison addressing the problem? How was spending money to do so good for the city? The town was drowning in heroin, and most of it was coming from the same source. He wanted to get tougher on drug dealers and track the suppliers down, but he got stonewalled or slowed down with red tape every time. The State Police had been conducting a RICO investigation with the feds for more than six months, and nearly every lead Wyatt got was swallowed up by them. They took all his work and intel and left him in the cold.

Nobody wanted him to do his job. He couldn't track down the heroin supply because the State Police pulled rank on him. He couldn't bust up the tent city full of addicts and degenerates because, heaven forbid, people might get upset. Sometimes he felt as if he were being strapped down and made to watch the town slowly die.

C'MON! YOU ALWAYS SNORT IT, DUDE! This is so much better," Tim said, tying a piece of cloth around Travis's right arm.

"Are you sure, bro?" Travis asked nervously.

"Yeah, man, it's *so* good!" Tim grabbed his arm and slapped it a few times to get his veins popping. "There you are," he said, grabbing the needle he had ready to go. "Relax, bro. Just breathe, it's going to be better than sex."

He slowly pushed the needle into Travis's vein and pulled the plunger back ever so gently. Blood filled the syringe, mixing with the heroin to purposely dilute it. Then he pushed the plunger in, sending the heroin-mixed blood into Travis's vein. Travis sat up a little and his eyes nearly rolled back into his head. He smiled as the euphoria washed over him. He felt weightless and relaxed. Tim released the tourniquet.

"Woow!" Travis managed to say as he slumped back into his couch.

"I told you, bro!" Tim laughed, shaking him as he began to nod off.

Tim then tied off his own arm and shot a second syringe he had prepared for himself. Soon both boys were passed out on the couch together, which was not their intent, and not what Travis's parents expected to find when they came home.

Travis came to when his father yanked him off the couch and into the air by his shirt, screaming angrily in his face. Travis couldn't make out what he was saying or why he was mad.

Tim slowly opened his eyes to see Travis's father smacking Travis around, but fell back to sleep. He tried to open his eyes again, knowing that what he had just seen was important, but by the time he did, Travis's father was gone and Travis was lying on the floor in pain. Tim looked up and saw Travis's mother crying, but then fell back asleep.

"Come on! Come on! We gotta go!!" Travis said, shaking him awake moments later. Tim began to recognize where he was and what was happening, albeit slowly. Travis continued to yell and pull at him. "My dad is calling the cops, come on!!!"

The thought of cops caused Tim to sober up a bit. He shook his head, and tried to stand up, but nearly fell. Travis helped him, and the two made their way down the stairs and out the front door. As they got to the end of the drive, Tim brushed off Travis's help and the two began jogging away.

"And don't fucking come back, either!" Travis's dad shouted from the front door. *"Fucking junkies!!"*

THE TRIVOTY HOUSE ON RECKON AVENUE was packed and raucous that evening. Andrew and Caesar had returned from Hartford earlier with a whole car full of girls following them.

Despite Andrew's best efforts, Eddie was not in the mood for partying. The giant sat alone, staring grimly at the ground. Occasionally Andrew would bring a pretty girl over to him, and he would smile and wave his hand to decline.

"C'mon, man, you got to get that fuckin' puta off your mind," Andrew told him.

"Just not feeling it tonight," Eddie replied. He wasn't the only one. Michael was noticeably down, too.

"What the hell is wrong with you two?" Andrew asked, laughing and shaking his head. "Don't tell me you're going soft on me!"

"I'm just not in the mood," Eddie said gruffly.

"I've been trying to get ahold of Maegan all day," Michael said, showing his brother the phone in his hand.

The truth was that Michael was still haunted by the image of the girl Eddie had beaten and smothered, but he didn't want his brother to know that. He could see the way he was looking at Eddie as if he was a disgrace. It was better that Andrew believed Maegan was all that was on his mind.

"Man, fuck that puta. We've got fine bitches right here," Andrew said, grabbing his brother's arm and shaking him. Michael just shook his head. "Man, you two are crazy," Andrew said with a dismissive laugh, turning back to Caesar and the girls dancing in the backyard.

"Doesn't even faze him," Eddie said.

"Huh?" Michael asked, shocked anyone would utter such a thing out loud. *Was he criticizing Andrew?*

"No, I'm just saying. Boy's hard as nails," Eddie replied.

"Damn right," Michael said, the image of the girl's swollen, broken face in his head.

He shook the thought away and tried to text message Maegan yet again. After a few minutes, he tried to call her. She didn't answer so he decided to leave a message.

"Maegan, girl why you do this to me? Don't be like this. After everything we've been through, you're going to pull this shit? Running around with some white bread pussy-ass bitch, pretending you're something you're not. Don't forget what you are, Maegan! Don't forget what you are. You're no better than me. When you're ready to admit that, you call me. You call me, Meg. I love you, girl."

"THAT WAS A GREAT MOVIE!" Maegan exclaimed as she and Jason walked out of the theater toward his car. .

"I definitely agree. Way better than the second one," Jason replied.

"No, for sure. The second one sucked," Maegan laughed, stopping to smile affectionately at him before getting into the car.

For all her faults, she could not understand how someone like him had fallen for her. Surely, she thought, such a caring and kind man could find someone that didn't have the demons and baggage she had. Yet he looked at her as no other man had. He looked at her like she deserved his best. It was a nice thought, even if she didn't completely believe it.

They drove for a while until they hit dirt roads, where Jason found a pullover nestled among some pines near a brook. Once parked, he popped the hatch so they could sit and smoke. She snuggled in close to him, and he put his arm around her, handing her the joint to light.

"It's beautiful here," she said, listening to the crickets chirp.

She wondered if he'd brought other girls to this spot.

"Yeah, a little-known place I like to come and think," he replied.

They smoked for a bit in silence, just enjoying each other's company. She felt as if she should say something—anything—to break the silence. Before she had a chance, he put a finger under her chin and delicately turned her head toward his. He kissed her softly. She smiled and wrapped her arms around his neck, tossing the joint to the darkness. Nudging closer, she threw her leg over him as he pulled her onto his lap. Passionately, their mouths interlocked and their hands grabbed for each other, their breath growing heavier as he slid his hand up the back of her shirt, massaging and caressing her.

She pulled away and lifted her shirt off, tossing it into the car with a laugh. He looked at her, drunk with desire, and pulled her close. She slid his shirt off and sunk her fingers into the flesh of his back as he slowly kissed her breasts and worked his way up to her neck with his mouth.

He stopped to admire her beauty, lightly brushing the back of his fingers along her neck, down her breasts, and over her stomach. He unbuttoned her jeans, teasingly running his fingertips beneath the top of her panties.

She laughed slightly, tickled from the touch, and pushed him gently onto his back. Standing up outside the car as he laid in the back, she pulled his pants off with haste before falling to her knees. Jason moaned as she used her mouth to pleasure and tease him. Then she stood up, slid her pants off, and climbed into the back of the station wagon on her knees. Jason laid flat on his back and allowed her to straddle him.

"This is where you take all the girls, isn't?" she asked with a grin.

"This is where I take the pretty ones, at least," he smirked.

They kissed and she tried to sit up, but hit her head.

"Careful," he laughed. "Here, lay down," Jason said, pulling her down and turning her around so she was on her back.

He lifted her leg and softly kissed her inner thigh, then he did so again with more force, letting his teeth lightly grabbed at her flesh. He kissed his way up to her labia and licked it gently. She shivered ever so slightly.

Jason continued to use his tongue to please her. After some time, Maegan moaned and her legs jerked uncontrollably. She grabbed the back of the seat and sunk in her nails.

"Oh God! Don't stop!" she pleaded with him.

He obliged, and her moaning became louder. Then with what sounded almost like a whimper, her body tensed up and then went completely limp. She let out a sigh of relief as her breathing raced to catch up with her.

Jason laid beside her and kissed her on her forehead. "Was it good?" he asked.

"Mmmm," was all she could manage to say.

He rolled her over onto her side and adjusted himself. With a firm but slow thrust, he entered her from the back. She moaned with delight as he fucked her from behind, his arm embracing her tightly until he too had climaxed.

Afterward, they laid still on their sides—Jason caressing her while gently running his fingers through her hair.

"I wish we could stay like this," she said. "I wish we could freeze time right here, right now."

"But then we would miss all the good times we have to come," Jason replied.

"No, this is perfect. Right now. Life will only fuck it up if given a chance—like it does with everything."

"Not this time," he promised.

She wanted to believe him, but she knew better.

ASPIRIN WASN'T CUTTING IT ANYMORE. Dwight had called in the big guns: Dilaudid washed down with a lot of whiskey. The ringing in his head was enough to drive him mad, but at least that was something with which he could live. The pain, however, seemed to be getting worse with each passing day. He sat on the back porch, Max lying by his feet, and set to finishing his fifth of Jack Daniels.

Is this it? Am I dying?

He closed his eyes for what seemed like just a moment. When he opened them, his pain was gone. Oddly, he could still hear the ringing, which now somehow seemed to be coming from afar. A thick fog had rolled in, so thick that Dwight couldn't see his yard. He cautiously moved through the fog, following the ringing.

Soon, he was on the road. The ringing ceased, and Dwight became irrationally concerned. Suddenly, a flash of lightning revealed a shadowy figure on the road. The figure whistled at him antagonistically—a whistle almost identical in tone to the ringing that haunted him. Thunder bellowed, shaking the ground beneath Dwight's feet. The figure laughed menacingly, and Dwight felt paralyzed with fear. Lightning flashed again, illuminating the street and everything around them brightly as day. Except for the figure, he remained black as night.

Before Dwight could understand what was happening to him, the figure began to quickly advance on him. Dwight reached for his gun, but his holster was empty. He retreated frantically toward the house, desperately trying to remember where he had left his gun. Was he drunk? He could barely think, let alone move his legs.

Thunder shook the house as Dwight approached it, followed by a blood-curdling scream. *Maegan!* He grabbed at the backdoor, but it was locked. He heard the dark figure's insidious laugh mocking him. He heard the awful whistling, this time from inside the house. Drawing upon all his might and concentration, he kicked the door in and rushed inside. The figure laughed, but was nowhere to be found. Maegan's lifeless body lied motionless on his couch. He collected her body in his arms and cried out in agony. Her face was blue, like those he had seen of so many young people who'd finally lost their battle to heroin.

That's when he awoke, still holding his fifth of Jack. Max was still asleep at his feet. The dream left him panicked and afraid. He took a hard swig of whiskey and sighed. Max stretched, rose to his feet, and laid his head in Dwight's lap. He rubbed his partner's ears affectionately before rising and heading inside.

The ringing of his kitchen telephone startled him. It was unexpected and too reminiscent of his dream. He checked his cell phone; it was after midnight. Any call at this time was not good news.

He picked up the receiver and held it to his ear.

"Evans,' he said.

"Dwight, this is Lynn at dispatch," the voice on the other end replied.

"Yes, Lynn, what is it?"

"DEP just called in. They found a body floating in the reservoir. Lieutenant requests you go secure the scene until detectives show up, then assist the detectives as needed."

Dwight sighed and set the bottle down on the counter.

"I'll need to make some coffee first, but I will head over."

"Sober up," Lynn told him. "DEP will maintain control of the scene till you arrive."

"We got a call, partner," Dwight informed Max, who promptly jumped onto the couch and laid down in protest. "Alright, bud. You hold down the fort then."

He didn't expect Maegan to come home that night, but he left the porch light on for her just in case.

THE BODY WAS SWOLLEN, pale, and dusky. The face of what was once a pretty girl, mangled beyond recognition. One eye was swollen shut, the other was open and bloodshot, coldly staring into the night.

"Victim's a female, approximately twenty to twenty-five years of age. She was found by a couple gentlemen illegally fishing the reservoir," the DEP officer told Dwight. "Doesn't look like she's been in the water too long," he added.

"Jesus Christ," Dwight said. He had fielded calls for dead bodies many times, but he'd never seen such brutality. "Looks like you've got this area cordoned off fairly well. I'll go park my car down by the entrance and keep people from coming in until the detectives get here."

He was eager to get away from the sight.

"Appreciate it," the DEP officer said, shaking Dwight's hand.

Before Dwight could reach his car, he was met by two well-dressed detectives.

"Detectives Carlyle and McAuliffe," the younger one said, extending his hand.

"Trooper Evans," Dwight said, shaking both their hands.

` "We need to limit foot traffic around these woods, Trooper," McAuliffe said. "So tape off the area... let's say four... five-hundred yards in each direction at least."

"And the parking lot, until forensics can go over it, please," Carlyle added. He was friendlier than his partner, who barked at Dwight like he was ordering fast food at a drive-through.

Dwight shook his head and muttered under his breath as he retrieved the yellow police tape from his trunk. Guys like that got under his skin; he could tell they thought less of him. Granted, his work was far less exciting than the detectives', but even Colebrook needed law enforcement. In part, he knew his dissatisfaction was with himself. He had always enjoyed the relative safety of his post, but what good had that done him? There was a good chance he was going to die now, anyway. Maybe he should have taken more risks, or a more exciting job, he thought. He wondered if he would have made a good detective.

Dwight played security guard while forensics, the coroner, and a couple more detectives showed up. He bummed a cigarette off of one of the detectives and smoked while he stood his post. About three hours later, the scene was wrapped up, the body removed, and he was relieved of his duty.

He got home after 4 AM, the first signs of dawn subtly peaking over the horizon. He found Max still lying on the couch. He rubbed his ears affectionately before pouring some food into his dish.

"Lieutenant says briefing at ten; then we can have the day off, Max," he informed his partner. Dwight then dug into the cupboard above the fridge and retrieved an old bottle of Scotch, pouring himself a drink and then sitting down with a long sigh. "That was a shit show, boy. Easily the most heinous crime scene I have ever seen."

Max's ears perked as his owner spoke, but his focus stayed with his food.

"Should have seen those detectives, Max. One looked like he's never even shaved. Baby-faced; real green behind the ears. The other one? A fat piece of shit. It's just a shame, ole boy. Guys like us, we missed all the glory—all the action. Played it too safe, ole boy. If they're what passes for murder police, we could have been something… something fierce, too. I tell you, in our prime—four, five years ago." He laughed boisterously. "I bet we could still fuck shit up, Max. I bet we'd give them hell. If we had to, we could still fuck those bastards up."

Max moaned, probably in protest to Dwight's ramblings, but Dwight took it as concurrence.

"Damn right, Max! God knows there's enough filth in this world. That poor girl today—you didn't see that call, boy. Terrible thing. Young girl—Maegan's age, maybe a little younger. Just beaten bloody and swollen, then drowned. Or maybe she died from the beating. I don't know, Max, but she's gone—someone's daughter... someone's niece." He took the final swig from his bottle and sighed, lighting a cigarette. "Years ago, something like that happened, people would be shocked. They'd be afraid. It would be the tragedy of the year in a town like this. Now, what's it matter? Who the fuck even cares? We've got the fucking world wide web streaming atrocities to us live from around the world, Maxie. We got violence in ultra-high definition, hundreds of damn channels of it. Now, this kind of stuff, well, I guess it's boring to people.

"We've become so comfortable with the filth, the grime, the fucking degenerate scum. We worship it. We want it in our faces. TV shows make heroes out of monsters. And it goes both ways, Maxie. Some cops are just as dirty as everyone else, maybe even more so. I tell you, it's a dog-eat-dog world. Hell, you know that. And dogs exert dominance through force, buddy. I know you understand that, too. We as a society, we cowered, and we let the thugs dominate us. We've let the filth become normal."

Chapter Four
The Storm

"Lieutenant?" a red-headed Trooper with big eyes asked. She peeked through the entrance of the lieutenant's office, a delightful smile on her face as she awaited his response.

"Yes, Mallory?" Lieutenant Leahy replied without looking up from his computer screen.

"They're ready for you, sir," she said dutifully.

Today was no normal day at the Canaan State Police Barracks. Reporters from all over the state had swarmed to their sparsely populated corner for the promise of a tantalizing tale of moral decay. A young woman was brutally murdered, and now all the state's attention was on them.

Of course, Colonel Hastings had already informed Leahy that Hartford would be taking the lead on the investigation. The brass wasn't going to leave such a high profile case to Canaan's under-staffed detective's unit. A decision he was sure Detective McAuliffe would welcome—you don't put in for a transfer to Canaan if you're the type who wants to see action. Hartford had already started to muscle them out, but the appearance that local police were handling the situation played well in the press. It kept residents from feeling the situation was out of their control.

"Thank you for coming here today," Leahy spoke into the microphones stacked on the podium. "We are at the very early stages of this investigation, and I am a man of few words. So, I won't take up much of your time."

Leahy had grown up in Virginia, and his accent was still slightly present. He was an older man with a hard demeanor. He was by no means elegant, but people listened when he spoke.

"Last night, fishermen alerted police to the presence of a body in the Colebrook reservoir. A DEP officer reported to the site and discovered the body of a young woman washed ashore on the lower west side of the reservoir, not far from the boat launch. The victim was a Hispanic female, approximately five-foot, four-inches, weighing around a hundred-fifteen pounds. The victim was beaten, stripped, and dumped in the water. The cause of death at this time is still unknown. We are asking for help identifying this young woman; approximately nineteen to twenty-four years of age. If anyone has a daughter, relative, or friend who is missing, or if anyone has any additional information, we urge you to call the phone number we have provided to the press."

After asking a myriad of questions Leahy had no answers to, the press reluctantly filed out of the barracks. There was some feeling among them that they had picked up on a dud of a story.

Leahy didn't have time to coddle the press and entertain their questions; his officers needed to be briefed. He ordered Master Sergeant Grant Harrison to lead the daily briefing while he took the men he needed for the Jane Doe murder.

"Of course, sir," Harrison said too eagerly. He was a perfect specimen of a lawman; tall, lean, and fit. His attitude often rubbed Leahy the wrong way. He tended not to like kiss-asses.

"Alright, troopers!" Leahy announced loudly from the head of the briefing room. "I need everyone involved in this murder investigation in my office. The rest stay here for a briefing with the Master Sergeant."

Dwight Evans had arrived a bit late and was just walking into the briefing room when Leahy made his announcement. Afraid his breath smelled of whiskey, he popped a piece of gum into his mouth before heading to Leahy's office.

"Trooper Evans," Leahy greeted him as he opened the door.

"Good morning, sir," Dwight replied. He exchanged friendly nods with Detective Carlyle. McAuliffe didn't acknowledge him.

"Thank you for coming, Trooper, but you can go home," Leahy continued, his wrinkled brow furrowed.

"I'm sorry, sir?" Dwight was confused. "You said to come in this morning for the briefing?"

"Detective McAuliffe assures me anything you have to provide to the record has already been provided. So, I can't imagine why I would have to take up any more of your time."

"Colebrook is my town. Shouldn't I be kept in the loop? I can help catch this guy."

McAuliffe chuckled at Dwight's assertion and defensively shot down the idea. "With all due respect, we don't need a uniform to help us track down a killer. There's a reason why there are separate departments for these things."

"Don't feel bad," Leahy told Dwight. "The brass has just as little faith in them as they do in you," he said, motioning to the two detectives.

"What's that mean?" Carlyle asked.

"It means that Hartford is going to be taking lead on this one. You two will play support, but command wants this one solved quickly. They're giving us investigators and supporting resources."

Carlyle and McAuliffe now shared the same indignant look as Dwight.

"I guess you hotshots are going to sit on the sidelines with me," Dwight smirked.

"Fine by me, "McAuliffe scoffed. "Less work, same pay."

Carlyle rolled his eyes, and Dwight shook his head.

"Let me know if you do need anything, Lieutenant," Dwight said, putting his trooper hat on as he left.

MARIE CALLOWAY PLACED her favorite stuffed bear down on her bed with care and lovingly adjusted his apron, which read "Mommy's Little Girl."

"I'm not going to be able to hang out today, Mr. Bear," Marie informed her stuffed friend. "I'm going to see my mommy." She patted Mr. Bear on the head and then did a turn to show off her flower-print dress. "Do you like my dress? It's important to look nice for Mommy."

"Do I look nice?" her little sister Stacey asked from the doorway of their bedroom.

"Yes, you do," Marie said confidently. "But come here," she instructed. Stacey slowly walked over, and Marie ran her hands over the sides of her head to smooth her hair. It didn't do much, but Marie enjoyed these moments where she was able to help her sister. It made her feel important.

"Does Mr. Bear think I look nice?" Stacey asked, a look of uncertainty imprinted on her adorable face.

"He says you're magnificent!" Marie relayed, kissing Stacey on the top of her head. Stacey beamed with approval.

"You ready, girls?" their father called as he came up the stairs. "Let's go see Mommy," he said as he reached their room. He was wearing black dress pants and a white collared shirt—the very things he had worn to Ellen's funeral.

THE GRAVEYARD WHERE ELLEN was laid to rest was in downtown Winsted, next to the city park. Dickey's feelings about the location were mixed. On one hand, it was nice to see families doing family stuff. On the other hand, it was extremely difficult to see families doing family stuff. On this particular Saturday, a little league baseball game was happening, which meant Dickey had to park down the street.

The three walked to the cemetery holding hands, Dickey holding three bouquets of flowers. This was their ritual, at least one Saturday a month since Ellen had passed. The girls enjoyed it, but for Dickey, it was always hard.

HERE LIES
ELLEN CALLOWAY
DEVOTED WIFE, LOVING MOTHER
GONE BUT NEVER FORGOTTEN
1986 – 2014

Dickey stared at the stone for some time, sorrow weighing on his heart. It felt heavy in his chest, making it more difficult to breathe. The girls placed their flowers down against the headstone. Dickey urged them to talk to their mother, but neither girl responded. Stacey clung to his leg, unsure of how to appropriately act. Marie just stared at the ground.

"What's wrong, sweetheart?" Dickey asked, kneeling down to his daughter's level.

"Can Mommy really hear us?" Marie asked.

"Yes, baby, she can. She always will. Whenever you want to, you can talk to her. I do it all the time," he said.

"Then why doesn't she answer me?" Marie said, tears welling up in her eyes.

"Oh, baby," Dickey said, his voice strained with grief. He pulled her close and hugged her, and she cried. Stacey reached in and joined the hug as tears began to roll down her cheeks as well. "Oh, my sweet girls. I am so sorry, but Mommy can't talk to us anymore. She's gone to live in heaven. But she's always with us and always listening."

"How do we know?" Marie asked.

"Well," Dickey said, searching for the strength not to break down in front of his girls. "You know when you're going about your day and suddenly you think of Mommy?"

Marie and Stacey both nodded in tearful agreement.

105

"Why do you think of her out of nowhere? It's because she's still with us, and a part of us, deep down inside, can recognize it. We feel her presence. Just like I do whenever I look at you girls."

"Because we're pretty like Mommy?" Stacey asked.

"Just like Mommy. You both have her smile and her eyes."

"I miss her," said Marie. "I miss her a lot."

"I know, baby," Dickey said, pulling them both close for another hug. "I do, too, girls. I really do."

"Daddy?" Marie asked.

"Yes, baby?" Dickey answered.

"If Mommy is with us always, why do we have to come here?"

Dickey smiled; she was a clever girl, just like her mother.

"It's our way of letting her know we haven't forgotten her... That we never will."

"I miss you, Mommy," Stacey said, slightly adjusting her flowers.

"I miss you, too, Mommy," Marie said, wiping the tears from her eyes. "I'm glad you're always with us."

Dickey teared up, but he held it back. "Girls," he said. "Go play on the swings for a minute. Let me have a minute with Mommy."

"Come on, they need to have an adult talk," Marie said knowingly, grabbing Stacey's hand and leading her to the swings nearby.

"Hey, darling," Dickey said as he laid his roses across the top of the stone. "I miss you really bad. It's just hard... the girls... my head... I'm a real mess sometimes." He started to sob. "I guess I just really need somebody. You know, we said 'until death do us part,' but you weren't supposed to check-out so quick." He gasped for air, tears leaking from his eyes. "I'm not going to lie to you, I resented you for it. I fucking did. I know that sounds terrible. But you *wouldn't fight*. Why wouldn't you fight for us? You just quit. You just gave up, and you thought you were giving up on yourself, but you weren't. You gave up on all of us!" He tried to calm himself and wiped the tears from his face. "Look at those little girls. They need you," he shook his head. "I just don't understand. I know you were
106

scared. I know, baby. I was scared when I was over there, but I fought like hell to get back to you. Why couldn't you fight for me? Why couldn't you fight for our girls? I guess I have been trying to forgive you. You know I love you more than anything in this world except those girls.

"Jason's been a big help, but he's in trouble, too. Drifting through this world, selling drugs for a living, dating addicts. He's like a brother to me, and just like my real brother, he's drowning. Why do I feel paralyzed as everyone around me is in need? How do I save them when I cannot even face my own thoughts?

"I'm haunted by some of the things I've seen. Things I've done. I get hit with anxiety out of nowhere—it's like I'm always in danger. Like the ax is going to drop at any time. I'm really trying, but I'm lost. Work isn't going so well, either. My anxiety, my temper... they don't let me fit in anywhere. Drugs and beer... Let's just say, I know you wouldn't approve of how much.

"I read the letter you wrote me before you died. I know you were scared. I know you thought chemo would have slowly killed you and you didn't want me or the girls to see you like that. But we would have supported you," his voice cracked, the tears returned. "No matter the odds, we could have fought together...

"I just don't know how I'm supposed to do this alone. I've been pushing the VA to get me some help, but the wait times for psychiatrists are so long. The country doesn't give a shit about guys like me once we've done our part. Discarded... just thrown away. I finally found out they'll pay for me to see someone local. I'll call tomorrow. I have to fight. Someone has to be there for our girls. As much as I want to end this life and be with you, I have to fight for them. I'll never stop."

He waited until he had regained his composure and his eyes were dry before collecting the girls and returning to the truck.

"Okay, who wants ice cream?" he asked with a smile.

"I do!" both girls yelled repeatedly.

"Alright, let's go get some!" he cheered as he dropped the shifter into gear.

IT WAS AN INORDINATELY HOT DAY for May in the northwest hills. The air was thick, and though there wasn't a cloud in sight, it felt like a storm was inevitable. Dwight, still bitter about the lieutenant sidelining him that morning, sat parked on the side of the road, the air conditioning cranked, watching cars speed down route 183 without care. To his boss and others at the Canaan station, this was all he was good for—enforcing traffic laws. That thought made him less inclined to do much of anything. His head hurt and the thought that he was spending what could be his final days writing speeding tickets was downright depressing.

Maybe it was the barometric pressure, or maybe it was the stress of knowing the tumor was ultimately killing him, but it felt like the world was about to explode. Even Max seemed to sense it; his ears perked and his eyes darted attentively out the back window of the cruiser.

"I'm probably losing my mind," Dwight said as he gazed at his partner in the rear-view mirror. It was a distinct possibility, from what the doctor had told him. The auditory hallucinations were only mild effects. Visual hallucinations, confusion, loss of bodily control, and speech impediments were all likely as the tumor progressed. All reasons cited as to why he should undergo an operation to remove the unwanted intruder as soon as possible.

The procedure, however, was more likely than not to kill him. This left him with a grim choice to either continue on for as long as he could, being slowly stripped of his cognitive and physical faculties, eventually dying a painful and confused death, or go under the knife and likely never wake up. The choice was so difficult, he avoided thinking about it, as if some other answer might present itself. He supposed the best option would be the one that allowed him to live the longest, though he was hard-pressed to guess which that would be.

Then there was the matter of his job. He could not keep the department in the dark for too long about his condition. They would undoubtedly yank him off duty as soon as they found out, and rightfully so. Just another reality he sought to avoid for now. There was also Max and Maegan, both of whom he worried would have trouble making it without him.

"Dispatch to Unit forty-three, come in," a woman's voice crackled through radio static.

"Unit forty-three to dispatch, go 'head," Dwight replied into the receiver.

"Code thirty-six. Lieutenant wants you to bring in a couple parents to possibly ID the Jane Doe," the dispatcher said.

"Alright, go ahead with the twenty," Dwight answered, requesting the address.

The parents were Mr. and Mrs. Martinez of Burrville, a Torrington suburb just over the Winsted line. They had reported their daughter missing that morning after she'd failed to come home or show up for her babysitting job. It was the lieutenant's unpleasant duty to inform them that they had a body of a young Latina girl that seemed to match her description.

Dwight took his hat off in respect when they answered the door. The solemn presence was underscored by the heavy bags beneath the father's eyes. Dwight could tell he had not slept. The mother was beside herself with grief, requiring both her husband and Dwight's aid to climb down the porch steps and make her way to the car. Dwight called Max out of the back so the two parents could ride together.

"C'mon, Maxie boy," Dwight called, slapping his hand against his thigh. Max climbed out of the car and slowly stretched. Dwight could tell that Max seemed to make Mrs. Martinez uneasy.

"Don't worry," Dwight reassured her. "This is my partner. He'll ride up front with me."

Mr. Martinez patted her hand to calm her and climbed into the back of the cruiser. She reluctantly followed, sniffling and trying to hold back tears.

There's no right thing to say to parents who are en route to ID the body of their only child. There is no appropriate conversation to have. Ignoring their pain was just as insulting as remarking on it, so Dwight focused on the road in silence like a sentry sworn to his duty. He wanted to express his regret—to tell them how sorry he was for them, but he knew better. They hadn't seen the body yet, and the reality was still deniable.

Dwight knew the body was most likely that of their daughter's—she fit the description. In an area that small, the chances of another missing Latina girl were less than slim. But he hoped, for their sake, that it wasn't her. He hoped they would see the body and cry in relief. He found himself fantasizing that their daughter had run off with a boy, or was out being irresponsible with a group of friends and would soon turn up. He didn't know Mr. and Mrs. Martinez, but he desperately wanted them spared of the pain that awaited them at the end of that ride.

Sadly, this was not the case, and Dwight could only watch through the glass window of the coroner's lab as Mrs. Martinez collapsed on the floor beside the battered body of her daughter. She cried in agony as her husband held her and rocked her back and forth on the floor. His face was expressionless as if someone had drained all the emotion from him. Dwight felt for the man; his daughter slain, his wife overcome with pain. He held her tightly as if his strength could somehow keep her whole.

"Hardest part of the job," Lieutenant Leahy said to Dwight with a shake of his head. "Thanks for bringing them in. Make sure they get home safe. See if there's anything you can do for them."

Leahy was typically a stern man, but even he seemed moved by the parents' grief. Dwight watched as the coroner covered the body with plastic He found himself thinking of Maegan and recalling his dream. The thought of losing her terrified him. It would destroy him. He could not begin to imagine the grief Mr. and Mrs. Martinez felt in that moment. Their lives would never be the same. A monster had stolen that from them. A monster Dwight wanted to pay for what he'd done.

CARSON TRAIVER TOOK ONE LAST PULL from his joint before extinguishing it in an ashtray full of roaches. His lakeside beach house was littered with garbage and smelled of stale cigarettes and weed—not that either fact bothered him. He was content to wait until his bastard roommate finally came home to help him clean it.

Carson was a child of privileged means. Born the son of the area's premier real estate broker, Carson's life was an ongoing disappointment which his parents were willing to subsidize out of shame and disregard. They paid his bills and provided him with a stipend. In exchange, he kept away from the family, particularly his younger siblings. All in all, it was a good deal for him.

His roommate and lifelong friend had gotten a similarly sweet deal from his parents; they gave him their house before retiring to Florida. But he had always had a sense of guilt about it—a feeling that he didn't deserve it. As such, he let his brother and nieces live there while he stayed with Carson in a cottage on Highland Lake.

The two shared a common outlook on life—that it was much better when they weren't sober. They had a simple life of drinking, smoking, and snorting whatever they wanted to and would often sit out on the porch and watch the lake life. Fishermen, boats, water skiers, girls in bikinis—they had plenty of entertainment. It was a simple life, but one they both enjoyed.

That was before his roommate had scored a connection and come into a large stash of Oxycontin. Then he got ditched like a girl who puts out on the first date. Carson was pissed, and when George finally came home, he was going to hear about it. He thought maybe he would charge him rent, or at least threaten to, just to make him pay for ditching him.

When he heard the front door open a few moments later, he was sure it was George finally coming home.

"It's about damn time you fucking back-stabbing son of a—"

As he rounded the corner to confront George, a black 9mm welcomed him and promptly pressed itself against his forehead. The visitor pushed him back, causing him to fall backward over the back of the couch. The man pointed the gun down at Carson and cocked back the hammer.

"Whoa! Whoa! Whoa!" Carson exclaimed, raising his hands in protest.

"Do you know who I am?" the man asked. Carson nodded hesitantly.

"You're Gary Augustine, right?" Carson asked. The man was infamous in the circles Carson ran with.

"And do you know why I am here?" Augustine asked, sweat slowly running down his pock-marked face. Carson just shook his head, afraid to even move. "Where's George Calloway?" he asked.

"Look, man, I have no idea!" Carson pleaded emphatically. "I swear to God. He owes me rent money…"

"He owes me eighteen grand!" Augustine snapped. He looked around the place and laughed. "What a fucking shit hole."

"Look, man, I haven't seen him in weeks," Carson said, his voice trembling with fear.

"You wouldn't lie to me, would you?" Augustine asked. Carson shook his head and made a whining sound. "Because if you did, I would have to punish you," Augustine explained. "And let's be honest, it's rather hard to punish someone who lives in shit and doesn't care about life. Junkie's curse…" Augustine uncocked his gun and lowered it slightly. "So, what I would do is go visit your family. Yes, I know who your family is and where they live. It isn't exactly a secret around here. Then I would tie your crooked pig of a father up and make him watch while I bury my cock up your mother's ass. Then I would take your little sister and make your parents watch as I fucked her brains out. Then I would kill them all… slowly."

"She's only twelve years old, man!"

"*Don't get me excited*!" Augustine roared. "I like 'em young."

"I swear to God!" Carson cried. "I have no idea where he is. Fucker took a bunch of pills and split town or something. He didn't even ask me to come with him. Left me here with this fucking mess," Carson said, gesturing to the clutter that covered his house.

"Okay, I believe you…. For now…" Augustine tucked his gun under his shirt and into the back of jeans. "When he does turn up, which he is bound to sooner or later, you be sure to give him a message for me. You tell him he had better find me with my money before I find him. Otherwise, it's not going to end so well for him or those he loves."

ANDREW TRVIOTY WAS NEVER the passive type. His aggressive nature was cemented in prison, where establishing himself as the alpha was the only way to survive. He always felt angry, and he was always ready for a fight.

Mounted on his back porch was on old Everlast punching bag that had been re-stuffed and taped so many times that you could no longer see the original leather. That was where you would find him most mornings, or whenever he was bored—beating that bag like it owed him money.

He never taped his hands or wore gloves, just pummeling the bag until his knuckles split, leaving blood stains on the gray duct tape. He would punish that bag—unloading combos, roundhouses, and uppercuts while he thought about every person who had ever wronged him, every person he had beaten, and every person he wished he could beat: his father, the first kids who ever beat him up as a boy, the gang members who jumped him into their circle of trust, the prison guards who raped him and used him as a mule, and that little punk who he had beaten and stabbed. He would strike and grunt, strike and growl.

That's where Travis and Tim found him when they came looking to score another bundle of heroin. As the two rounded the corner of the house, Dexter stood at attention and growled. Both boys froze in fear.

"Down, boy!" Andrew barked, striking the bag with all his might two last times.

The sight of Andrew, hulked-out, sweat glistening on his bronze, prison-sculpted body, his knuckles busted, and blood splattered across his chest and face, terrified Tim. Andrew wiped his bloody hands on his jeans without concern and smiled a wild grin, his green eyes burning with adrenaline.

"Back again? Damn, you boys selling this shit like I told you?" He grabbed the shirt he had draped over the porch rail and wiped the sweat and blood from his head and body. "You making some money?"

"No,", Travis said, looking down at the ground timidly.

"But you do have my money?" Andrew asked, his eyes narrowing with concern.

"Yes," Travis replied, pulling a wad of bills out of his pocket.

"Good, good," Andrew said with a laugh. "I got nervous for a second. Thought you were going to tell me you didn't have my money."

He took the money and counted it, motioning for the boys to follow him inside. They hesitated.

"Don't worry about him," Andrew said, nodding toward Dexter. "He won't fuck with you… Unless I tell him to." Andrew laughed again. He loved scaring the shit out of these two.

Inside, Andrew retrieved another bundle of dope. While they were waiting, Tim and Travis stared at the naked woman who was passed out on Andrew's couch. When Andrew returned, he saw their fixated glances and chuckled.

"Bitch fucked a whole squad of us last night. Let us run a train on her for a few bags," he recalled with a shake of his head. "Fuckin' whore. You want a go? I'll wake her up."

"No, that's alright," Tim said. He felt embarrassed for the girl.

Andrew handed them the bundle, and the two immediately headed for the door.

"Hey!" Andrew called after them. They froze and turned back slowly. "Be careful," he said with the slightest tone of caution and amusement. "That shit is addictive. You guys look like shit."

MAEGAN CRIED AND GRABBED her purse from Jason's bedside table. She had to get out of there—away from his judgment.

"I just don't understand," Jason said with anger. "You're not going to group anymore. You aren't seeing a doctor. So, why are you still using Suboxone?"

"Because I'm a fucking addict, Jason!" she bellowed. "Because I fucking need it or I will relapse!"

"But aren't you supposed to wean off of it at some point? You can't use that forever."

"Why the fuck do you care?" she asked, heading for the door.

"Because you take it and then you're not here anymore. I can see it in your eyes, hear it your voice," he said, sitting down upon his bed, defeated. "Because I care about you."

"If you cared you wouldn't make me feel so bad about something I need."

"If you still need it, then shouldn't you still be going to group? I was reading—"

"That's the fucking problem right there. Reading? What were you reading? What am I, a fucking research project for you? What, do you think you can read a few articles on the internet and know what's best for me? I'm trying my best goddamnit! I still feel withdrawals; I still feel the urge to shoot-up. I wake up in the middle of the night and all I can think about is dope. Are you happy to hear that? There you go. Now you know, I am still a fucking addict. Sorry to burst your bubble. Now you know, no more illusions—now you know I'm still scum, and you can leave me. It will be for the best if you do!"

She walked out, slamming the door behind her, leaving Jason in shock. He had never had any expectations of her. He knew her struggle was a daily one and that she would never completely break free of the hold that dope had on her. But he also knew that to win that fight she needed support, and he knew continuing to use Suboxone was a crutch that kept her body wanting the next high. He had done a lot of research on addiction since meeting her, and he believed that if she still needed Suboxone, she should still be seeing *someone* for help.

He felt helpless. At this point, he cared for her too much, yet he didn't know how to help her. Her actions terrified him. The last thing he wanted was for her to relapse. Everything they were building together would come crashing down if she did, and then how could he ever trust her again?

Every woman he ever cared for had left him, starting with his own mother. He longed for someone to share his heart with; someone who would stay. Though he feared no one would. He believed he would be alone.

He rolled a joint and took it out to the porch to smoke. The afternoon was warm, and the breeze was soothing. He choked back his tears and breathed the pot smoke in deeply. His grief was disrupted by the sound of footsteps coming up his porch stairs. His heart leaped in anticipation, assuming Maegan had returned to make up. His heart fell, and the sadness returned when he saw Mrs. Williams making her way up the stairs.

"Hello there, darling," she greeted him warmly.

"Hi, Mrs. Williams," he said with a smile, handing her the joint.

She took it with a smile and sat in the chair beside him. "You forgot to stop in yesterday," she told him.

"Oh, I'm sorry. My girlfriend and I… Well, I just got busy and forgot."

"That's alright, dear," she said, inhaling a hit of weed and passing the joint back to him. "Damn, that's good," she said.

"Only the best," Jason replied, his eyes staring off into the distance.

"What's the matter, dear?" Mrs. Williams asked.

"Girl problems," Jason said with a shrug.

"Well, darling, that's just a part of life. Love is just another contrary human emotion," she said with a laugh. "Humans are, by nature, social creatures. Yet at the same time, we build walls to protect ourselves from others. We need companionship yet we don't want to let anyone in."

"Yeah, walls. This girl has some major walls. I just don't know what to do… to keep her in my life. She's got some serious problems."

"Might be more trouble than she's worth," she replied. "Plenty of fish in the sea, or so they say."

Mrs. Williams had the wisdom you would expect of someone her age, with a no-nonsense directness that she told him some people couldn't handle. "I'm too old to beat around the bush," she would always say.

"Maybe she is more trouble than she's worth," Jason sadly agreed.

"Do you love her?" Mrs. Williams asked, taking the joint from him and drawing from it like the seasoned smoker she was.

The question took Jason off guard. He stopped for a moment to contemplate it and sighed. "I suppose so," he finally answered.

"Does she know?" she asked through wafts of smoke.

"No, I don't believe she does... I don't know... Maybe. It's all fucked up now, anyway."

"Honey, relationships always get fucked up. My husband, God rest his soul, knew that first hand. It was me who fucked up our relationship... Well, nearly fucked it up, I guess."

"How did you do that?" Jason asked, surprised at her candid confession.

"I cheated on him with my ex while he was on one of his extended business trips. I don't know why I did it. I met my ex at a bar to tell him he had to stop contacting me, but I still wanted him. I guess I went there with the idea in the back of my head. After a few drinks, one thing led to another."

"But he forgave you?" Jason asked, hitting the joint before dabbing it out on the porch rail.

"Eventually. I confessed as soon as he came home—I knew I had screwed up so badly. He packed his things and went to stay at the Brass Horse," she told him, her voice pained with regret. "It was the single most foolish thing I ever did. Anyway, about a month later we reconciled. He apologized for leaving me alone so often, and I swore that it was the biggest mistake of my life—one I would never allow myself to repeat."

"And you two were happy after that?"

"No relationship is perfect, dear. But we got past that because we did love each other. Love can overcome the imperfections we have in our souls. If we want it to."

Jason nodded. "Let me grab you a bag," he said after a moment.

She smiled at him thankfully.

SHE WAS A CUTE LITTLE THING; dyed-blonde hair, perky breasts, and a little round ass which she always showed off. Her bangs hung just low enough to kiss her eyelashes, which were long and dark with daring green eyes peeking out from underneath.

"It's fine, sweetheart," Rachel assured her, running her red fingernails through her soft, blonde hair. "We're just going to have a little fun."

Her name was Allison, a freshman at the local community college that Rachel had met through a mutual friend. Rachel knew George would like her and, truth be told, she was exactly Rachel's type.

"I mean... I've just never..." Allison said pensively, twisting a few strands of hair around her finger anxiously.

Rachel gently grabbed her hand and pulled her closer. "What, you don't think I'm pretty?" she asked. Allison blushed.

"No... I mean, yes... I mean... You are," she smiled shyly at Rachel, but then shot George a look of unease.

"Here," Rachel urged, holding a pill up to her mouth and slowly inserting it along with her finger.

Allison reluctantly allowed the pill and Rachel's finger into her mouth and felt a slight rush of excitement. However, hesitation and guilt followed. *This wasn't who she was. Wasn't she better than this?*

"We're just a few friends having fun," Rachel said encouragingly. She pulled Allison down beside her on the hotel bed.

"And we are going to have lots of fun," George assured her, flashing a baggie full of pills.

"I just... It feels wrong..." Allison said. She thought about getting up and leaving, but she really wanted those pills and, though she was ashamed to admit it, the feeling that it was indeed wrong was turning her on.

"Just come here," Rachel said, taking her head in her hands and softly kissing her.

Allison felt Rachel's soft lips against hers and allowed her tongue to enter her mouth. Reluctantly, she kissed Rachel back. Then she kissed her again, with more eagerness. She felt Rachel's fingers brush down her neck and over her breasts. She pulled back instinctively, but Rachel followed, kissing her and unbuttoning her blouse.

"Just let it happen," George urged, his eyes wide with anticipation.

Allison smiled an unsure smile and lied back as Rachel undid her shirt and began kissing her chest and stomach.

"I just don't know… I don't know how… I don't think I can…" Allison said in protest, but Rachel was already undoing her pants.

"I'll show you," Rachel said, taking Allison's hand and placing it on her breast. "Do you like that?"

"I don't know," Allison said with a laugh. But she didn't move her hand.

Rachel slid down to the floor and pulled Allison's pants off. Allison was embarrassed but also felt very hot. She wanted to do it but felt ashamed.

Rachel felt the hesitation and grabbed a mirror with crushed pills on it from the bedside table. "Here," she said. "This will help."

Allison smiled slightly, then took the rolled-up bill and snorted a large line. The euphoria washed over her as she lied back on the bed, her anxiety melting away. She didn't have a care in the world anymore, not even that Rachel was on her knees eating her out while George watched.

She glanced over at George, who was transfixed on her, slowly jerking off, though he wasn't fully erect. He grabbed a handful of pills and tossed them onto the bed. "There ya go!" he cheered.

Allison moaned as Rachel worked her tongue over her clit.

Soon she was on her knees, her inhibitions gone, face buried in Rachel's crotch, while George fucked her from behind. She had fleeting thoughts about him not wearing a condom, or the fact that she was essentially prostituting herself, but she shook them away. George fucked her till he came, then retired to his chair to watch her and Rachel continue.

They occasionally stopped to snort more Oxy and then continued to fuck around for more than an hour until they all fell asleep.

She awoke later that day feeling sore, violated, and ashamed of herself. The reality of what she had done set in quickly and left her scrambling for her clothes. Both Rachel and George were asleep. She dressed hurriedly and headed for the door. Then she stopped, went back to the bed and picked up as many pills as she could find. Seeing a baggie with more than thirty pills in it next to a pile of cash on the table beside George. She quietly walked over and lifted the bag and the cash before leaving.

She found her boyfriend, Rick, asleep in his Jeep outside the hotel.

"Christ, took you long enough," he said groggily as she slammed the passenger door. She dropped the bag of pills and around three grand in cash into his lap and he smiled. "Hot damn! Holy shit, baby! Good job!"

"Just get me the fuck out of here," she said.

He looked at her—makeup smeared and the unmistakable look of regret in her eyes.

"Okay, baby," he said before starting the engine. "Let's get out of here."

She stared out the window into the distance, wishing she could somehow forget what she had just done.

"You want to go grab some food?" he asked, as he navigated the highway onramp.

"No," she said curtly. "I want to go home and take a long, hot shower."

Rick nodded and lit up a cigarette, feeling ta slight tinge of guilt coupled with jealousy.

They didn't speak for the entire ride home. Both knew what neither would say; they had just crossed a line from which they could never return.

DAVE SILVERS TAPPED HIS HARD HAT twice to make sure it was secure before fastening the rope to his saddle with a carabiner. Just as he was about to climb the fifty-foot oak, a firm hand grabbed him by the shoulder.

"Whoa, whoa, hold on there," Dickey scolded him.

Dave, the boss's son, didn't take well to anyone second-guessing him, especially Dickey, with whom he'd had repeated confrontations.

"Damn it, Calloway!" he snapped. "I don't need you checking up on me. I've been climbing trees since I was a boy."

Dickey looked at him incredulously and scoffed. "Then what the hell is this?" He grabbed hold of the rope Dave had just tied onto and pointed to a fray.

"That?!" Dave laughed in disbelief. "That's fine. Barely a fray."

"Bullshit it is!" Dickey said, his pulse quickening. Conflict of any sort would send him from zero to ten in no time flat, and Dave had a way of setting him off. He had already faced a suspension for fighting with the bastard.

"Fine," Dave said with contempt. "Hey everyone, hold on!" he called to the crew. "Dickey's got his panties in a knot. We have to run a new line."

"Listen, asshole," Dickey snapped. "As much as I would love to see you plummet to your death, I would prefer it not happen at a job site."

Dave wasn't going to let some green-behind-the-ears climber talk to him that way in front of his men. He shoved Dickey and shook his head. "You wouldn't know your dick from a tree limb," he charged. "Mind your fucking business. Or do I have to remind you of the pecking order here?"

Dickey felt his muscles tense and his fist ball up. The anxiety swept over him like a wave of hatred. With a sudden and swift movement, he grabbed Dave by his shirt and yanked him close. In an instant, Dave's smirk was transformed into fear as Dickey growled.

"Listen, mother fucker," Dickey said sternly and quietly so no one else could hear. "If this were Iraq, I would slit your fucking throat right now and walk away like it was nothing. I wouldn't think twice about it. Killing you would be just another part of my day. Like taking a shit."

He released his grip and Dave stumbled backward, falling square on his ass.

"Climb however the fuck you want," Dickey said, turning to walk away.

A couple of crew members came to help Dave up, shooting Dickey looks of scorn and contempt.

"Pyscho threatened to kill me!" he heard Dave cry.

With anger still surging through his veins, Dickey lit a smoke and walked back to his truck to cool down.

In his truck, Dickey attempted to call his brother, George, yet again. Once again, he received no answer. He hated worrying about him; he was a complete fuck-up and didn't deserve his concern. At the end of the day, however, he was still his brother.

"Hey, asshole, where the hell are you? Call me… I mean it," Dickey said gruffly in the voice message for George.

Dickey held his head in his hand and sighed. His hands trembled from the recent conflict. Suddenly, there was a rapping on his window. He jumped, then saw Dave standing outside.

"Hey, asshole," Dave smirked. "Report to the office. My dad wants to talk to you," he ordered through the window.

Dave smugly walked off, and Dickey punched his steering wheel in frustration.

A few moments later Dickey called Jason.

"Hey, buddy, can you grab the girls from their grandparents' and cook them dinner?"

"Of course," Jason answered.

"Thanks, bro. Still no word from the babysitter. I have to drive back to Lakeview and deal with shit at the office. I'll see you when I finish up."

OLD MAN SILVERS WAS A STERN MAN, but aside for the blind spot he had for his son Dave, he was a fair man.

"Come in, have a seat," the old man told Dickey in his trailer office. Dickey obliged him and prepared to be fired. "Now, what is this I hear about you and Dave fighting again?"

"Sir, can I be honest?" Dickey asked.

"Of course," the old man replied.

"Your son is a dick, and he's going to get someone killed. Hopefully, it's himself and not somebody else."

The old man let out a little chortle then caught himself. He smiled and shook his head slowly. "Maybe you're right," he said, to Dickey's surprise. "But that doesn't change the matter of your temper. We have had three incidents now where it's been a problem."

"Are you firing me?" Dickey asked glumly.

"No," the old man answered. "I respect you for your service and don't want to put a veteran widower out of a job. But you have to get help, son."

Dickey nodded painfully and lowered his eyes in shame.

"Your head's not right, son. *It's* you who's going to end up hurtin' someone. Now I don't know what you gotta do, but you have to see someone and start getting some help. When you do, you can come back to work. Until then, you're on paid leave."

Dickey wanted to protest, but the old man's request was reasonable.

"Okay," he replied in defeat.

"Go home. Get some help. Once you've seen a doctor, bring proof and I will put you back on the schedule."

RANDY SANDUSFIELD CAREFULLY PRUNED the leaves from around his plants' colas, leaving perfectly shaped buds ready to harvest. It was an art form—one which he had perfected over the years. Too much leaf and the appearance and taste would suffer. Take away too much, and he would be cutting into his profits.

He finished up, checked his phone for the time, and then retired to the house to count the latest drop, locking the barn behind him on his way out. In the kitchen he took stacks of hundreds out from a black duffel bag, counting it twice, and then placing ten percent in a separate bag. It took him over an hour to count. After he was done, he retrieved a small red ledger from behind his fridge and wrote, '350,000' in the 'RECEIVED' column and '35,000' in the 'PROFIT' column.

"Mark!" he called out. A moment later his son appeared. "Take this bag up to the spot and add it to the rest."

Mark carried the bag and a shovel a half mile into the woods until he came across a few large rocks. He put the bag down and used the shovel as a lever to move the rocks. Then he proceeded to dig away the dirt and leaves, revealing a wooden hatchway. Carefully, he took out his keys and unlocked the padlock on the hatch. Then ever so slightly, he lifted the hatch and slid his fingers underneath. Carefully, he removed the trip wire attached to a hand grenade—a nice surprise for any unwanted visitors.

With the booby-trap disabled, he opened the hatch and proceeded down a ladder with the bag. The stash spot was a reinforced bunker he and his father had made together. Mark climbed down about ten feet and then through a twelve-foot tunnel. At the end of the tunnel was another booby-trapped hatch. Beneath that was their money stash. Three large duffel bags lined with plastic contained well over twenty million dollars. Mark opened the bag that was sitting on top and transferred the contents of the small bag into it. He then sealed the plastic lining, zipped the bag shut, closed the hatch, and rearmed the booby-trap. He did the same with the top hatch, then set about rolling the large rocks back into place and burying them halfway with dirt and leaves.

JASON PUSHED A SHOPPING CARRIAGE down an aisle of the Winsted Save N' Shop. Stacey Calloway was seated securely in the child seat while her sister Marie walked alongside, holding Jason's pant leg.

"Can we have this?" Marie asked, pointing to a box of Oreo cookies.

"No, your father would kill me," Jason replied.

"Can we have this?" she asked a moment later, pointing to a box of fruit snacks.

"No, sweetie," he answered with a laugh. "We're here to buy stuff for dinner."

"Can we have this?" she said, ignoring his logic and grabbing hold of a package of chocolate pudding snacks.

"No, baby, just dinner," Jason said.

"Can we have ice cream?" Stacey asked from the child seat.

"Yeah! Can we have ice cream?!" Marie joined in concurrence. He was outnumbered.

He looked at Stacey's big brown eyes, then down to her sister who was pulling at his pant leg eagerly.

"Fine," he said with an exaggerated sigh. "We will get ice cream, but it's for after dinner. Agreed?"

Both girls were happy with the agreement, so he picked up a carton of mint chocolate chip ice cream after grabbing some chicken breasts and spaghetti.

"What's for dinner?" Marie asked they headed for the checkout.

"My famous chicken parmesan!" he told them enthusiastically.

"What's a chicken parms me on?" Marie asked earnestly.

"It's like cheesy chicken," he said. Both girls looked at him skeptically.

"It's good. Trust me," he said as he stacked the ingredients onto the checkout counter. "It's like a big chicken nugget with spaghetti sauce and cheese."

"Okay," Marie said, sold on anything having to do with chicken nuggets.

"Your girls are just so pretty," the clerk at the checkout told Jason. She was an older woman with white hair and soft features.

"We look like my mommy!" Marie proclaimed proudly, a fact she often informed anyone who complimented their looks.

"Well, I bet your mommy is a beautiful woman," the clerk said, smiling warmly. "You have lovely girls," she added to Jason.

"Thanks, but they're not my girls," he replied, rubbing Stacey's head affectionately.

"He's our uncle," Marie asserted. She was at that age where she would proudly proclaim just about anything she knew.

"Well, they're very sweet," the clerk smiled.

"Thank you," Jason replied.

"Our mommy is in heaven," Marie informed her in a matter-of-fact tone. "We visit her sometimes, but Daddy says she's always with us."

Visibly taken back, the clerk smiled an uneasy smile and nodded. "I'm sorry, I didn't..." she said to Jason.

"It's fine," Jason assured her. "Don't worry about it." He smiled to ease the clerk's guilt and handed her a twenty dollar bill.

OUTSIDE THE SUN HAD QUICKLY VANISHED. Dark storm clouds were on the horizon, and the wind was picking up. Jason could smell the rain on the air.

"Look at that," Jason said to the girls, Stacey and the groceries secure on his right arm, Marie holding his left hand. "Looks like we have to go through a storm."

"Do we have to? It's scary," Marie asked, looking up at the dark clouds in the distance.

"Yup, no other way," Jason said as he secured Stacey in her booster seat.

"But I'm scared," Marie protested.

"I know, sweetheart," he said, kneeling down to her level. "But that's life. Sometimes it's scary. Sometimes you have to go through the storm to get home. But I promise, I won't let anything happen to you. We have to be brave together. Will you help me be brave?"

Marie nodded and wrapped her arms around his neck. "I will," she said as they hugged. He helped her into the back seat and fastened her seat belt.

"Let's get home and get supper started for daddy," he said as he closed the door.

On the way home, they did hit some heavy rain, even a little thunder, and lightning, but Marie stayed brave. By the time they pulled into the driveway, the worst had passed. Once they had settled in, the girls played in the living room while he prepared dinner.

"*Daddy!*" Stacey shrieked with joy when Dickey's truck pulled into the driveway.

The two girls eagerly greeted their father as he came through the door soaking wet, looking tired and sad.

"What's wrong?" Marie asked as he hugged her and her sister. Dickey shot Jason a serious look and then shook his head. "Nothing, baby. Go play," he told them, patting her lightly on her butt as they ran off. "I need to talk to you," he said to Jason.

"Alright, well come into the kitchen, I have to watch the sauce," Jason said, throwing a dish towel over his shoulder and wiping his hands on it.

Dickey followed him to the kitchen and grabbed two beers from the fridge, popping the caps off on the counter and handing one to Jason.

"What's up, brother?" Jason asked, concerned.

"You hear about the body they found in the reservoir?"

"Yeah, I saw something about it on the news but I turned it off quick because the girls were there," he answered, sipping the beer and stirring the sauce."

"It was Jennifer; the girls' babysitter," Dickey said, his voice heavy. "Beaten to a pulp and ditched in the water." He took a large swig from his beer and shook his head.

"Oh, man," Jason said. His immediate thoughts were of concern for the girls.

"I just got a call from her parents," Dickey added. "Poor folks are devastated."

"Wow... Do they have any idea what happened?"

"No, not really. I guess she was hanging out with some shady types a lot. Fell in with a bad crowd, I guess."

"That's a damn shame; such a lovely girl," said Jason. He shook his head in disgust. "What are you going to tell the girls?"

"I don't know, man. Honestly, I'm not sure if I should say anything to them."

"They're bound to ask," Jason said. "Especially Marie, she was fond of her."

"I just don't know how they'll handle that. They've already lost their mother for fuck's sake," Dickey said, sitting down at the table in exasperation.

"I thought I had problems," Jason said with a sigh.

"What's up with you?" Dickey asked.

"Nothing, just some girl bullshit," Jason said. His anxiety had been ramped-up all day. He couldn't stop thinking about how he and Maegan had left things. His problems, however, suddenly seemed small in light of such a tragedy. "Well, I think you should tell them," he added.

"I don't know," Dickey said, shaking his head. "They've got enough to worry about. What the fuck is happening to this town? Jesus Christ...."

"It's getting pretty fucked up, that's for sure," Jason said. "Really fucked up."

"I got suspended today," Dickey added nonchalantly.

"Oh man, did you punch Dave Silvers?" asked Jason.

Dickey laughed at the suggestion. "No, but I should have. Anyway, the old man's making me see someone."

"A therapist?"

"Yeah, I have to get proof I am seeking help before he'll let me back on the job."

"Probably not the worst thing, brother. I think you could benefit from that," Jason replied candidly.

"Yeah, I am well aware that you do," Dickey said in an indignant huff.

"So, what are you going to tell the girls?"

"I don't know... Maybe that Jennifer moved away. The less specific, the better."

"Until they see her face on a newspaper or in the news," Jason warned.

"If that happens, I will deal with it then. I can't lay this on them. I don't want them to think about this kind of shit... I mean, the brutality of it all. They shouldn't have to think about that kind of thing," Dickey said, finishing his beer. "Put that on simmer, let's go out back quick and burn a joint."

Jason nodded slowly, thoughts of Jennifer being beaten and drowned swirling in his head.

They headed outside, where Jason crushed up some bud and rolled a joint.

"It's just really fucked up," Dickey said before lighting the joint, his thoughts lingering on Jennifer and her fate. "This sort of thing happening here."

"Yeah, it is," Jason concurred.

"No, you don't understand. I've seen real violence, Jay. I've committed real violence. You tell yourself you're leaving that behind." He puffed on the joint a few times and passed it to Jason.

"Doesn't change that I think it's messed up," Jason countered.

"My last tour, things were already getting to me," Dickey recalled. "We were just outside of Fallujah, sweeping homes to find insurgent weapon caches. This young sergeant, a real hot-headed piece of shit. He was always pushing the line with these folks—going that extra mile to be a total dick. Time comes to roll out, I notice he isn't around. So, I go looking for him. I find him in a hovel down the block from where we're clearing houses. The girl must have been no older than thirteen. He'd killed her father and raped her next to his body."

"Jesus Christ…"

"When I found him he just laughed about it. She was huddled in the corner, terrorized. That son of a bitch was no better than the monsters we were fighting, and I killed monsters without a second thought. It was the only way to survive. It was the only way to give some feeling of righteousness to what we were doing every day." Dickey grabbed the joint back from Jason and took a deep pull. He ran his hand through his curly brown hair and sighed as he let the smoke out.

"We would carry drop weapons; unregistered guns we picked up off of hajis," he continued. "A lot of shit happened over there. Sometimes you had to make quick decisions. Sometimes you'd drop someone, and maybe they weren't the threat you thought; maybe they were unarmed. The drop weapons were an insurance policy. They made sure we didn't face life in prison for deciding to kill in a hostile war zone. Was it right? I don't know. But we did it because it was better than the alternative. There was no black and white there, no real right or wrong. It was just us trying our best to be the line between the monsters and the innocent. Sometimes that line got blurred.

129

"So, I find this guy, I see what he had done, and everything else was just pure response. I didn't even think; it wasn't calculated or rationalized. I just pulled out my drop gun from under my flak jacket and shot him in the face. In seconds, his smiling face was gone and half his head was splattered on the wall. I dropped the gun by the father's body and told the girl to get out of there."

"Jesus, what happened?" Jason asked, his mouth agape in shock.

"I radioed it in. Squad didn't think anything of it. Just another KIA Marine with a dead haji. To this day, it's not what I did that bothers me—he deserved it. It's the fact that I reacted that way, without a second thought, like a machine... a killing machine."

"You killed an American soldier?" Jason asked, stunned.

"I killed a monster. A rapist. A murderer. And yeah, he was a soldier. I have to live with that, and sometimes it's hard. Sometimes it bothers me. A lot of things I did over there do," Dickey admitted. "But I left that all behind. The nerves, the feeling of suddenly being under attack. That shit doesn't go away. I thought about slicing Silvers' throat today. I would never do it, but I thought about what it would be like. You tell yourself, though, that those feelings—those types of actions—they aren't needed here. There's no monsters here... I want my girls to be able to believe that."

MAEGAN HUNG AN ARMFUL OF CLOTHING up in the closet of her new bedroom, and smiled as her Uncle Dwight brought in the last box of her stuff from downstairs.

"You all set, kiddo?" he asked, putting his arm around her and smiling.

"Yeah, I think so," she said, leaning up and kissing him on the cheek. "Thank you so much," she said.

"No need," he replied. "It's great having you here. If your brother decides he wants to come, we can fix up the basement," he added.

"Give him time, he just might," she said.

"Well, I am going to get some sleep if you're all set," Dwight said. She gave him one last hug before he retired. Soon after, she was in bed herself, trying to rest. She couldn't help but feel annoyed when Jason called.

"Hey," she said into the phone.

"I'm sorry," Jason replied, his voice somber and low.

"I am, too," she replied. She lied on her bed and stared out the window into the blackness of the Colebrook woods.

"I just care about you a lot," he added.

"I know you do. Thank you," Maegan said. She felt bad about the way they had left things. Jason was a good man—perhaps too good. She felt a lot of pressure to live up to how he saw her. She didn't want to hurt him or, worse, disappoint him. She wanted so badly to be the girl he thought she was. "I'm going to get some sleep. We'll talk tomorrow," she said.

"Sweet dreams," Jason replied.

"You, too."

She put her phone down on her chest and closed her eyes. Soon after, Max found his way into her room and joined her on her bed. He laid his head down on her stomach and closed his eyes. The two were soon fast asleep.

Sometime later, the vibration of her phone woke Max first and then Maegan. She answered it without looking, expecting it to be Jason again.

"What do you want, silly?" she said sleepily.

"Hey, baby girl," the voice on the other end of call replied. It was Michael Trivoty. She froze, unsure of what to say.

"Why are you calling me?" she asked sternly.

"Because I miss you, baby girl. I can't stop thinking of you."

"Please don't call me again," she said, hanging up the phone and tossing it onto her nightstand. The phone came to life again, vibrating and lighting up. Michael's name was on the screen. Maegan sat in distress, staring at her phone. Soon it stopped. She turned the phone off and turned over to cuddle with Max.

GUILLERMO GARCIA LIT TWO SMOKES and handed one to his partner, Detective Wyatt Mayhew. The two sat silently in the dark inside of a black Crown Victoria, eyes trained on the dope house ahead. Guillermo reached around his back and pulled out his Sig Sauer .45, racked a round into the chamber, and tucked the gun neatly into the front of his tactical bullet-proof vest. He pulled down around the neckline of the vest and cursed in Spanish.

"These fucking things are so uncomfortable," he grumbled.

"Better than catching a bullet," Wyatt replied, running his fingers over his bald scalp.

"There's no room. I always feel like it's choking me," he complained.

"Then take it off," Wyatt suggested with a laugh.

"Fuck that," Guillermo cackled. "Where the fuck is everybody? They're late."

"Probably jerking themselves off at the station," Wyatt quipped, pulling deeply from his cigarette.

Guillermo's demeanor changed when he saw a string of headlights coming up the road. "Here we go! Here we go!"

The two climbed out of the Crown Victoria and tossed their smokes. Wyatt readied his Glock 17 and tucked it into his vest. Four unmarked cars parked down the road and eight officers in tactical gear converged on them.

"Where's SWAT?" Wyatt asked the lead detective.

"They parked a block over, they're en route now," he answered.

Wyatt nodded and pulled out his gun. His partner followed suit.

"Higgs, Blackman, Dreyfus, you're with Garcia and me. We'll take the back. SWAT goes in the front. Collins and Matthews, back them up. The rest of you guys establish a perimeter," Wyatt directed.

"We could just set up shop out back in case any try and run. Let SWAT deal with the raid," Blackman suggested. He was a young kid and this was his first time seeing action.

"And miss all the fun?" Guillermo asked with a laugh.

Wyatt began a beeline for the backyard as a small SWAT team in full tactical gear approached the house quickly from the front. The house was a rundown multifamily; their target was the upstairs apartment.

Wyatt held his gun in the SUL position—close to his chest and pointed down, as he quickly ascended the back steps of the domicile, Guillermo and the others close behind. The back steps were poorly built and not well maintained; they swayed under the weight as the men made their way to the second floor.

"In position," SWAT radioed from the front hallway. "Going on 3,2..."

As Wyatt and his team made it to the second-floor porch, they heard the front door crashing in and shouts of *"Police! Police! Down on the ground!"*

Seconds later, two men came bolting out the back door. Wyatt grabbed one of them by the shirt collar, positioned his leg behind the perp's, and pushed him down onto his back. Guillermo pistol-whipped the other man as he attempted to push past the team. Both men hit the ground hard. Higgs and Blackman quickly landed on top of them and proceeded to cuff and search them as Wyatt and Guillermo entered the home.

The kitchen table was littered with heroin, baggies, needles, and a scale.

Children cried from the front of the house where SWAT was apprehending their parents.

Wyatt pointed to a stairway leading up to the third floor from the kitchen. Guillermo nodded, and the two proceeded up, their guns ready.

The third-floor had two bedrooms. They carefully entered the first, Wyatt breaking right, Guillermo left. They found a pill press; a machine used to turn fentanyl and heroin into counterfeit pain pills. Wyatt shook his head, knowing just how deadly an operation of this sort could be.

Having cleared the first room, they proceeded to the second, where the bedroom door was locked. Wyatt and Guillermo positioned themselves on opposite ends of the door. Two members of SWAT made their way up the stairs and stopped when Wyatt held his hand out.

"Come on out with your hands up!" Wyatt called through the door. "No point in making this dangerous. Just come on out!"

A couple of moments later the door handle began to turn slowly. The SWAT members crouched down in the stairwell, guns ready. Guillermo and

Wyatt pressed themselves against the walls on each side of the door. The door flew open and a young man with a revolver charged out, screaming.

Before anyone could react, Wyatt grabbed the arm that brandished the gun and forcibly pointed it at the ceiling. A swift punch to the assailant's gut dropped him to his knees and caused the revolver to tumble from his grasp. SWAT pounced on the man.

"Superman!" Guillermo laughed, patting Wyatt on the back.

"These little shits never have firearm training. They never know how to even hold a gun, let alone shoot one," Wyatt said as they walked down the stairs, moving aside for a couple more SWAT members.

"Alright!" Wyatt called out once downstairs. "They got a pill press upstairs, so you know what that means."

"Fuck!" exclaimed Higgs.

"Don't touch anything!" Guillermo ordered. "Don't be stupid," he said, looking at the younger officers. They all remembered the officer who had nearly died after merely brushing fentanyl off his uniform earlier that year. The whole house was toxic.

"Get a HAZMAT team down here. SWAT, secure the perps and get out!" Wyatt shouted so the men upstairs could hear. "Good work, everybody."

BACK AT THE STATION, Wyatt pressed one of the two individuals who had been running the operation at the drug house. He was a sickly looking man with rotten teeth and pockmarks on his face.

"We could do that," Wyatt said. "We could get you an attorney. But that's just going to drag this out and the longer I have to wait, the less generous I'm going to be feeling. It's in my nature; I'm an impatient person."

The perp, Richard Nelson, stared at the table, refusing to look Wyatt in the eye.

"See, I know you've seen on TV," Wyatt continued, "that a lawyer is going to come in and help you. But the truth is, they're not. It's only going to piss me off, drag this out, and then in the end, you know what they're going to tell you? They're going to tell you to make a deal with us—to tell me what I want to know. In exchange, we'll see that you don't serve the maximum time."

"But I'll still go to prison. Some deal," Nelson scoffed.

"We got you running a heroin and fentanyl operation out of the same house your children were living in. We found a pill press with deadly fentanyl dust all over it. You're going to prison, Richard. There is absolutely no outcome here where you don't end up behind bars. Question is, do you want to serve ten years or twenty?"

Wyatt approached Nelson and sat down on the edge of the interrogation table. He glared at him with his steely blue eyes and shook his head. "Here's the thing. I don't think you're the prison type. Not made for it. You won't survive twenty years. Tell me what I want to know, you'll get ten years and be out in five if you play your cards right."

Nelson's eyes welled up with tears. He finally looked Wyatt in the eye and sighed. "What do you want to know?" he asked.

"That-a-boy. What do you think I want to know, Richie?" Wyatt asked.

"My supplier is connected. If I give you his name, he will make sure I am dead," Nelson said, desperation in his voice.

"Well, chances are if he's that dangerous, he'll have you killed either way. Best bet is to tell me what you know and we can try and get you protective custody."

"Goddamn it," Nelson said, shaking his head. "Everything moves through a house in Winsted. Trivoty—Andrew Trivoty."

"That's your supplier?"

"No, he's the middleman. That's where most of this town's dope has been coming from."

"Okay, and who's the supplier?" Wyatt pressed.

"You're going to get me killed, man. No Way. Look into Trivoty. Investigate! Do your job."

"Alright," Wyatt said, rising from the table and heading to the door. He knocked on the door and waited to be let out. "I guess you don't want to make a deal."

"Fucking goddamn it!" Nelson exclaimed. "Fine! Jesus Christ."

"Give me a name!" Wyatt barked.

"Augustine! Gary fucking Augustine!"

ANOTHER STORM WAS NEARBY that night, and it made the wind fierce. Dickey Calloway sat on his porch sipping his beer, watching the enormously tall pine trees in his front yard sway in the wind. He liked storms; he enjoyed the chaos and the noise, even if the thunder made him jump sometimes. War had taken a toll on his nerves, that much was true. Even still, he felt more normal in the midst of the storm.

He gazed up at the pines, watching them sway. Many years of wind and rain had made them strong and able to withstand almost anything. However, like anything else, someday the pressure would be too much and they would snap. He considered again whether he should take them down before they wound up crashing through his house or hurting someone.

As he contemplated the method by which he'd drop them, a car pulled into his driveway. He didn't recognize the headlights or the sound of the engine. With his nerves already on edge, he arose from his seat and went inside. He came back out a moment later, his Sig Sauer .40 tucked into the back of his jeans.

Gary Augustine emerged from a black Impala smoking a cigarette, a revolver in his hand, and walked up to the base of the stairs. "I'm looking for George," he said, the wind hollowing behind him, lightning brightening the night.

"He don't live here," Dickey said sternly. "You take what you have to up with him, but you leave this house and never come back."

Lightning struck again, turning the sky a violent green. A loud crash of thunder followed. This time, Dickey didn't flinch. His nerves were as steady as could be as he stared coldly at Augustine.

"I know he doesn't live here," Gary said, eyeing the house behind Dickey. "But he's been hiding out somewhere. Mind if I come take a look?"

Dickey pulled his Sig out and held it by his side, pointed at the ground. "Can't have you waking my girls. George isn't here, and he isn't welcome here. Neither are you." Dickey said.

The two calmly stared at each other for a few moments. The rain began to fall, and Gary laughed.

"Alright then, no need for things to escalate here. I'm just looking for George. Tell him Gary stopped by, if you see him."

Gary tucked his pistol away. Dickey did not.

"He owes me quite a bit of money," Gary added.

"I'm not surprised," Dickey replied. "He owes me plenty more than that."

Gary nodded then slowly walked back to his car, got in, and started the engine.

Dickey stared at the car, his finger curled around the trigger of his gun. Gary rolled down the window and said to him with a smile, "If I find out you're lying to me, I'll burn your house down with your kids in it."

Dickey stared back without saying a word as Gary reversed out of his driveway and pulled away.

The wind howled and the trees swayed. Dickey gazed up at the pines and wondered how long they'd hold.

Chapter 5
The Fix

George stared out the motel window, his eyes scanning the parking lot with paranoia. Every car was his potential doom. Sooner or later he would find him; the town was too small and he had too many connections. *If only that whore hadn't run off with his money.*

He lit a smoke and wiped his face on his dingy, yellowed tank top. He smelled, but no worse than the rundown motel known to locals as the fuck-hole did. Steam from the bathroom filled the room.

Rachel, fresh from the shower, groaned in disgust as she plunked down onto the motel bed. "This place is such a fucking shithole!"

"Yeah, well, it's all we can afford after your little girlfriend fucked us over," George shot back. "You just had to have her, didn't you?" He locked the door and hurriedly drew the shades, peering out the window with paranoia.

"Fuck you!" Rachel yelled, sitting up and throwing her lighter at George, striking him in the head. "You wanted her, too. Kept talking about 'my friend with the cute ass.' Don't lay that on me!"

138

"Ow! Fuck! Yeah, well she fucked us good. That ass wasn't six grand in cash and pills," he said in a huff.

"I'll find that bitch, I swear to God. I'll cut her little throat," Rachel promised.

"We've got bigger problems than that," George reminded her. "Little Miss sweet ass ran off with all the money I had for Gary and most of our pills. I've been off the grid long enough; he's bound to be pissed the fuck off." He peered out the window again, examining every car in the parking lot with suspicion.

"So, what the hell are we going to do?" Rachel asked, afraid. "I'm starting to feel like shit." It had been hours since they'd last gotten high.

"Here, baby," he said, grabbing a couple of pills out of his cigarette pack and giving them to her. "First things first—I need to score us some dope to get us through."

"Heroin? Jesus Christ, George."

"It's the same shit, Rache. We'll use it to wean off the pills. We've gotten too used to doing them; can't just stop."

"What are you going to do about Augustine?"

"I don't know. I can't think straight. Might have to sell my car or something." He lit a smoke and sat down on the bed beside her. "But I'll figure it out. I always do. I'll come up with some money, pay Gary, and get more pills. Then we can start partying again."

"This time, let's not get robbed," Rachel suggested, rolling her eyes.

"Yeah, yeah. Keep your girlfriend away from our shit."

"How are you going to score?" she asked, her concern turning to their next high.

"I'll call Carson, see if he can help us out," he replied, pulling his phone from his pocket to call his roommate.

DWIGHT WINCED AS THE RINGING in his head grew louder. He took out a bottle of Ibuprofen, popped four pills into his mouth, and chewed them. Max sat loyally beside him in the waiting room. Dwight rubbed him behind his ears and sighed. *How long were they going to be kept waiting?*

"Mr. Evans?" the doctor finally called sometime later. "Why don't you two c'mon back," he said invitingly.

"Well, I'm not going to sugar coat things, Mr. Evans; it's not the greatest prognosis," Doctor Humphrey said, running his hand affectionately down Max's back. "His hips are degenerating, as are his eyes. While there is nothing immediately concerning, Maxie here is getting towards that time."

"How long do you think, doc?" Dwight asked with a sigh.

"Could be six months, could be a couple years. But you'll know when the time has come. I know you love him, so I know when it does come, you'll make the right choice," he said. Dr. Humphrey had been Max's vet for twelve years. He was a good man who had always been there for Max, and Dwight appreciated that.

"Thank you, doctor," Dwight said, shaking his hand.

"In the meantime, spoil the fella a little. He deserves it," Humphrey teased.

"Oh, believe me," Dwight laughed. "He lives better than I do."

"Let him take it easy. No more morning runs, alright?" the doc added as they left.

Dwight nodded regretfully and then brought Max back to his truck. Inside the cab, he hugged his best friend and rubbed him generously. "You're a good boy, Maxie. You're a damn good boy," he repeated. He choked back tears and lit a smoke. "Guess we're both past our prime, hey, buddy?"

He dropped the gear shift into drive and headed home.

"…AND PARKING WILL BE AVAILABLE on Franklin Street for any who want to come down to the arts fair on Sunday," Mrs. Hayes, the director of Torrington's arts commission, reported to the City Council and all residents in attendance.

The council meeting was held biweekly in the large conference room of the newly remodeled City Hall. The seal of the city, depicting the house where hometown icon and abolitionist John Brown was born, hung with prominence behind the council. Beneath the seal, each council member sat in a leather chair before a microphone.

There were maybe a dozen residents scattered throughout the large room, few of whom seemed to be paying any attention.

"Thank you, Mrs. Hayes," the presiding officer said. A placard in front of his microphone displayed his name: Councilman Bowe. "Is there anything else before we move to adjourn?"

A younger petite woman who was noticeably pregnant stood up and raised her arm.

"Yes, ma'am," Bowe said, motioning to her with his gavel.

"I was wondering when you were all planning on doing something about the shantytown in the woods behind what used to be A-Mart? You know, there's gotta be a hundred people living there. They do drugs, they burn trash, they rummage through people's cars, and steal anything they can get their hands on…."

"Ma'am," Bowe interrupted. "Let me stop you there. Okay, we are aware of this problem, but there is no easy fix. Those people have rights," he said cautiously. "They have to go somewhere. We can't just throw them out of town."

"Sure you can," a gruff voice came from the back of the room. Detective Wyatt Mayhew stepped forward. He wore jeans and a plain white t-shirt. If not for the City Police badge hanging by a chain around his neck, no one would have guessed he was law enforcement. "Hell, I bet more than half of them aren't even from Torrington. You don't want to admit that this city has become a go-to destination for derelicts and a dumping ground for surrounding towns to get rid of their homeless and addicted."

"Detective Mayhew," Bowe said, clearing his throat. "Thank you for your opinion…"

"I'm sorry, ma'am," Wyatt said to the young woman. "This guy's not going to address your problems. In fact, they won't let me or any other police address it, either. Too many political motivations to keep in mind.

"Fact is," he continued, turning his attention to the residents and councilors who were listening. "This town has a lot of charity, a lot of programs to aid people, and a lot of compassionate people. We also have lots of liquor stores and easy channels to score hard drugs through. We can pat ourselves on the back, talk about how compassionate we are, but that tent town in the woods on the north end is what we get. Hundreds of people with untreated mental health and addiction issues living in subhuman conditions, stealing whatever they can, spreading disease, and harmful substances."

"Detective Mayhew, we thank you for your remarks. We will take them into consideration," Bowe said, ready to bang his gavel.

Wyatt laughed. "You guys aren't going to do anything until something bad happens. We got kids who live in that neighborhood. Many of them cut through by the entrance to your shantytown."

"Thank you, everyone, for coming," Bowe said. "I will take a motion to adjourn."

"Moved," one Councilman said.

"Second!" another followed quickly.

Bowe slammed the hammer down on the table. "Meeting is adjourned!" he declared.

BOWE KNEW HE WOULD FIND WYATT in his office when he entered it minutes later.

"How many cases of scotch do I have to buy you to keep you away from these meetings?" he asked the detective, disarmingly.

"More than you could afford," Wyatt snickered, shutting the door to the councilman's office.

"Did you come here to put on a show or to put public pressure on me?"

"Does it have to be one or the other?" Wyatt asked with the hint of a grin. He took a seat. "You know that shantytown has been on my radar for a while."

"I've told you, between the ACLU and the Project Cleanway people, the mayor doesn't want a shakeup with elections coming in the fall. Maybe after…"

"Too many political motives here for my tastes. You're giving too much power to people who don't know what it's really like out there. They have no idea how bad it is, let alone how to fix it. You want me to clean up the streets, let me do my job."

"Listen, it's out of my hands. This is an election year, Wyatt. Besides, the shantytown is just a symptom of the problem," Bowe said, grabbing a bottle of scotch and two glasses from his bottom desk drawer. "Unemployment, addiction…"

"Another problem the city has tied my hands on," Wyatt griped, grabbing the bottle and pouring his own glass. "Too many political concerns over locking drug dealers up, I suppose."

"Wyatt, lock the dealers up! Go ahead. We've been over this." Bowe took a sip of his drink and exhaled loudly.

"You know what I am saying. Don't dick me around. There's a flow—a direct vein of heroin coming into this town. The lab says most of the dope we recover is coming from the same place, yet I can't get the green light to put an investigation together, or to even move on anyone involved."

"It's out of our hands, as I have told you. Goes too high and out of Torrington. State Police need to handle that."

"Call them in! Let me coordinate with them! They don't seem to give a shit about what I know."

"Wyatt, State has been made aware of what you know. Several times."

"Through reports and emails. I want an actual person to come down here and explain to me why they aren't doing shit."

"Listen, Wyatt. I've told you, there is a RICO investigation..."

"Right, the feds are working a RICO case and don't want cooperation from detectives on the ground? It's bullshit, Larry. Something doesn't add up."

"I would be careful what you're insinuating, old friend. I've asked as many questions as I can. I'm not on the police board, I have no business pushing the brass, and I have no contacts at the State PD."

"Look, I'm going to do some digging on my own," Wyatt insisted.

"Be careful. Don't piss off the wrong people," Bowe warned. "Oh, and Wyatt?"

"Yeah?" Wyatt replied before leaving.

"Don't come here anymore. I can't have someone in the mayor's office seeing you here any more than you would want the brass seeing you with me."

Wyatt's eyes looked to the floor and he sighed. "You're right, old friend. Take care of yourself."

Bowe sniffed hard and took a sip from his drink as Wyatt shut the door behind him on his way out. Bowe sighed and scratched at his beard. The man was his friend, but the realities of their respective jobs were more pressing for both of them.

WYATT MAYHEW'S REALITY was all but defined by his job. He had known that sooner or later, that would end his friendship with Bowe. It was inevitable, though part of him felt a tinge of sadness. Maybe even a hint of regret. There was a time when he valued personal relationships. Now, when he wasn't working (which was less and less these days), he preferred isolation. He lived alone, drinking scotch and beer, smoking cigarettes, and eating frozen dinners.

He came home to his apartment that evening, just as his did every evening, and poured himself a tall glass of Scotch. He microwaved a frozen steak dinner and sat down to drink and smoke while he waited for it.

It was a relatively nice apartment, though it hadn't been cared for in quite some time. Wyatt had leased the place with his fiancée, Carla, two years prior, but after living with him for three months, she became miserable. She hated his career—the way it made him act, the hours, the risks he took.

In 2011, he was involved in a shootout with two home invaders. He killed both men and saved the family they were terrorizing. The papers lauded him as a hero but for Carla, it was too much. She left him without warning one evening while he was at work.

That was the last time he had tried to have a meaningful relationship with anyone. Heartbroken, he poured himself into his work. The shooting had earned him the nickname 'Wyatt Earp,' but the event had changed him. Taking a life was something with which he had never come to terms. An inner loathing and societal dissatisfaction turned to rage. He pushed the boundaries; sometimes he stepped over the line.

He had more complaints lodged against him than any other member of the force. The only reason he had kept his job was that the claims were hard to prove. Nor did it hurt that he was a pretty damn good detective. He got results, so the department was often willing to look the other way.

Mayhew knew he had a temper but he aimed it at the most deserving filth he could find. He took his job seriously and, as far as he was concerned, you couldn't clean things up without getting dirty.

THE NAUSEA WAS UNBEARABLE. Maegan lurched over, gripping her stomach, her body aching in fits of betrayal for not getting its fix. She didn't want to cry but cry she did, feeling all her progress slipping away. She had not come nearly as far as she had led herself to believe. She was still dependent; still needing that fix. Her prescription had expired, and having not seen a doctor or returned to counseling, she was forced to seek alternative avenues to make the sickness stop. Her mother's dealer, Dennis, had agreed to sell her some Suboxone but he was over an hour late.

She sat on her mother's porch and looked at her phone anxiously. She had three unanswered messages from Jason. Thinking about him stressed her out. His love just made her feel guilty. How could she talk to him now? She couldn't tell him the truth or stand the thought of lying to him. She felt helpless and destined to disappoint him and break his heart.

Finally, after what seemed like an eternity, Dennis showed up and gave her what she had been dying to have. After popping the strip under her tongue, she felt instantly better.

"Let me know if you need anything else," Dennis said with a sly smile.

Maegan shot him a look of contempt and lit a cigarette. He then went inside, presumably to sell April something. Maegan knew her mother's use was getting worse; the house was a disaster, and she was always asleep when Maegan would visit. Danny told her she was high all the time and had nearly set fire to the kitchen trying to cook him dinner the other night.

"I don't know," he'd told her. "Maybe it would be okay to come live with you and Uncle Dwight."

She hoped he would. This house was toxic, and yet here she was— the only place she felt safe and unjudged for her weakness.

"Thanks, darling!" April called from the door as Dennis left.

"Anytime, honey," he said through rotten teeth and a twisted smile.

"You're fucking disgusting," Maegan chided her mother.

"What the fuck was that for?!" April scoffed.

"Just remembering how many times you've fucked that skeevy piece of shit," Maegan snapped through a haze of cigarette smoke.

"I'm not ashamed of anything I've done," April said defiantly.

"You're disgusting. You have no standards. No morals. Simply disgusting," Maegan said sharply.

Her words were meant to hurt, as if she could rebuke herself by cutting her mother down. Somewhere inside, she saw herself standing in her mother's shoes. She saw her own future and she detested it. She wished her mother would just go away so she would never have to see her again and never have to be reminded of her fate.

"You think you're so goddamn great?" April sneered. "You think you're better than me? Just because you got a new place and fooled that boy into dating you? You're a fucking fraud," she said with a laugh as she retreated into the house.

The screen door smacked against the outside wall from the force with which Maegan opened it. She pursued her mother like a beast on the scent of blood.

146

"At least I have people who love me!" she yelled, blood coursing through her veins, her face red with anger. "At least I haven't fucked up everyone's life that ever depended on me!"

"You will. Just give it time," her mother said calmly, lighting a smoke and sitting at the kitchen table, fully satisfied she had gotten under Maegan's skin. "You'll ruin everything you touch because you have the disease and that's what it does. Pretend to be whatever you want. You're just like me, and you will never escape that."

Maegan smacked her mother's face as hard as she could, exploding the head of her cigarette into a thousand burning embers. April stared back at her coldly, a handprint forming on her face. Then she laughed. "Did I hit a nerve, sweetheart?"

Maegan began to cry, her rage and sadness melding into a feeling of hopelessness.

"Just like your mother," April said with satisfaction, lighting another smoke.

"I hope you die!" Maegan shouted in her face. She grabbed her purse and headed for the door. "I hope you fucking die you vile, disgusting whore!"

The door slammed, and April was left alone. Her daughter gone, it was safe for her to cry. She held her face in her hands and sobbed uncontrollably. She would never let her know it, but Maegan had wounded her, and she had never felt so low. She grabbed the bag of heroin Dennis had sold her and retreated to her bedroom.

THE DOCTOR PURSED HIS LIPS and tapped his fingers on his desk in consideration.

"What's wrong?" Dickey asked, anxiously curving the brim of his John Deere hat in his hands.

"Nothing at all, Richard," Doctor Spencer replied. "Just considering something."

"Call me Dickey, please. Richard was my father," Dickey requested.

147

"Very well," Spencer said with a nod. He sat up in his chair and leaned across his desk. "This is only our first time speaking, and I don't presume to be able to know you or your problems after speaking for only an hour, but you seem to have a savior complex."

"A savior complex? Like, I think I'm Jesus?"

"No," Spencer replied with a slight laugh. "No, this is rather common among veterans and law enforcement. They take the responsibilities of their job or service, and they try to transfer that to personal relationships. They believe they can save everyone—solve their problems or fix their lives."

Dickey sat in silence contemplating Spencer's words. He supposed he did have an urge to save people and fix their problems, but he never considered that to be a bad thing.

"What's wrong with helping people?" he asked.

"Nothing, to a point," Spencer answered. "But at some point, it becomes unhealthy to yourself and your relationships. These tendencies can often signal a need for control as well as a need to feel needed."

"Guess I never much considered it that way," Dickey said, genuinely surprised at the logic.

"I also think you suffer from a lot of bottled up resentment, possibly even rage, stemming from your wife's death. The PTSD from your service just compounds that."

"So, what do I do?" Dickey asked. "How do I start to fix myself and get back to being normal."

"I wouldn't say normal," Spencer corrected him. "There's nothing particularly abnormal about the reactions you're having to these traumas."

"Okay, well how do I get better?"

"Coming here is a good first step," Spencer said with a smile. "Let's do this once a week. As far as the anxiety, I will probably prescribe you something once I am able to learn more about you and your symptoms."

"What do I do until then?"

"Tell me, are you or your girls allergic to dogs?"

"Not that I know of," Dickey said confusedly.

"There's been a lot of research to back up the benefit of having a therapy dog, or an emotional support dog. Whatever you want to call it."

"Like a service dog?"

"Sort of… There are places that train animals for this purpose, but really, in a case like yours, any dog will do, as long as it has a good disposition. The dog becomes a companion; it offers comfort, affection, even a listening ear when you need to vent."

"You want me to get a dog…. To talk to?"

"Well, you don't have to talk to it, Dickey, but the effect they have on anxiety is documented. I am prescribing this for you. Go get a dog. It will be something you can do with your girls. They'll benefit from it, too."

"A dog? That's your prescription?"

"Trust me," Spencer said with a smile, rising to shake Dickey's hand. "Get a nice dog; a lab or something. Your kids will love it, and it will help you."

Dickey shook his hand skeptically but agreed he would get a dog.

"I guess the girls will be happy," he said before leaving.

IT WAS LATE AFTERNOON when the party started ramping up. The Toros had rolled into town, and Andrew wanted to make sure they were properly welcomed. His house and yard were full of Toros, easily identifiable from their tatted faces and golden bull necklaces. Decked out, flashy cars lined both sides of Reckon Avenue. Scantily clad Latina women— there mostly for eye candy and the enjoyment of the members— mixed with the Toros.

Michael pulled his car into the front yard where Eddie helped him unload two kegs of beer.

"Think this will be enough?" Eddie asked. The bald giant grunted and lifted one of the barrels himself. Michael tried to follow suit but could only laugh in defeat when he was unable move it.

"Yo, I can't move this shit on my own, Hercules!" Michael called after him. Eddie placed the keg he was carrying on the front porch and then returned to grab the other one.

"I got it, ese. Go tell your brother we're back, see what else he wants done."

"Yeah, yeah… fuckin' love these parties. Just love being everyone's fuckin' bitch and running errands all day."

Andrew generally treated Michael and Eddie as equals but when the Toros came around, that all changed. They were unaffiliated, and as such, they were at the bottom of the pecking order.

Michael found his brother in the backyard smoking a blunt with Gary Augustine, a group of Toros, and a couple of women.

Andrew welcomed his brother. "What's up, hermano?!" he asked, putting his arm firmly around his shoulders and handing him the blunt.

Michael smiled and took a couple of puffs from before passing it to his left.

"Nothing, bro. Just got back with the beer. You guys need anything else?" he asked, glancing around at the Toros' mean mugs. They all acted real hard when an outsider was around.

"Nah, bro. Just relax! Enjoy the fucking party, man!" Andrew said with a laugh.

Michael looked at Gary, the whitest guy at the party. Andrew and Michael's mother was white, but they both took after their father. Gary was pale as snow and stood out at any Toros event. Nonetheless, the Toros treated him with the utmost respect. They knew he was connected. More importantly, he was one of their suppliers.

"What's up, Gary?" Michael asked, lifting his chin in respect.

"Little Michael," Gary said with a laugh, taking the blunt from the Toro on his right. "Not so little anymore, though. Heard you're making all kind of moves these days," he added.

"You know, I'm keeping it real," Michael said with pride.

"I'll keep that in mind," Gary said with a grin.

"For real," Michael said. "You ever need someone to roll with you for something, you just let me know."

Gary looked to Andrew for his reaction before responding. Andrew raised his eyebrows and shrugged as if to say he was indifferent on the matter.

"Alright, Mikey. I'll keep that in mind," Gary replied.

Gary's cell phone rang, prompting him to step out of the circle. He held the phone up to his right ear and plugged his left to block out the noise from the party.

"Who this?" he asked when he answered the call. He paused a moment then smiled widely. "Connor, buddy, I had a feeling you would be calling."

JASON WAS RELIEVED to see Maegan. She had not been responding to his messages all day and he'd become quite concerned. As a result, he'd wrestled with his anxiety until she messaged him with apologies, asking if they were still on for dinner at Dickey's that night.

They were all waiting on the porch when Maegan pulled into Dickey's driveway in her uncle's pickup truck. She extinguished a cigarette as she climbed out. Jason greeted her with a big hug and a kiss.

The girls were eagerly awaiting their introduction.

"Maegan, baby, these are my nieces, Marie and Stacey," Jason said.

"Hi!" Maegan said with a warm smile. "Aren't you two pretty!"

"Thank you," Marie said with a bashful smile. Her sister Stacey shied away behind Jason's leg.

"Is she your girlfriend, Uncle Jay?" Stacey asked.

"Yes, Stacey. She's the lady I told you about," he said, rubbing her head softly. Stacey flashed Maegan a big smile.

"Hi," Stacey said with a laugh.

"Hello, sweetie," Maegan said, kneeling down to the girls' level.

"You're pretty," Marie said.

"Aw, thank you! You're very pretty, also," Maegan said, delicately placing her hand on Marie's shoulder. "And so are you, Stacey."

"Thank you," Marie said, blushing.

"Thank you," Stacey said, always following her sister's lead in new situations.

"You must be Maegan," Dickey said as he emerged from the house, extending his hand.

Maegan rose and shook his hand with a warm smile. "That's me," she said with a laugh. "And you must be Dickey. Jason has told me so much about you," she added.

"Hopefully not too much," Dickey replied with a chuckle.

"Only good stuff so far," Maegan said.

"Yeah, I'm saving the bad stuff for after she gets to know you," Jason joked.

"Well, I hope you're hungry," Dickey said. "I've got a roast on. Should be ready in about an hour."

FOR THE NEXT HOUR, Maegan found herself playing dolls with the girls as Jason and Dickey tinkered in the kitchen.

"A girl's gotta have a nice wardrobe," Maegan told the girls as she helped them pick out doll clothes.

Hearing her interactions from the kitchen, Dickey smiled.

"What?" Jason asked quietly.

"She's good with the girls. It's nice seeing them have a woman to play with. I don't know, maybe I misjudged her. She seems nice, brother."

"Thanks, man. She's really a great girl. I'm in love with her."

"That's great, brother. Have you told her yet?" Dickey asked, checking the temperature on the roast.

"It's complicated," Jason replied.

"It always is," he said, wiping his hands on a paper towel and tossing it in the trash. He walked over to the living room to offer Maegan a reprieve. "Hey girls, why don't you go upstairs, gather all your doll clothes to show Maegan?" They enthusiastically agreed. "Maegan is going to come out back with Uncle Jay and me for a few minutes for some adult conversation. Then we'll eat, and after dinner, you can play some more," he suggested.

The girls ran upstairs to search for their doll clothes, and Maegan followed Jason and Dickey onto the back porch to smoke.

"You have great girls," Maegan said.

"Thanks," Dickey beamed. He lit the joint and shook his head. "It's hard by myself, but I give it my all. Jason here is a godsend. He's always been there for me. Especially lately, stepping up and helping me until I find a new sitter."

"I heard about that!" Maegan said empathically. "Such a tragedy. I'm so sorry. What kind of monster would do something like that?"

"It's scary to think about," Jason said, hitting the joint then passing it to Maegan.

"Thanks," Maegan said as she took it.

"Yeah, hard to imagine," Dickey said.

He exchanged a quick look with Jason. They both knew that it wasn't hard for him to imagine at all. He knew the ugliness and brutality of the world all too well. But that wasn't a conversation to have in front of his guest.

"I gotta say, Maegan," Dickey said, shifting the conversation. "I haven't seen Jason this happy in quite some time. From what he says, that's because of you."

Maegan smiled and batted her eyes. "Aw, well I try my best. He is a great guy, for sure. He deserves to be happy."

Dickey's words made her feel good, but at the same time they cut into her like knives. In some way she couldn't fully understand, she felt guilty. She felt like a fraud. Her mother's words from earlier that day still echoed in her head. All she wanted was to be the woman both of these men saw her as, yet more and more she felt like that was impossible. This was a good, wholesome life with lovely people. She wanted to belong so badly but deep down, for some reason, she felt she never could.

After dinner, she played with the girls some more and found herself having a great time. She started to feel ill again but took another Suboxone in the bathroom. That only made her feel guiltier. She took Jason for a drive up to the lake in the pickup, where they had sex in the bed and smoked another joint. She always felt better about their relationship in the throes of passion. That's when it felt right to her; when the doubts and the guilt seemed to fade. That's when she truly felt equal to him.

"I love you," he said to her as they laid in truck bed, their naked bodies huddled together under a thin blanket he'd taken from Dickey's linen closet.

Maegan's heart sank. She froze. She didn't know what to do or what to say. She wanted to cry out to Jason—to tell him she loved him too. She wanted to allow herself to be overjoyed at this moment. Such an amazing and caring man loved *her*. Of all people, he loved her! Instead her guilt washed over her and made her panic. *Surely, he didn't love the real her, only the woman he thought she was.* The reality was that she was an addict. *A filthy addict.* She carried the disease and always would. She would never be good enough for him.

He waited for her response, and she found herself unable to speak for what seemed like an eternity.

"I'm sorry," she finally managed to say. "I just—it's a lot—I'm just not ready—I can't."

He looked at her with hurt eyes. Perplexed, he sat up and a stared into the distance. She sat up and hugged him from behind.

"I'm sorry," she said again. "I'm just really fucked up. It's hard to sort out sometimes."

He told her he understood and kissed her softly. They got dressed, and she drove him back to Dickey's.

"I'm sorry. I just can't yet..." she said to him as he got out. "I had a really nice time tonight," she added, trying to soften the blow.

"It's okay, really," he said, but she could tell he was crushed. "I'll see you tomorrow," he said before shutting the truck door.

She cried the whole way as she drove back to her new home. Once there, she took another Suboxone and cried some more. She cuddled with Max, as had become her routine, and cried herself to sleep. *Why couldn't she be a better person? Why couldn't she be the person she wanted so badly to be?*

BANG! BANG! BANG! THE SHOTS rang out across the range as Dwight unloaded his .45, striking the target with deadly accuracy. When he finished, he punched the red button and recalled his target.

"DAMN!" the range master remarked as he walked past. "Dirty fucking Harry over here!"

"Dirty Harry carried a 44 magnum," Dwight said with a chuckle.

"You know, I never see any of the local boys in here. You've probably put in hundreds of more hours than them."

"Well, Steve, it gets boring up in the sticks where I work. This is all the action I ever get."

"Ain't nothing wrong with that. These targets don't shoot back!" Steve joked as he swept up brass.

"Think that's it for me today," Dwight concluded, folding his target and sticking it into his ammo bag. He removed his ear muffs and paused, unable to tell if the ringing in his ears was from shooting or his tumor. He shook the thought way, and continued to pack up, thankful he hadn't had a headache in days.

"You got Maxie with you?"

"Nah, don't dare leave him in the car in this heat," Dwight replied.

"Well when you can, you bring him down again. He can come inside and hang out behind the counter with me while you shoot."

"That would be great. Thanks, Steve. He hates being left home."

"A dutiful partner," Steve said, hanging the broom up on a hook on the wall.

Dwight emerged from the gun shop and was pleased to see the rain had stopped. The early evening sun was already baking the rain off Torrington's streets, glimmering and dancing on the wet surface.

He locked his ammo bag safely in the trunk of his car and was about to leave when he saw a disheveled man acting sketchy at the gas station across the street. He watched as the man approached a busted Ford Taurus and leaned in the driver's side window. From his vantage, Dwight could see the man take something from the driver and put it in his pocket.

"Son of a bitch…" Dwight said, shaking his head.

Before he could react, the Taurus drove off. He reached for his radio, forgetting he was in civilian clothes. The disheveled man hurried away. Dwight sprinted after him. He came up quickly behind and drew his .45.

"Police! Hands in the air!" Dwight commanded.

"What? Oh, fuck! C'mon!" Swamp yelled, throwing his hands in the air with a sigh.

"Down on the ground!"

"Man, this is fucking bullshit! What's your probable cause?" Swamp asked as he complied.

"Just saw you buying drugs, asshole," Dwight scoffed as he searched him for weapons. He retrieved the baggie of dope from his jeans pocket and shook his head. "There's just no end to this shit, is there?"

Not having his cuffs on him, Dwight led Swamp to his car at gunpoint and put him securely in the back. He then radioed Torrington PD to request they allow him to book the suspect there. The man smelled like shit and Dwight did not want to ride with him for forty-five minutes to the Canaan Barracks. As usual, TPD was more than happy to accommodate State Police requests and the dispatcher cheerfully told him to "head on over."

Once there, Dwight went through the process of booking Swamp with assistance from a local officer.

"Name?" the local officer asked Swamp as Dwight fingerprinted him.

"John Pryor," Swamp answered. He was sullen and despondent that he would be facing jail time once again. To top it off, he hadn't been able to shoot up and would soon be quite sick. "Yo, I need detox!" he said forcefully.

"Yeah, yeah, after you're booked. You know the drill," the officer told him.

"Been through this before, huh?" Dwight asked, finishing up his prints.

"Oh, yeah. Pryor's got a bunch of priors," the officer joked.

"You think that's funny, huh?" Swamp asked. The officer simply winked at him.

"Trooper, we just need you to fill out the arresting officer's report. You can use any empty desk upstairs," the officer told him.

Dwight nodded. "Appreciate the help," he said before heading upstairs.

About twenty minutes later, as Dwight was filling out the paperwork, a burly bald man with steely eyes walked up to the desk where he was working and extended his hand.

"Trooper Evans? Detective Mayhew," he introduced himself. "Pleased to meet you."

"Detective," Dwight said, rising to his feet and firmly shaking his hand.

"Could you step into my office for a moment? I wanted to have a little talk with you," Wyatt asked.

"Of course," Dwight said.

Wyatt's office was small and his desk was littered with stacks of paper. A laptop he hadn't touched in some time peeked out from under the mess. He pushed the papers aside and sat on the edge of his desk.

"Is this about the Taurus?" Dwight asked.

"Excuse me?" Wyatt asked, confused. Then he realized what Dwight was talking about and shook his head. "Oh, no. No, we have a good idea who that was. Don't worry about that. Listen, I wanted to tell you—professional courtesy and all—the guy you just picked up…"

"Yeah?"

"We're cutting him lose," Wyatt said, raising his eyebrows and shrugging.

"Excuse me?" Dwight said, his hands placed on his hips in indignation. "Mind telling me why?"

"The guy you picked up is an asset of mine. I get a lot of information from him and frankly, he does me no good if he's off the streets." Wyatt rubbed his head, aware the news was not going to be understood or taken well by a Trooper from Colebrook.

"Wow, so just let the dope heads roam free? Is that how they do things in Torrington?"

"Listen, buddy, I am aware this might seem... well... strange. Where you come from, I'm sure you take what busts you can make. Down here I have to play things a bit more diplomatically."

"Is that what you call letting heroin addicts go scot-free? Diplomacy? Where I come from may seem like the sticks to you, but heroin is destroying my community. I don't regard users as people to negotiate with."

"Heroin is destroying all our communities. That's the point," Wyatt told him. "Swamp is my inside man., I have leverage on him. In fact, today you helped me gain a little more. So, thank you. And you better wise up to the fact that users are often the victims in this world."

"Unreal," Dwight said in disbelief.

"Look, that's how we have to play it down here. We let the small fish go, and they help us bring in the big fish."

"How's that working for you?" Dwight asked sarcastically.

"I've brought down six dope houses based on information from Swamp alone, Trooper. I've saved lives. Don't you dare come into my house and act like you're morally superior. We're fighting the same damn war. You just don't understand what the war looks like on the front lines."

"Guess I shouldn't have bothered. I'll look the other way next time. Won't even waste my time," Dwight chortled.

He turned to leave but Wyatt stopped him.

"Listen, Trooper," he said, rising to his feet and stepping closer. "I can tell you want to help," he said slowly. "There is something I can use your help with if you want to really have an impact on the heroin supply running through our towns."

Dwight didn't respond but looked Wyatt straight in the eyes and waited.

"Have you ever heard of a man by the name of Gary Augustine?" Wyatt asked.

"No, why?" asked Dwight.

"How about Andrew Trivoty?"

"Sounds familiar, but I can't place it," Dwight said.

"More than eighty percent of the dope we find lately has the same makeup. It's likely coming from the same source. A major vein running right through our towns."

"What does this have to do with me?" Dwight asked.

"I believe it's all being run through a house in Winsted. You have jurisdiction there, I don't."

"So, call Winsted PD. Tell Hartford about it. The state has a massive task force…"

"Yeah, yeah, I know all about their jerk-off task force. All it does is confiscate my evidence and block me from doing what I have to do. Look, this is a major operation, and Winsted is full of crooked cops—likely the state police too."

Dwight's brow furrowed disapprovingly. *Was this guy serious? Crooked cops?*

"What could you possibly need me for?" Dwight asked hesitantly.

"I need someone I can trust. Someone who has some authority to poke around in Winsted."

"And what makes you think you can trust me?" Dwight asked.

"Your outrage here today. Crooked cops aren't going to care about some shithead holding a dime bag."

"Look," Dwight said with a sigh. "If what you say is true then I wish you all the luck, but I'm just a resident trooper from the sticks. I am not the guy you need to take down a major operation."

Wyatt put his hand firmly on Dwight's shoulder and looked him square in the eye. "You're exactly who I need." He could see something in Dwight; he could tell he wanted to say yes. "Look, think about it. If you want to make a difference, meet me at O'Malley's on 44 in Winsted tonight at midnight."

"And if not?"

"If not, then have a nice life in the sticks," Wyatt said. He opened his office door and nodded for Dwight to leave. "Don't worry about finishing that paperwork."

THE IRON HORSE MOTEL in Barkhamsted was about as run down and lowly as you'd expect for a place that still advertised their color TV in 2016. A few brave travelers and a slew of permanent residents were its typical inhabitants. The Iron Horse had a reputation for being a go-to hold up for anyone hiding out or on the run. Of course, this fame had stemmed from several news stories that, while differing in circumstance, all shared one common theme: the person hiding or running had always been caught, or in one case, killed. A rightful legacy for the Iron Horse should have been a place to avoid when hiding out, but such was not the logic that brought George and Rachel to room 4 of the famed motel.

"Baby, get me some cigs when you go out," George called out to Rachel.

"Okay, but I need money," she replied.

"It's on the dresser," he called out from the bathroom as he urinated. He heard the door shut a few moments later. He washed his hands and examined his face in the mirror. He was pale and his eyes were dull. He'd probably lost twenty pounds over the past few weeks.

He pushed the bathroom door open and gasped. Gary Augustine was sitting next to the bed, his gun trained on him.

160

"George, George, George… What are you thinking? What are you doing? I thought you were smarter than this," Gary teased. "To throw it all away for so little, and for that ugly whore? Dude, we could have been bros. We could have nailed hot high school girls together and had free primo drugs all the time. Instead, I have to fucking murder you in this shit hole. Why, George? Why did you let me down?"

Augustine's demeanor was cold and flippant. His long, black hair was tied back, displaying a tattoo of a reaper on his neck.

"Gary, let me explain!" George stammered, sitting down on the foot of the bed, his eyes unable to see anything but the pistol aimed at his head.

"Do you have my money?"

"No."

"Of course not. If you did, why would you be here?" He laughed. George remained frozen.

"This girl, she robbed me!" he tried to explain.

"There's always an excuse, George!" Gary replied. "I thought you were better than this. You got anything you can do to make this right for me?" he asked, lowering his gun slightly.

"I—I don't know…Maybe, I mean, I could come up with something!" George insisted.

"Well, come up with something. You'd better come up with something to make this right and soon, or I'm going to shoot you in the head and go get a drink."

George began to panic, his breath drew shorter and he felt faint.

"I—I—I can find a way… I mean, just a little time—something, I mean… I'll do anything, just please!" George stammered.

"Then what's it going to be? What are you going to do?" Gary asked, aiming the gun at George's head. "C'mon, George! What's the solution?!"

Right as Augustine was about to pull the trigger, George looked up and said confidently, "I got it. I know what to do."

Chapter Six
The Catalyst

Travis Madison was one of his mother's three children, but he was the odd son out. The other two boys were the sons of his drunken stepfather, Rick. They generally had free range while Rick rode Travis hard.

He was just seven years old the first time Rick kicked his ass using a sock with a roll of quarters in it. There'd been many beatings over the years. Two weeks ago, Rick had pummeled him bloody with his bare hands. That was the last beating Travis intended to take. He packed his things and moved out. His mother couldn't care less; she had pill habit and was terrified of Rick.

Tim, his best friend since grade school, had convinced his mother to let him stay there for the time being. The two were together nearly all day, every day anyway. As of recently, however, those days were filled with two tasks: finding the cash for dope and doing dope.

"This isn't a real good idea," Tim cautioned.

"Shut up and keep your voice down," Travis said in a hushed, urgent tone.

They crept along the driveway of Rick's house, slowly approaching the garage. The night was clear, the moon was full, and the street was quiet save the sound of crickets.

"He's gonna hear it!" Tim stressed in a whisper.

"Trust me," Travis allayed. "I used to sneak out and back in all the time. He sleeps like a rock, anyway—fuckin' drunk."

He punched the four-digit code into the code box, and the door began to lift. The horrid noise of the mechanical motor seemed even louder against the still, quiet backdrop of his street at three-thirty in the morning.

Travis hit a button, stopping the door about three feet off the ground.

"Let's go," he said, ducking down and under the door.

"Jesus Christ…"

"Look, we're just grabbing the coin collection and that's it. Easy in, easy out," he reassured him as they slowly felt their way through the darkness.

Travis carefully opened the door that led into the raised ranch, and the two walked inside. Tim followed as Travis made a left turn into the first room. Inside, Travis pulled out a pocket flashlight and shined it on a nearby mantle. A book of coins rested upon it.

Tim grabbed the coins but as he turned to leave he brushed into something in the darkness. A broom slid across the wall and fell to the wood floor, making a loud smacking sound.

"Shit…" Tim whispered. They heard heavy steps above their heads.

"Go!" Travis commanded.

The two hustled out the garage and under the door. By the time they hit the road they were in full sprint.

"Holy shit!" Tim said when they stopped around the corner.

"His lights are on, now…" Travis said, peeking back through the bushes. "Shit, we didn't close the garage door. He's going to know!"

"Fuck it, man. Let's go to the car and get out of here! We can pawn those down in Waterbury so he won't find them. Then we can get a few bundles from Trivoty."

"SEEMS LIKE A GOOD RAIN STORM would wash some of these roads right out and you'd be stuck," Greg Hostetler chuckled, sweat running down from under his wide-brimmed Stetson hat. His Ford pickup with Maine plates was the newest thing on Randy Sandusfield's property.

"A couple storms have tried but we always get out," Sandusfield chuckled. He was a scruffy man with thick stubble, a wiry mustache, and long graying eyebrows.

"Gotta say, you keep a pretty low profile out here," Hostetler observed. "You'd think you were living hungry. I know you must have made quite a bit of money. Sorry for asking, but what do you do with it all?"

Hostetler lit a pipe and passed it to Sandusfield. His visits were always a matter of business, but he would usually stay and visit for a few hours. Randy would oblige him only because he felt for the man having to make such long drives.

"I've got it stashed away somewhere safe. Not here. It's for my boy," Randy answered, motioning to Mark who was in the shed hanging up plants.

"How old is he now? Getting big."

"Fourteen."

"Funny, though, you know?"

"What's that?"

"Oh, nothing. Just I was reading about Juarez, earlier. I'm sure you've heard. You know, it's a bloody fucking mess down there. They just found another one of these body-houses… Abandoned addresses where the cartels dump their victims. Awful mess—women and children, even. Hundred or more of them just rotting in there."

"Savages."

"That's it. They are. And yet here we sit in peace with your son hanging marijuana plants in the shed like it was tobacco."

"If tobacco was illegal, people would kill for tobacco," Randy said as he drew from the pipe.

"Indeed. But then there would also be a lot more money in growing tobacco."

"Damn right."

"But here we are in New England. We've got weed and—shit— we've got plenty of dope, blow, and speed. Anything you need. Yet you and

I conduct business civilly. I don't need armed guards. What makes us different?"

"It's the middle-class suburban drug world, friend. People just want to get high. They don't want to associate with drug lords, gang members, or get shot at for trying to cop a joint."

"But that's just it, friend," Hostetler argued. "That's where you and I come in. It is the same here as anywhere else. That blood in Mexico may not be tied directly to our operation, but it's still blood for control of a market we help to thrive. We pretend it's a different world; that it's not connected. But it's all one big, ugly black market, Randy. We just don't allow problems like that up here. Got to maintain the illusion, if only for the customer's sake."

"Mark!" Randy called down, interrupting the conversation. "Make sure you check those timers downstairs, too."

"Yeah, Dad," Mark answered with a wave.

"You served," Hostetler noted. "Desert Storm, Iraq. I saw the bumper sticker on your truck."

"Yeah, I served," Randy said before lighting the pipe.

"Ever kill a man?" Hostetler asked, his eyes wide with intrigue.

"Have you, Greg?" Randy asked coolly in reply.

"I'm just a driver, friend. I carry a gun but I mostly see nice folks like yourself."

"Maybe you shouldn't ask questions you wouldn't understand the answers to," Randy advised.

"Alright! Easy, now," Hostetler chuckled. "I just wondered if you had it in you."

"Killing a man is the easy the part," Randy said. "Living with it is harder."

With that, Randy rose from his seat and went inside. He came back out with a large black duffel bag slung over his shoulder. He dropped it on the porch, making a loud thud. Hostetler understood this meant it was time to go. He grabbed the bag and groaned as he lifted it up.

"Shit never gets lighter," he chuckled as he stumbled forward.

166

"There's three-hundred-fifty thousand dollars in there. If it gets lighter, I'm screwing you," Randy joked.

Hostetler slid the duffel into the back of his covered truck bed. Soon after, he was pulling away, headed north for Maine.

Randy set to preparing breakfast for him and Mark. He didn't see George Calloway's Pontiac Le Mans pull into sight and then slowly back away.

MAEGAN CAME BEARING COFFEE, cigarettes, and a rehearsed apology, though she didn't feel like her mother deserved it. For as long as she could remember they had fought, and her mother had never accepted any of the blame. Maegan resented always having to be the bigger person. Nonetheless, she felt the weight was on her to maintain the relationship.

She found the front door open and no one in the living room or kitchen.

"Hello?!" she called through the house.

Her brother likely hadn't come home, she thought.

She knocked on her mother's bedroom door, where she assumed she would find her sleeping off a hard night. She started to open the door but hesitated. *What if she wasn't alone?*

"Mom?" she asked softly.

She cracked open the door and peered inside. Seeing only her mother in the bed, she entered the room.

"Rise and shine, bitch!" she said with a smile.

Then she gasped and recoiled in shock. The coffees dropped from her hands and crashed onto the floor. Her mother was dead, the needle still hanging in her arm. Her skin was stiff and pale, her face swollen and blue.

She had been gone for some time. First the sight and then the smell hit Maegan, dropping her to her knees and causing her to vomit onto the coffee-soaked carpet.

"ANY ALLERGIES?" the man asked Dickey as he led him through the kennel.

167

"I'm sorry?" Dickey asked.

"You or your girls have any allergies to animals?" he clarified.

He led Dickey past several empty kennels to a room full of dogs. The barking and yapping were enough to drive anyone mad. Dickey didn't want to be there any longer than necessary.

"I honestly don't know. The girls haven't been around dogs, really," he admitted.

"Well, the reason I ask is we have these doodle puppies," the man said, leading Dickey to a pen at the end of the room, where he showed him a mother and her eight puppies. "They are hypoallergenic, so you don't have to worry about your kids being allergic. Great family dogs. Usually they're expensive, but the mother was abandoned, and we're just trying to place the pups."

Dickey picked up one of the little pups by the scruff of its neck and held it up to give it a look over.

"So, you're supposed to fix my broken brain, little guy," Dickey said to the pup. "I don't see it, but we'll give it a try. The girls will love you."

Dickey placed the puppy into his arms and pulled out his wallet.

"How much?" he asked.

"Just the filing fees and vet costs. We can take care of that up front."

"THE ODDS ARE NOT GOOD," Doctor Aedesh Singh said with a smile. "A typical doctor would probably fail and you would die. I am not a typical doctor, however."

"You certainly don't have typical costs," Dwight said, reviewing the pamphlet Singh had given him.

"Mr. Evans, if you have one at-bat to hit a home run, you need the best hitter you can find. I'm confident I can do this for you, remove the tumor, and save your life. Will you let me?"

Dwight sighed, taking a moment to consider before answering, "Yes."

"Great, when can we schedule the appointment? Let's see; I have two days next week…"

"I just need a little time, first," Dwight interrupted. "I have to take care of a couple things before I make that appointment."

"I'm obligated to advise you that you cannot afford to wait long. This is a ticking time bomb. You could have a stroke or even die. Take care of your affairs, Mr. Evans, but do it soon."

Dwight nodded, the gravity of his situation still sinking in. His phone rang, breaking his train of thought. He thanked the doctor and promised to soon be in touch, then rushed out to answer the call.

"What's the matter? What happened?" he asked, leaving the building. "Jesus Christ… Okay, stay calm. I'm on my way now."

BY THE TIME DWIGHT ARRIVED at the house, the coroner's office had already removed April's body. He exchanged brief words with the local cops who had responded, then hurried to his niece.

She was smoking a cigarette on the porch, staring blankly off into nothingness. It was clear she'd been crying. Dwight wrapped her in his arms and she began to cry again.

"I'm so sorry," he told her, holding her tightly. He remembered how Mr. Martinez had held Mrs. Martinez when they identified their daughter's body—as if he were physically holding her together. Dwight squeezed his niece and wished his love could hold her together. "I'm sorry."

"I want to go home," she said after a few moments.

"Where's your brother?" Dwight asked.

"I talked to him. He's at a friend's… I told him to get dropped off at your place. I hope that's okay…"

"Yes, of course," Dwight said, helping her to her feet.

They drove home in relative silence, both contemplating their loss. For Dwight, this moment had been a long time coming. It was almost bittersweet to be over the constant worry. He had mourned his sister long ago. Now he could begin to move on, though he worried about Maegan. Such a tragedy could put her recovery at risk.

"Is it bad that I blame her for the pain I'm feeling right now?" Maegan asked as they neared the house.

"I think you're allowed to feel however you feel," Dwight told her.

He lit a smoke and handed the pack to her.

"Still smoking, huh? Is that my fault?" she asked, taking one for herself and lighting it.

"Life's short, right?' Dwight said, exhaling smoke through his nostrils. He parked the truck in front of the yard.

"Yeah, I guess it is."

SWAMP MADE HIS WAY to the ally outside his backdoor where Tim and Travis had been waiting.

"Here you go, ladies. Forty dollars, please," Swamp told the boys.

Tim took the dope and inspected it.

"Shit, man. We'll give you twenty," Travis said.

"That's what I paid. I told you I wasn't doing this shit for free," Swamp barked, grabbing the baggie back from Tim.

"Alright, whatever. Nobody has shit anyway, man. Just give him the forty," Tim told Travis.

"Alright, fine," Travis said with a huff. "It's bullshit, though."

He held out two twenties for Swamp to grab then pulled them back.

"Maybe we give you forty," Travis said. "Or maybe we just rob your junky ass and give you shit."

"Well," Swamp said, throwing his hands up defensively. "Well, now, alright. Let's just calm down."

"Travis, fucking chill!" Tim pleaded.

"Just relax. You can have it for twenty," Swamp said.

He held the dope out for Travis to take. Travis smiled and reached for it but just as he was about to grab it, Swamp punched him in the nose and then kicked him in the balls. Travis dropped to the ground in pain and Swamp snatched the forty dollars from his hand.

Swamp looked at Tim, who threw his arms up and stepped back in submission.

"Take it easy!" Tim yelled.

"Don't ever let me see you trying to score around here again," Swamp said. He threw the dope on the ground and walked inside his apartment.

Tim helped Travis to his feet. *Now where were they going to score?*

DARKNESS CAME SOMETIME AFTER 9 PM, the last vestiges

of twilight disappearing into the trees as Mark and Randy finished dinner.

"Quiet tonight," Mark said. "Usually you talk my ear off."

"Just thinking, I suppose," Randy replied. The sound of displacing gravel and the hum of an engine caught their attention.

"Maybe Greg forgot something?" Mark wondered.

"No," Randy said, rising to his feet and heading to the kitchen cabinet. "Go to your room, get your shotgun, and stay there!" He pulled out a 357 magnum revolver and headed out the door.

Outside, the Pontiac crept slowly down the dirt road, its lights off.

"You ready to step up with the big dogs, little Michael?" Augustine asked from the front seat.

"Hell yes! You ready?" Michael Trivoty asked George as he slapped him on the shoulder.

George took a deep breath and checked his shotgun.

"Nobody gets hurt," George said.

Michael laughed, pulled his ski mask down over his face, and racked his 12-gauge shotgun. Gary and George did the same.

"Alright, let's get in and get out, no dicking around," Augustine instructed from the passenger seat.

Randy met his visitors in his driveway, gun in hand. The three masked men emerged from the car, shotguns trained on him. Seeing he was outnumbered, Randy threw his gun into the dirt and raised his arms.

"Smart man," Augustine said.

"No problems here, guys," Randy said. "Nothing here is worth me or anyone dying over. Just so you know, this whole thing you're stepping into is much bigger than me. You are going to be causing yourselves a lot of pain. Now, if you just leave now…"

"Shut up!" Augustine said, menacingly shaking his shotgun at Randy.

"It's all in the shed!" George exclaimed, heading for the backyard with Michael.

"On your knees, man!" Augustine instructed Randy.

Randy obeyed. "Just stay cool, bro. This will all be over soon."

Randy looked away from the shotgun and stared at the Pontiac. It had no front plate, but he burned its image into his head.

Michael blasted the lock off the shed and George pulled the door open. The smell was overwhelming. The sight was nothing short of amazing. Hundreds of plants were hanging upside down drying. On shelves lining the far wall, there were hundreds of vacuum sealed bags of finished product.

"Grab what you can and hurry," George instructed. "Finished product only!"

"What's the rush?" Michael asked.

"I told you! His neighbors. He pays them for security and shit."

"Just take what you want and go," Randy pleaded with Augustine. "No one else has to get involved."

"Hurry the hell up!" Augustine called out to Michael and George.

George grabbed two huge black trash bags stuffed full of cured and ready weed over his shoulder and headed for the car. Michael continued to stuff bags full. George returned for two more. On the final trip, Michael handed George two bags, then took two himself and followed him out.

Just as George rounded the corner, the sound of a shotgun chambering a round caused Michael to freeze. Mark stood at the base of the back steps, a 12-gauge trembling in his hands

"Easy, kid," Michael said, dropping the bags of weed, his right hand tightly clenching the stock of his gun.

"Put the gun down!" Mark ordered, his voice shaky with fear.

"Alright, alright, boss."

Michael began lowering the gun to the ground but kept his finger on the trigger. When Mark moved closer, Michael swung the barrel upwards and fired.

GEORGE SLAMMED THE TRUNK shut and called for Gary.

"Let's go!"

Randy looked into Gary's eyes with contempt. Gary grunted and struck Randy in the head with the butt of his gun. Randy toppled over, and Gary jumped in the front seat of the Pontiac as George started the engine.

"Where the fuck is Trivoty?!" Gary yelled.

A shot rang out from behind the house and echoed through the woods. George gave Gary a look of terror.

Before Gary could react, Michael was pounding on the trunk. "Open the trunk!" he commanded.

Gary opened the glove box and popped the trunk. Michael loaded his two bags into the trunk then slammed it shut. He jumped in the back seat, slamming the door behind him. "Let's go!"

George needed no further motivation. He punched the gas, sending dirt and rocks flying into the air as they fled from the scene. Randy's body laid face down in the dirt and leaves, blood spilling from his head.

At the end of the dirt road, the silhouette of a man emerged from the wood line and fired a rifle shot at the moving car, then another. The second round shattered the back window of George's Pontiac.

"Holy shit!" Gary shouted.

"Woo-hoo!" Michael yelled out the window as they left the woods and the darkness behind them.

"What happened?" George asked, his voice trembling.

"We just stole a shit load of weed, that's what happened!" Michael laughed.

"No, why did you shoot? What happened?!" George asked.

"Farmer's boy drew down on me," Michael answered, lighting a cigarette.

"What?! Are you fucking kidding?! You shot him?"

173

"Well, I wasn't going to let him shoot me, Calloway."

"What's done is done. It's over," Gary declared. "Drop it."

"This is unbelievable," George muttered. "What the fuck have we done? This is fucked up. Is he dead?!"

"George, he did what he had to. And we did what we had to do to save your fucking life," Gary said. "Better that boy than you, right? Now we're even."

"Right?" Michael chimed in from the back.

"Yeah, right…" George said, feeling sick to his stomach. Michael slapped him on the shoulders and laughed.

"We can trust you, right George?" Michael asked, glaring at him in the rearview mirror.

"Yeah, yeah of course. Just give me a fucking cigarette, would ya?" George asked.

The Pontiac drove unmolested back to Colebrook.

THE SMOKING WAS ILLEGAL but ignored by local cops; everyone wanted at least one bar you could go to and smoke while you drank. Plenty of more serious laws were broken at O'Malley's on any given night.

Dwight felt odd and out of place there. He didn't get out much, nor had he ever done police business in plain clothes. He wore a black leather jacket, a t-shirt, and a blue baseball cap to look discrete, which only caused Wyatt to laugh.

"You look like a cop," Wyatt said. "I don't know why, but you do."

The two snagged a table at the back of the bar and ordered a couple of drinks. Wyatt didn't waste time getting to the point. He pulled out a file and laid out papers detailing Andrew and Michael Trivoty, Gary Augustine, and their known associates.

"Andrew is technically in charge of his operation and crew, but he has to stay in good with the Toros and keep Augustine happy. Augustine is the real target here; he leads to a larger network of big players. He's just using Andrew and his crew to distribute, but I'm not sure who he is working for."

"And the brother?" Dwight asked.

174

"Michael is the one we need to worry about. He's reckless. Trying to prove something. He'll do something stupid."

"Maybe that will be our chance," Dwight replied, lighting a cigarette and sipping his drink.

Wyatt raised his eyebrows and nodded, then helped himself to one of Dwight's smokes.

"No, I think we need to play the long game here," Wyatt replied.

"Why not just bust the guys now?"

"I need to put more pieces together so I can take down as many of them at once." Wyatt stopped and furrowed his brow. "You should know," he continued. "What I said before about crooked cops—I wasn't kidding. I don't know who we can trust on this one. So, I need to be able to move on Augustine and then get my time with him immediately before state or anyone else finds out."

"And that's why you need me," Dwight said. It made sense now, he thought. Here he thought Mayhew saw a real cop in him. *He was just a way for this guy to get around the bounds of his authority.*

"Listen, there is way more going on here than we understand. Moving on Augustine is going to make the rats scramble, and desperate people do desperate things."

"What exactly do you need me to do?"

"Help me watch the house and establish a pattern. Then when the time comes, you will need to say I came to you with a tip and you checked it out with me. We move on them, take Augustine into custody, and I handle the rest."

"This will hurt the heroin trade in Colebrook and Winsted?"

"Evans, we're going to hurt the heroin trade for the entire state. Maybe more. We are going to shut this vein down and take down as many big players as we can."

"When do we start?" Dwight asked.

He thought of his sister and his niece. It was time to take a stand.

"RANDY! RANDY!" THE VOICE CALLED.

175

It took a moment, but Randy recognized the voice as belonging to his best friend and neighbor, Albert Redding. Albert called for him again, but Randy could not understand where he was calling from, or why. It was dark; he couldn't see where he was.

"Randy! Randy! Goddammit, wake up, Randy!"

Red—all Randy could see was dark red. Then he saw the hazy outline of a person through the darkness. Slowly he became aware of the pain. His head and face hurt badly.

"Albert?" he groaned.

"Randy! Yes, Randy, it's me! Come on now, buddy, wake up." The older, portly man in overalls and plaid knelt beside Randy and gently patted him on the chest.

"What—what's the matter?" Randy asked. He could now see Albert hovering over him, a rifle in his hand.

"Randy, you've been robbed—knocked out cold."

"Ahh, shit!" Randy yelled, the memory flooding back to him. He winced as he touched his head, then used his shirt to wipe some of the blood from his face. "How bad is it?"

"It's split open, Randy. You've got to get to a hospital."

"No hospital," Randy insisted.

The shotgun butt had split his forehead. He'd split his lip and scraped his cheek when he hit the ground.

"Alright, Loretta can fix you up. Let's go," Albert suggested.

"My boy… where's my boy?"

"Christ, he was home?"

"Mark!" Randy called. He tried to rise but fell again.

"You're concussed, Randy, take it easy. He's probably hiding somewhere."

"Mark!" Randy tried to get up again, this time Albert caught him. He helped Randy up the front steps and into the house, both calling for the boy.

"Something's wrong!" Randy cried, pushing Albert away and mustering his balance. He got to the back door and gasped. "No, no, no, no…..” he muttered frantically as he flung the screen door open and exploded down the back steps. “Mark!!!”

Albert followed, afraid of what he would find.

“Mark!!” Randy cried, cradling his boy’s body, lifeless and full of buckshot. “He was just a boy, you fucking savages!! Just a boy!” He sobbed. The shot had torn the boy’s torso apart.

“Jesus…. Randy, I’m—I’m so sorry…” Albert shook his head. “I am going to head back to the house and call the police, Randy…”

“No!” Randy snapped. He set Mark’s body down upon the ground and with it, his sorrow. “You can’t. I’ll call it in tomorrow when I know who is going to come out here and handle it.”

Albert seemed hesitant.

“I pay you good money, Albert.”

“Yeah and I took two shots at the bastards as they were leaving!” Albert said in his defense. “And I got their plate number.”

“Nice work, Albert,” he patted his neighbor on the shoulder. “I’ll throw you a bonus… let’s say fifteen grand. Just keep this between us for now. I’m going to want to take care of a few things as soon as possible.”

“What are you going to do with Mark till then?”

“Open the shed. He’ll keep till tomorrow night.”

“Randy…” Albert was shocked. “This is your boy. You can’t just throw him in the shed.”

“Listen to me, Albert! I’m not burying him in the backyard like some secret, and I am not calling the cops until I take care of some things.”

“What are you going to do?”

“Kill the bastards,” Randy said as he lit a cigarette. “And secure my getaway plan.”

“Cashing out?”

“Blood’s in the water, Albert. The sharks will be coming now. I might be able to hold them off, but if not, I have to be ready.”

“Fucking shit! Alright, let’s move him. And, for the record, I don’t have your back because you pay me. I’ve had your back since Grenada.”

"Yeah, well, this isn't the Marine Corp, Albert. Kids shouldn't be dying."

Randy lifted his son's body into his arms, tears welling up in his eyes. By the time he reached the shed, he was sobbing, his tears mixing with the blood from his head wound and running down his cheeks.

"I'm sorry, son," he said as he laid his body down.

They locked the shed and headed over to Albert's place where his wife Loretta examined him and cleaned him up.

"Lucky your skull is intact," she told him. "Just going to be one hell of a lump," she said as she stitched him up. He winced as she jabbed the sewing needle into his flesh.

Once she'd finished up, he went to wash his hands and face off in their bathroom. He stared into the mirror and saw both rage and guilt.

"I'm ready," Albert said, tucking a Remington .45 into his waistband.

"Albert, no!" Loretta yelled from the kitchen.

"You stay here, old man. This is my score to settle," Randy told him.

"Then what?"

"Then the chips fall where they may…."

The two men embraced at the door. When they pulled away, Randy could see the tears in Albert's eyes.

"You come back in one piece," Albert said, holding back his tears.

"The way I see it," Randy said. "Part of me was killed bit by bit in foreign lands and part of me just died in that backyard. What's left is a bitter, hateful man. But I ain't going anywhere till I make those bastards feel it."

"May God bless and watch over you."

"I have no business with him where I'm going," Randy said shaking his head slowly. "If you don't hear from me by tomorrow night, call the police. See that Mark gets a proper burial."

"So this really is goodbye," Albert noted. "You are my only friend, Randy."

The two embraced again. Randy slapped Albert affectionately on the back with firmness.

"Albert, one more thing. The money…." Randy said before he left.

"It's there. Right where you told me. Every cent."

"That's… that's a lot of money."

"Probably around one and a half million and some change. Three duffel bags in the boathouse where you told me."

"I will leave you one bag, friend. That's your final bonus."

Albert nodded, smiled wryly, then shut the door and sighed.

Loretta lovingly placed her hand on her husband's shoulder and told him, "Some wars you have to fight on your own, darling."

RANDY HAD ONE FRIENDLY OFFICER working the skeleton crew that night at the Canaan State Police Barracks whom he trusted, Tommy Delnero. Randy had played softball with his older brothers for years. As far as crooked cops, Tommy was always dependable for a fair price.

"I'm looking for a Pontiac Bonneville, beige and brown, between 1978 and 1981," Randy told Delnero through the bulletproof glass. He handed him a piece of paper with the plate number on it through the slot.

"Alright, just go wait outside in your truck," the officer said, looking around to make sure they were alone.

Randy went to his truck and chewed a handful of aspirin. His head hurt so bad it was making him nauseous. He kept thinking of the eyes of the man who'd struck him. He wasn't the one who shot Mark, but he seemed to be the leader of the crew.

"Jesus, you look like shit," Delnero remarked when he came out nearly an hour later.

"Whatta ya got?" Randy asked gruffly.

"Car's registered to a George Calloway, sixteen twenty-two Meadowview Road, in Colebrook." He dropped a printout into Randy's lap. "Got his picture and details on there…."

"Thanks," Randy muttered, studying the photo.

"Whatcha gettin' into this time, Randy?" Delnero inquired, examining Randy's head wound.

"Mark's dead…. They killed him."

"Jesus Christ."

"I'm going to track them down and I'm going to kill them all."

"Now, Randy," Delnero said, laughing anxiously. "You have to be smart here…."

"Little late for that, don't you think?" Randy started his truck, the tail pipe coughed black smoke.

"Randy?" Delnero said, putting his hand on the steering wheel. "My money?"

"Right…" Randy said, digging into his pocket and handing a wad of twenties to the officer. "Should be about three hundred, just keep your mouth shut about all this. Don't let Leahy hear about it till I'm done."

But before the truck was out of sight, Delnero was on his cellphone, smiling widely.

"I think we have a very unique opportunity that just presented itself to us…. Yes, I fucking know you're in South Carolina. Vacation's over, buddy. Come home now… Then fucking leave the family, man. I need you here. This is big. If we don't move now, we might miss it… Yes, mother fucker, right fucking now! Put your pants on and drive your ass to the airport. Okay. Good. I will get things ready. I'll explain everything when you get here… It'll be worth it, I promise! Alright… See you soon."

Chapter Seven
Blood In the Water

The morning brought thunderstorms and heavy rain. Dickey dropped the girls at school and then grabbed a coffee from Rachel's before returning home. He was surprised and relieved to find George's Pontiac parked out front.

He found his brother starring into the bottom of a cup of coffee, smoking a cigarette at the kitchen table.

"Well, I see you aren't fucking dead, at least," Dickey said. "But you look like shit."

"Good to see you, too, brother," George answered. He was pale and unshaven. Smoke billowed from a cigarette filter burning in his fingers.

"Is there booze in there?" Dickey asked, motioning to George's cup and taking a seat.

"Nope."

"Jesus Christ, this is serious. You alright?"

"Just trying to get my shit together a little—sober up." He looked as if he were about to collapse.

"What are you into, George?"

"Quite the mess, Dick…. Quite the fuckin' mess." He stared into his coffee.

"What is it?"

"Don't worry about it," he said, shaking his head a little and discarding his smoke into the ashtray.

"Listen, big brother, you come around here, you bring your problems with you. That means it's my business…"

"I don't bring my problems here!" George snapped. He shook anxiously.

"Augustine came here. I nearly had to shoot the man in my driveway. You think that's my business?"

"Jesus Christ." George was stunned.

"You know, when dad used to sit us down, he would tell us the first step to fixing any problem is coming clean."

"Don't give me that shit!" George barked, grabbing at his smokes with anger to light another. "You were the golden boy! I was the whipping post. You goddamn know it."

"You were a fuck up," Dickey said plainly. "Maybe that's why you got the belt a bit more than I did."

"Or his fists," George retorted.

"Oh, you did fucking not! What world are you living in, man? You're fucking delusional!"

"Of course," George laughed. "You could never be bothered to notice. Just blanked it out. I remember…"

Dickey gasped a couple of times and stammered to find the right words. "Jesus Christ," he said, rising to get himself coffee. "So what are you into now? This guy still after you?"

"No."

"So what's the matter?"

"Nothing."

"George, do you have a gun?"

"No." George laughed. "I never have. I'm not like you, Dickey. I don't do well under pressure. I could never kill anyone. I'm not a killer,

182

Dickey.... I don't kill people!" Tears welled up in his eyes and began to leak down his face. "It's not okay, you know?" he cried. "I'm not a killer!"

"No one is... until they have to be." He remembered his first time; the man had taken so long to die. That was the worst part, having to listen to the moans of a dying man. "I have a gun; you can have it. It isn't registered. But I have to ask you to take it and leave here. I wish I could do more for you, brother, but I can't get sucked into this...whatever it is. I have the girls. You can't come back till this over with. You understand?"

"Augustine isn't even after me anymore," he pled. "I have nowhere else to go."

"Why isn't he after you?"

"I made it right."

"You made it right?" Dickey stared at his brother, trying to determine if he was lying.

"Yes."

"How?"

"Paid him."

"How?" Dickey asked skeptically.

"Don't worry about it... Everything is good."

"So why are you here shaking over your coffee? What's with the whole getting sober bit? You must have fucked up real good."

"Forget it," George said as he stood to leave.

"George!" Dickey called after him.

"What?" he asked from the door.

"Take the gun."

George laughed, shook his head, and walked out the door. He climbed into his Pontiac, the events from the night before playing endlessly through his mind. *Fuck sobriety!* He combed his ashtray and found a half-smoked joint. He lit the joint and peeled out of his driveway. He didn't see the Ford pickup truck that followed him as he left.

Soon after, Jason arrived with joints and a heavy heart. He told Dickey how Maegan's mother had died and how Maegan had been the one to find the body.

"That's awful, man," Dickey said as the two smoked on the back porch. "Be sure to tell her how sorry I am."

"I will," Jason replied. "Whenever I talk to her next. She said she needs space. Whatever that means."

"Considering her mother just died, I would give it to her," Dickey recommended. "Don't panic or read into it."

"Seems like she should want to be around me. Maybe we don't have what I thought we did. Things got weird the other night."

"How so?" Dickey asked, inhaling his hit and passing the joint back to Jason.

"I told her. Just like you told me to do. I told her I loved her and it didn't go over so well."

"Oh man. I'm sorry, Jay. Give her some time, she'll probably come back around," said Dickey. "I saw George, bro," he added, happy to change the subject.

"No shit. Well, at least he's alive," Jason said.

"He's into some serious shit," Dickey said with a heavy sigh. "A man came by here looking for him the other day, brandishing a gun in the fucking driveway."

"Holy shit."

"Ever hear of a guy named Gary Augustine?"

"Yeah, actually," Jason recalled. "Word is he moves a lot of heavy stuff around the area."

"What kind of stuff?"

"Heroin. Oxy. Pills and shit. He's looking for George?"

"He was. George says it isn't a problem anymore," Dickey said, checking his phone messages. "Hey, I gotta take a ride and pick up my new puppy from the vet, you want to come?"

"You got a puppy?!" Jason couldn't believe it. "What made you do that?"

"Doc thinks it will help me emotionally or some shit," he said with a laugh. "Had to have the bastard dewormed and get all his shots, but he's ready now."

They picked up the puppy in Jason's Subaru. Dickey affectionately tended to the pup while Jason drove back to his house.

"So, you believe George; that he fixed the problem with Augustine?" Jason asked.

"I don't know." Dickey paused. "The thing about George is that I have never known him to fix any of the problems he caused. Usually, he just finds some way to make things worse."

DWIGHT KNOCKED TWICE on Maegan's door before pushing it open with his foot. In his hands was an old TV tray with a bowl of soup, a can of soda, and some crackers.

"Hey, Uncle Dwight," Maegan said from beneath her blankets.

"Hey, sweetheart. I brought you some chicken soup. They say it's good for the soul, I think."

His awkward humor brought a smile to her face. She sat up in bed and took the tray from him.

"Thank you," she said meekly. Her eyes were sunken and red from crying.

"Is there anything I can do for you?" he asked, running his fingers gently over the top of her head.

"I just keep thinking, if I hadn't left... If we hadn't fought..."

"I know how you must feel," Dwight said, kneeling down beside her bed. "But the truth is your mother chose this path long ago."

"Did she? Or did it choose her?" Maegan asked. "You don't know what it's like. The scary part is that I do. I can't dismiss her like that. I haven't just walked in her shoes; we have the same shoes."

"I'm sorry, honey," Dwight replied, looking down at the floor in shame. "Maybe I'm afraid to see that because then I would have to explain why I gave up on her but would never give up on you. Maybe I owed her better. Maybe I let her down. I'm afraid that when it came to your mother— my sister—my disappointment turned to resentment. I suppose that's something I have to come to terms with."

"I keep telling myself if I had been a better daughter...."

"Stop," Dwight interrupted her. "It just isn't true."

185

"Our relationship was very contentious, and I contributed to that. It wasn't just her," Maegan tried to explain.

"You were a child, Maegan. She was the adult. You do see that?"

Maegan nodded slowly.

"You're right," she said. "Thank you for the soup."

"You need anything else," Dwight said as he rose to his feet. "Just let me know."

"I DON'T KNOW ABOUT THIS," Tim told Travis—a phrase he was getting way too used to muttering.

"Listen, I know we can score here, and they'll let us pitch a tent," Travis told him as the two passed the old A-Mart building in Torrington.

They had hitched a ride down route 8 with a pervy old guy who had kept trying to touch Travis's leg. He'd finally cut the shit and dropped them off at McDonald's after they threatened to stab him.

"How much money we have?" Travis asked as they passed what was once the outdoor lawn and garden center.

NO TRESPASSING OR LOITERING, the large sign read. It had gang tags spray painted over it.

"Twenty dollars and some change," Tim said, following Travis past the lawn and garden center and into the woods. The trail led up a short hill where you could either continue straight on to a residential street, or follow the trail left or right. Left led you back North Main Street. Right led you to what was known as Shantytown.

A turned over shopping cart with used condoms hanging from it marked the way. Tim clenched his backpack tightly. Inside was their tourniquet, a phone charger, a sweater, and an old tent they had stolen from Travis's house.

"I just want to sleep," Tim said.

"You don't feel sick, man? I just want to get high."

"Of course I do. I'm walking in the woods out here with you, ain't I? But I am fucking tired," Tim moaned.

"You gonna pass out and waste your high? *Shit man!* That's dumb," Travis laughed.

"I didn't say that," Tim muttered. "Just haven't slept in days…"

When the two first came around a bend, all they saw was one tent with two men sleeping in it. Then they passed through the brush and saw dozens upon dozens of tents next to shanties made of tarps, plywood, and even sheets.

It being morning, most of the inhabitants were asleep, though some were milling about. One man stood by a barrel fire near the middle of the camp, covered in dirt, grime, and grease. He was skin and bones with a long, stringy beard. He wore an old, torn up NASCAR hat and an old Mickey Mouse t-shirt that was equally tattered.

"Excuse me, sir?" Travis asked the man.

"Ten dollars a bag, but it's fucking strong. Don't fuck around with it," the man said. He smiled, revealing a mouth of rotted and broken teeth.

The refuse burning in the barrel stank horribly. Travis saw the remains of an old projection television and a tire among the ashes beneath the flames. They gladly bought the dope and went on their way.

About a half hour later the two had successfully claimed a spot and erected their tent.

"There sure are a lot of them," Travis said while Tim readied the dope.

"Yeah, man. Fucking economy sucks, what do you expect?" Tim said, drawing the dope through a cotton swab on the spoon into the syringe.

"There's gotta be a hundred fucking people here, man… It smells awful."

"Yeah, well, seems like a good place to me. There's dope, a place we can sleep and get high, it's close to downtown, and from what I hear, cops don't even bother coming back here."

"Yeah, can't blame them. Look around. We're all damned…"

"Shut the fuck up and take this hit or I will."

"Look at that girl, bro. She's younger than us and lookin' fuckin' rough!" Travis exclaimed with disgust.

187

"Maybe she'll blow you for a hit of this dope," Tim said with a snide laugh, nudging Travis and holding the needle out for him.

"You think?" Travis said with a devious grin.

"Look at her, bro! She'd probably blow you for free but I wouldn't let her. That's how you get bumps on your pecker."

"I wonder if we know anyone here... Like maybe that guy right there sold me shoes at A-Mart once, and maybe she worked at the Chinese place next door that closed shortly after. That's neat to think about..." Travis lit a cigarette and stared out at the crowd of hobos, addicts, and destitute lost souls.

"You're fucking killing me. Don't you want to get high? Been fixing for it all fucking day," Tim complained.

"Shit, man. I'm just having a smoke and takin' in the new environment before I go nodding out in front of all these people... I don't want to wake up and freak out or some shit, man. Come on."

"Whatever, I'm shooting this load."

"You do what you have to, brother," Travis said, laughing it off. "I'm going to go take a shit behind that tree over there, and I'll do mine when I get back. I fucking shit myself last time I shot up with a gut full of crap."

"Yeah, good. Go. Jesus Christ," Tim said. He wrapped his belt around his arm and sank his teeth into it to maintain the pressure.

Travis found his tree—a thick oak set about twenty-five feet back from the shantytown. He leaned against it and had a smoke while he did his business. He was about to get up when he realized he hadn't brought the toilet paper with him. Always the problem solver, Travis grabbed some nearby leaves and used them to wipe his ass.

After answering nature's call, Travis returned to the shantytown, where he smelled something phenomenal. The smell reminded him of his mother's homemade stew. Then he smelled something even better accompanying the food: marijuana.

The aromas led him to a nearby lean-to where a man with a white beard and long bushy eyebrows stirred a cauldron over a small fire.

"Whoa, dude. How did you set this up?" Travis asked with excitement.

The old man took a long hit from his joint and eyed Travis suspiciously. "Cauldron was left out on the road. I rigged up this here frame to hang it on from wood I took from crates."

"Smells good, man!" Travis said eagerly. "You got a lot?"

"You talking about my smoke or my stew, boy?" the man said sternly.

"Both?"

"Sit down, grab a rock," the man said, handing Travis the joint. "You don't look well, boy. You on the dope?"

"Huh? No!" Travis hit the joint, and the man gave him a stern look. "Okay, yeah. I am."

"Drop that habit, son," the man said, stirring his cauldron. "Or it will drop you."

"What's your deal? What's your name?"

"Name's Tigs and my deal is my own concern."

"Were you a cook?" Travis asked, passing the joint back. The old man seemed to ignore the question. "Sorry, I like talking to people. Tim always tells me to shut up."

"I *am* a cook, boy. No *was* about it."

"I see," Travis said. "And what is that you're making?"

"A little bit of everything…"

"A bit of everything?"

"Yeah. Squirrel and raccoon meat, mostly… You don't want to know the rest, as far as meat goes. Then I stole some turnips and onions from a garden up the street. Added some salt and spices I stole from the grocery store. I've been cooking it since before sunup. Gotta get coon meat really hot to kill the parasites."

"I want some, but you kind of grossed me out. It does smell good."

"Boy, you fairly young for this world. But since you here, you best learn to survive. Now you gonna eat this."

"There's not much there?"

"There's enough for you, me, and me again later," Tigs said.

189

"What about everyone else? They'll leave you alone?"

Tigs lifted his shirt, revealing a pistol.

"So what's your name, boy?" Tigs said, as he took a dirty, stained bowl and scooped some hobo stew into it for the kid.

"Travis," he said, taking the bowl with a smile. He decided he didn't care what was in it at that point. He was starving.

"Well, Travis, eat up. Then get the fuck out of here so I can sleep," Tigs said gruffly.

Travis finished his bowl; it wasn't half bad. Some of the tougher chicken-like meat was a bit off-putting, but he ate it nonetheless. When he was finished, Tigs invited him for dinner. "You and your friend, you can come by late tonight. I should have something cooking."

Travis felt a little better having eaten and smoked some weed, but he still jonesed for his next high. With that in mind, he strolled happily back to find Tim in their tent. When he got there he saw Tim's shoes sticking straight out the tent door, his toes pointed at the sky. Travis laughed, assuming he had passed out. He climbed into the tent and patted Tim's leg.

"Out like a light, huh, bro?" he laughed and gathered the dope and supplies to prepare his own load. Then he glanced at Tim's face. It was lifeless and swollen, and his mouth was full of vomit, which ran down his face and neck.

"Tim!" Travis yelled, shaking his friend. His body was already stiffening up. "Tim!!!"

Travis rolled his friend over on his side and used his finger to clear his mouth. He then rolled him onto his back and tried to resuscitate him using CPR.

"Tim!!!" he screamed, pounding on his chest. But Tim remained lifeless, his eyes staring straight off into nothing. He was gone.

Tigs swung the flap of the tent door open and scoffed.

"So, that's the yelling. Well, I'm sorry, boy, but you are going to have to get him out of here," Tigs told him sternly and went to leave.

"Wait! What do you mean?" Travis cried.

"Can't have him here anymore. Cops need to find him, can't let it happen here," the old man explained. He knelt down closer to Travis and whispered. "Don't wait till these people decide to do it for you because they'll toss your ass right out of here, too."

"What am I supposed to do, huh?" Travis stammered. "What is it you want me to do?"

"Grab a shopping cart from down the trail, put him in it, and get him the fuck out of here. Leave him behind that closed down sandwich place at the end of the trail. Back by the dumpster. Someone will find him in the morning."

With that Tigs rose and again went to leave. He stopped, compelled by the sounds of Travis sobbing.

"Alright," Tigs said with a heavy sigh. "You get the fucking the cart. I will take care of it."

"Really?" Travis asked, his eyes streaming tears. "You—you would do that?"

"Hurry the fuck up before I change my mind," Tigs barked at him. "You can fucking cry later while you cleaning your tent."

With that Travis let go of his best friend and went to get a shopping carriage so Tigs could dispose of the body behind a dumpster.

"WHAT UP, GANGSTA!?" Michael cheered victoriously when he saw George. "Can't believe we had George in full-blown g-mode! Shit was crazy! What a fun night!"

Michael exchanged a handshake with George and then tossed him a bag of dope.

"Here you go, playa. Shit is fucking far out, too. Real good. We've been partying all day," Michael bragged, motioning to a house full of his boys.

"Where's Andrew?" George asked.

"He's away on some business with some of the crew. Down in New Jersey," Michael answer, then nodded to the needles on the table. "You wanna lace up, playa?"

"No, I have to go."

"You pay me for that later?" Michael asked as George dashed out the door. "Kid's shook," Michael said to one of his boys with a laugh. "Shit got real last night. I don't think Georgie boy can hang."

George left the Trivotys' in a hurry. The rain had been persisting most of the day, but for the moment it was clear, and George wanted to take advantage of it. He jumped back into his Pontiac and cruised to his favorite spot to get high, Alice In Chains blaring on the stereo.

George didn't notice Randy following behind in his pickup.

The Pontiac pulled into the parking lot of the old Mill Street dam, then proceeded down a trail that hooked into the woods. Randy's truck followed soon after.

George found a spot to park among the trees and retrieved his tools: a tourniquet, a spoon, cotton wads, a bottle of water, and a needle. He sprinkled some dope onto the spoon and added a little water. He used his lighter to bring the dope to a boil, breathing heavily through his nose as he focused. He then placed a cotton ball in the dope and the syringe onto the cotton ball. After he had drawn the fluid into the syringe, he set it on the dash with care.

He tightened his tourniquet around his left arm and reached for the needle. If he had looked in his rearview at that moment, he would have seen Randy's Ford pickup parked at the trail's mouth. George was soon released from his torment; all his problems seemed, for the moment, to fade away into bliss and euphoria with the easy push of the needle. He never saw Randy Sandusfield approaching the side of his car, a 357-magnum in his hand.

DETECTIVE WYATT MAYHEW RUBBED HIS EYES and winced. He opened the glove box of his department-issued Ford Crown Victoria and grabbed a nipper of Jim Bean, which he poured into his gas station coffee. He replaced the lid, took a sip, and cursed; he had burned his tongue.

"Dispatch to unit three-three-nine, come in three-three-nine," the radio called.

"Three-three-nine, go 'head," Wyatt responded into the handset.

"Got a ten-forty-six, young white male, approximately sixteen years of age, in a shopping cart behind the dumpster of the old Uno Sandwich building."

"Roger that. Three-three-nine responding," Wyatt said, starting his car. "Fucking too early for this shit," he said as he sipped his coffee.

"Anonymous tip came into dispatch. They sent me out here to check it out, but I didn't touch anything. I just told dispatch to get Violent Crimes out here," the young uniformed patrolman explained to Wyatt at the scene.

"Thanks, but it's probably just another O.D.," Wyatt said with a sigh.

"Kid O.D.'s in a shopping cart?" the patrolmen asked skeptically.

"No. Ten to one, I bet you this kid overdosed up at the shantytown and they dumped him down here to avoid the police."

"You seem awfully sure about this," the younger cop said.

"Because this is the fifth time this has happened this year," Wyatt said, lighting a cigarette and walking away. "Stay here. Wait for the coroner and forensics."

"You smell like whiskey, Detective. You should probably do something about that before you head back to the station."

"Yeah, well, no one there will be surprised, I assure you," he said with a laugh.

Ten minutes later he was in his chief's office.

"Look, how many people are going to die up there before you let me do something about it?" Wyatt asked.

"They're heroin addicts for Christ sakes, Wyatt. They're going to die somewhere. Might as well have them away from the rest of the town. At least they keep to themselves up there," Chief Roberts responded. "The mayor has made it clear that for now, this is the way we are going to regard the situation in those woods."

"Burning waste, plastic, tires… they're killing and skinning cats."

"What?" the chief asked, appalled at the suggestion. "Don't be ridiculous."

"Go ask animal control. She'll tell you there are missing cats in surrounding areas and almost no strays. It's unheard of."

193

"Stray cats? Sounds like they're solving a problem," the chief said with a scoff.

"Except they ran out of strays. Now they're stealing Fluffy and Mr. Buttons from up the road."

"Conjecture. Look, what do you want to do?" the chief asked. "We can't arrest them all."

"Organize a sweep, pull them all out, screen them through mental health services and get them cleared medically. Get the addicts to detox, charge the ones who don't want to go with whatever you can. Find out which ones are from Torrington and which ones aren't. The natives we have to deal with. The rest you send back to their respective cities. And you level the shantytown to the ground."

"Been drinking, Wyatt?" Roberts said with a smirk.

"Not since last night, why?"

"You've got that unfocused glare you get…"

"Let's do this before it gets worse, and allow me to leverage the ones we catch holding and put together a case to take down this heroin distribution line that is destroying this city."

"You just don't seem to listen, do you?" Roberts said with indignation. "I told you. Mayor's office said no, and it isn't just them. Project Safeway is pushing for the methadone clinic as a solution. They will not stand by if we go in there like it's the 1920s and break down tents. As far as the rest of it, State is investigating the heroin line. Now, do your job."

"I am doing my job!" Wyatt yelled. "What needs to happen? We need to find a dead kid in that shantytown because it's going to happen. Kids play there, damn it."

"Why don't you take the rest of the day off and sober the fuck up!" Roberts ordered him. "Now! Get out of my sight."

"This is bullshit. You're punishing me because I won't walk the line on this."

"Get out!" Roberts said, rising to his feet and pointing at the door. "You're a goddamn mess."

"It's a serious public health liability but who the fuck am I to say otherwise? Tell the fucking mayor I said hello!" he barked. "Maybe you could ask him why the fuck I am not being allowed to move to shut down the heroin pipeline. How many more dead bodies I am going to have to ignore?"

"You're way out of line, Wyatt," Roberts warned.

"They get to you too, Ben?" Wyatt asked, his eyes heavy with disappointment. "Is that what this is? Are you a part of this?"

"You're insane," Roberts replied dismissively. "Go home. Sleep it off."

DWIGHT PEERED THROUGH THE BINOCULARS and leaned forward, resting his elbows on the dash of his truck. On the receiving end of his gaze, down the road, Michael Trivoty was hosting some of his crew. Dwight had been watching the house since he'd left Maegan that morning.

A sudden rapping on the driver-side window startled him, causing him to drop the binoculars. To his relief, it was only Wyatt and not a Toro.

"You're horrible at this," Wyatt said with a chuckle. He went around to the passenger side door and climbed into the cab. "How's it going?"

"Off work early?" Dwight asked.

"Yeah, they gave me the day off because I'm an asshole."

"Is that so?"

"Well, a drunk asshole," Wyatt replied, sipping his coffee. "So, what's happening at de casa de scumbags?"

"A lot of guys with ink and plenty of buyers rolling through. This one guy, though…" Dwight grabbed his pad from his breast pocket, where he had written down two license plate numbers. "A local guy I know named George Calloway came through. Interesting thing is he had a tail."

Wyatt's eyebrows raised.

"That *is* interesting," Wyatt said.

"Here's the plate numbers. Like I said, one should come back as George, but I would sure like to know who was following him and why."

"Did it look like a cop?"

"Maybe," Dwight said. "It could have been, to be honest. I figured we would want to know either way."

"You're right. I'll get the plate run and see what comes back," Wyatt said. "Hey, why don't you take off and let me finish the day?"

"That's a long shift, man. You sure?" Dwight asked. "I want to help."

"Listen, you're not great at this. You're in a terrible spot here. I appreciate the help but if you get made, we're screwed. Let me deal with this for now and I will keep you updated."

Dwight couldn't help but laugh. Pushed aside again, he thought.

"No, it's not like that," Wyatt said. He sighed and rubbed his eyes. "Listen, man, I just want some time to myself, and I would rather spend it doing something than sitting on my ass in my apartment."

Dwight nodded, his pride assuaged.

"You did good work today," Wyatt reassured him.

"Let me know what comes back with that plate," Dwight said as he started the engine of his truck.

"I will," said Wyatt as he climbed out of the truck.

As Dwight drove by the Trivotys', he saw Michael on the porch with his brother's mangy bull. The amount of criminality that Dwight had witnessed in just one day was astounding to him. He thought about what Wyatt had told him—it made sense. Something had to be wrong for such a large and open operation to continue for so long.

GEORGE AWAKENED TO FIND himself tied to a large oak tree, his face pressed tightly against its bark, his hands bound together with rope around its massive trunk. He groaned a little but found himself unable to move. *Was this real?* The heroin high was still strong.

"There ya go," Randy said, pouring a bottle of water over George's head. "Wake up you useless junky."

"What's happening? Let me go… who are?" George grumbled. He stopped when he recognized Randy's face. "Oh, Jesus! Jesus Christ!"

Reality hit George like a bag of sobering bricks.

"I didn't shoot your kid! It was Trivoty! Michael Trivoty!" he pleaded. "And I didn't have anything to do with planning it, either! That was Augustine! They made me drive them! I didn't want anything to do with it!"

"And you were the only one who knew where I lived. I remember you."

"I'm sorry! It wasn't supposed to go down like that!" George cried. He pulled against the restraints as hard as he could but to no avail.

"Who else? Was your brother involved?"

"No! Dickey would kill me if he knew!"

"Jason Terry?!" Randy pulled hard on George's curly hair. "Did that little shit sell me out?"

"The only ones involved were Augustine, Trivoty, and me! Jason wouldn't do that!"

"You're sure? I need to make sure you know the consequence of lying to me here."

"Mr. Sandusfield, I swear to God, it was only us three."

"And where can I find Augustine and Trivoty?" he asked.

"Look, man, they'll fucking kill you."

"Thanks for your concern." He pushed the muzzle of his revolver into George's throat.

"Michael lives on Reckon Ave in Winsted!"

"Where you just came from?"

"Yes!"

"And Augustine?"

"Lives in Hartland, above an old run-down US-Gas station."

"Thank you." He took a step back from the tree and aimed his revolver at George's head.

"Wait, what are you doing? I told you—"

The shot echoed through the woods.

Randy stood and glared with cold eyes at George's decimated skull. Chunks of bloody pulp dripped from the tree. He breathed a sigh of relief and headed back to his truck.

Before he could start the truck, his phone rang. It was Albert calling.

"What's wrong, buddy?" Randy asked as he turned the key and tucked his revolver into his pants.

"Hey, Randal. There's a small problem back here. I think you're going to need to…"

There was the sound of a scuffle and someone forcibly taking the phone from Albert.

"Hey, buddy," a gruff voice said.

Randy shook his head in disbelief. He recognized the voice; it was Tommy Delnero.

"Tommy?"

"I think it is best you come home now. We have some things to discuss," Tommy said. "You wouldn't want anything to happen to Albert or the missus here, would you?"

"No, of course not. I will be right there and we can work this out, Tommy."

"Sure, whatever you say, Randy. Just come unarmed or there will be trouble. I know what you're capable of and we are not taking any chances."

"I got it. No games. You can have what you want and be on the way. I've seen enough bloodshed."

ALBERT'S HOUSE LOOKED JUST AS PEACEFUL as it had when Randy left. The only change was the Canaan State Police SUV now parked out front.

Likely only two men.

Randy approached the door slowly, his hands behind his head. Tommy came outside, his 9mm trained on Randy. Albert stood in the doorway, another trooper behind him with a gun to his back.

"Everybody just relax," Randy said. "No need for this."

"We leave mister and missus alone here and you take us to the money," Tommy demanded. "That's the deal. Anything else and you all die now."

Get them away from the house. Then take them to the money tunnel. Whatever happens, the Reddings will be safe.

"That's fine by me," said Randy.

The other officer pushed Albert back into the house and the arms of his wife, then turned his gun on Randy. The name above his badge read "Gowan."

Randy walked along the wooded trail behind his house at gunpoint, contemplating his options.

They'll kill you once they have the money.

"Boss-man know you're playing this card?" Randy asked.

"I wouldn't worry about that," Gowan sneered.

"Fact is, you people are just tenants," Tommy laughed. "You think you own all this but you don't. We're the landlords. We're the reason you were ever able to operate to begin with. And that means, when things go south, we reserve the right to evict your ass."

"So, what's the play here?" Randy asked, trying to stall for time.

"We responded to a tip about a weed operation that had been robbed. You, unable to handle the death of your son, opened fire. Forcing us to kill you," Tommy explained.

The sad part was Randy knew it would work.

"My tunnel is over here," Randy said. "You'll have to help me."

Randy got onto the ground and began pushing boulders out of the way.

"No fucking way, man," Gowan scoffed. "You do it." He waved his gun at Randy and smirked.

Randy moved the rocks one by one and began to dig with his hands into the ground.

"This could take a while unless you help," Randy informed them.

"Fine, Jesus Christ," Tommy said. "Keep your gun on him!" he ordered Gowan. "How deep is it, Sandusfield?"

"I've got a lot of money down here; you think I keep the entrance a couple inches below ground?" Randy replied. "I told you we needed shovels. You didn't want to let me grab them."

"You said we 'should probably' grab shovels. That made it sound fucking optional," Tommy retorted. "Jesus fucking Christ! Adam, go get the fucking shovels from the shed."

"Are you serious?" Gowan protested.

"It's not that far, just fucking do it!" whined Tommy. "Hurry up while it's still daylight."

Gowan tucked his gun into the back of his pants and grumbled as his made his way back down the trail.

"For fuck's sake!" Randy yelled. "Can you two get your shit together?"

"Oh, you in a hurry to die?" Tommy asked, leaning against a nearby tree, his gun still aimed at Randy.

"Don't see much point in waiting," Randy said defiantly.

"As soon as we have your money and we get out of here in one piece," Tommy said, scanning the woods. "That old man better not try anything."

"He won't. His wife wouldn't let him. This doesn't involve him anymore," Randy said, taking a seat on the ground. "Can I light a smoke?"

"I don't give a fuck."

A few minutes later Gowan reappeared with a shovel and handed it to Randy. The two officers watched while Randy dug out the entrance to the tunnel at gunpoint. Finally, Randy reached down, brushed away the dirt, revealing a padlock. He pulled the key from his pocket and tossed it to Tommy.

"The money is down there," Randy said, closing his eyes.

Go ahead and shoot me you stupid fucks. I'll have the last laugh.

"Think we're fucking stupid?" Tommy asked. "Like you don't have that fucking thing booby-trapped."

Randy smiled and threw his hands up in the air.

"Well, you can't blame me for trying," he said.

Tommy handed him the key and gestured to the lock with his gun.

"Open the fucking door and get the fucking money," Tommy demanded.

Randy unlocked and removed the lock, then slid his fingers under the door and disarmed the booby-trap. He swung the door open and took a step back.

"You don't need me anymore," Randy said.

One booby-trap left. Just go down the fucking hole.

"Get down there and get the fucking—" Gowan started.

A loud shot rang out, and a .30-06 round exploded through the back of Gowan's neck and out his throat. He dropped in an instant, spraying blood across Tommy's face.

Now!

Randy grabbed Tommy while he was still stunned and pushed him down the tunnel shaft. He fell hard, smacking his head on the ladder rungs on the way down. From the bottom, he looked up at Randy, his vision blurred.

"Wait! What are you doing?!" Tommy yelled.

"Sealing your fate," Randy said before tossing a grenade from the booby-trap down the shaft and slamming the door shut. The grenade landed right next to Tommy's face.

The explosion kicked the door open and then brought the entire tunnel down on itself. Randy walked away as the ground behind him gave way, knowing he had one man to thank for his life.

"I told them you'd leave it alone," Randy said.

"That was their mistake to believe you," Albert replied, emerging from the wood line with his .30-06 rifle.

"Thank you, Albert."

"No problem. It was fun. Just like Granada."

Randy knelt beside Gowan's body and searched it for a phone.

"What are you doing?" Albert asked.

"Making a call," Randy answered.

He pulled Gowan's phone and keys out of his pants pocket and searched through the contacts. He found the number he was looking for and made the call.

"Hello?" the voice on the other end answered.

"Leahy, you slimy piece of shit. I've got two of your goons dead in my woods, a murdered son, and a hell of a lot of questions," Randy said.

"I should have known better," Leahy said with a laugh. "Alright, listen. You turn over the money, and I will let you and your neighbors live. You can run away to wherever the fuck you think you will be safe and hide away until you die. But the decision has been made. There is no more business for you. You've been shut down."

"You listen to me, you son of a bitch. You came after the wrong man. I'll be seeing you."

Randy hung up the phone and threw it into the woods.

"You guys better head out of town for a while," Randy advised Albert.

"Already ahead of you," he replied. "What are we going to do about Mark?"

"Give me ten minutes, call nine-one-one, and then leave. Tell them you heard shooting in the woods involving cops. They'll send in the whole cavalry and Leahy won't be able to control the scene. Give me your gun."

Albert complied.

"Goodbye again," Randy said.

"Randy," Albert said with a sigh. "Don't take this the wrong way, but this time I hope it is."

Randy drove away in the police SUV.

Get their vehicle away from the scene. Ditch it. Steal a new car. Find Trivoty and Augustine. Kill them both.

MAEGAN STARED AT HER PHONE and wrestled with her demons. For the first time in a long time, she just didn't feel strong enough. She was tired. Tired of pretending to be something she was not. Tired of the pressure from Jason to be a better person. In her mind, she knew what she really was, and she did not see the use in pretending.

She picked up the phone and made the worst call of her life.

Michael," she said into the phone. "Yeah, it's me... Michael, Mom's dead. Can you help me?"

202

She listened intently as she stood up from her bed and began to dress.

"I need you to pick me up then," she said.

Moments later, she hung up and sighed. Refusing to take the time to contemplate what she was really doing, Maegan grabbed her stuff and hustled past a sleeping Max on the couch. He raised his head alertedly, but she was already out the door, heading down the street.

After some time walking, the headlights of an approaching car veered off to the shoulder of the road in front of her.

"What's up, girl?" Michael said warmly.

"I just need to get right," Maegan said.

He nodded knowingly and told her to "Get in."

Chapter Eight
Hot Shots

Dwight pulled his car up a long driveway, past an elegant white Victorian house, and parked in front of the garage beside a green Subaru. This was the address on file for Jason Terry.

Dwight patted Max on the head and told him to stay put. It had been three days since he had seen or heard from Maegan. To make his concern worse, she hadn't shown up to her mother's funeral that morning. He was afraid she had relapsed. The ringing in his head was back, and so was the headache.

He checked his phone again before heading up the stairs to Terry's apartment. Wyatt had called several times, but he'd heard nothing from Maegan. He was late to meet Wyatt at the Trivoty house, but he would have to wait. Finding Maegan was his priority.

He knocked on the door. When Jason answered, he was noticeably distressed.

"Unbelievable," Jason said, shaking his head and letting out a wounded sigh. "What is it?"

"I'm looking for Maegan Riley," Dwight said. "I'm her uncle."

"Yeah, I know who you are," Jason replied. "She's not here."

"Bullshit."

"Search the place if you want, dude," Jason offered. "She hasn't spoken to me in days. I have no idea where she is or what she's doing. Though, I have a few guesses."

"And those would be?"

"What do you think, man? She's probably doping up somewhere."

Dwight could see the kid was hurting, but his words still pissed him off. The ringing in his head was growing louder, and he didn't have time for this shit.

"Maybe if she hadn't been hanging around with you, smoking pot and drinking, it wouldn't have been such a short step off the wagon," Dwight told him.

"Or maybe she was dirt all along, and it's time we all stop pretending otherwise," Jason snapped.

Dwight didn't make the conscious decision to hit him, but his fist found his jaw nonetheless. Jason dropped to the ground like he'd been hit by a train. The ringing in Dwight's head became almost deafening. The pain broke through Dwight's anger, and he froze, fist cocked back, ready to strike Jason again.

Jason was yelling. Cursing. All Dwight could hear was the ringing.

"If you-blee my bliece, you better calb blee," Dwight said, suddenly unable to properly speak.

He began to panic. The ringing was suddenly so loud, his headache so extreme, and his words were not forming right. His heart racing, gasping for breath, Dwight frantically stumbled down the steps, leaving an angry Jason rubbing his jaw. He locked himself inside his car and hugged his dog. *Was this it? Was he dying?*

After several minutes, Dwight began to feel better. The ringing seemed to fade as he calmed down. A few minutes later, he was satisfied that this was not the end. The writing was on the wall, though. He could no longer put off his surgery.

205

A BROWN VOLKSWAGEN RABBIT sputtered to a stop in front of a former US-Gas station. Randy Sandusfield glared through the windshield at the apartment windows above. He put the car in gear, and the engine backfired. A used car lot just down the road would be the perfect place to wait.

He had already gone to Trivoty's, but the house was full of bangers. Randy knew when he was outmatched. Better to try and catch Augustine off guard and then use him to get Trivoty alone. His emergency safety net awaited him in a boathouse in Goshen, but he had some scores to settle before he could cut ties and flee.

What would he do? Where would he go? Anywhere, he supposed. He had the money. He had the aliases and the fake passports. He could go anywhere and be anyone. And yet, that never appealed to him. He could have gotten out long ago and done just that. If he had, Mark would still be alive.

Whatever he had to do, he knew he was going to be bringing down a shitload of heat. Cops, feds, traffickers, cartels—they would all want him dead. His life as he knew it was over. Like it or not, Randy was going to be forced to start a new life. He would be goddamned if he weren't going to make these people pay first. Augustine. Trivoty. Leahy, too. As long as he was alive, they would never stop looking for him.

ANDREW TRIVOTY PULLED HIS LITTLE BROTHER aside by his ear.

"Look, man, I don't know these people. We've got Eddie and our crew coming in, so we need these people to clear out. Too much shit going down right now."

"Whatchu mean?" Michael asked.

"We got word that the staties got Eddie on that girl he choked out. DNA matched."

Andrew looked around at Michael's friends, disapprovingly.

"We just gotta get Eddie out of here. Proper sendoff party tonight with all the boys and hoes. Then he's going to go stay with our boys up in New Hampshire for a while," he explained to Michael.

"Alright, I'll get everyone out of here except Maegan."

Maegan waved at Andrew as she staggered by to use the bathroom.

"Alright, cool," Andrew said. "Our people say this can all go away. They're working on getting the investigation tanked."

"You talk to Gary?" Michael asked.

"Yeah, he's in Long Island, unloading the shit you guys scored. Nice work, bro," Andrew said, fist-bumping Michael.

"Ain't no thing," Michael said. He couldn't tell his brother he had been having trouble sleeping, or that whenever he closed his eyes, he saw the kid he had shot.

"Baby, we got anymore D?" Maegan asked. Her eyes were bloodshot and empty, surrounded by heavy bags. Michael kissed her and smiled.

"Andrew, you got more shit?" Michael asked his brother.

"Yeah, but the shit is fucking hot, bro. Tell whoever gets it to be careful," said Andrew. "I mean it. It's some real fire. Be careful." He handed a bundle of baggies to Michael, who gave it to Maegan.

"Let me just get these people out of here, and we'll lace up," Michael said to Maegan. She smiled, took the dope, and stuck it in her bra.

"You got a smoke for me, baby?" she asked, rubbing her hand on Michael's chest.

"There's a pack in the car," he said, handing her the keys.

DWIGHT CLIMBED INTO THE PASSENGER seat of Wyatt's car and handed him a coffee.

"Looks like you're the one having a rough day today," Wyatt remarked. "Busy day here, lots of hood rats."

"Listen, I can't do this," Dwight said. "I came here to tell you."

"Wait, you turning Boy Scout on me?" Wyatt scoffed.

"No, it's not about that," Dwight replied. "I have a condition... A brain tumor."

"Shit, you serious?"

"I thought I had more time—well, I hoped I did, but I don't. I'm going to have to have surgery very soon and chances are I won't make it out."

Wyatt shook his head.

"I guess there's nothing I can say. I'm sorry to hear that," Wyatt said after a few moments.

"I'm sorry, I want to help. I just can't."

"Looks like the crowd's leaving. I'm going to get some pictures then I suppose I'm out of here. Without your help, I don't even have the veneer of authority to be here."

Dwight felt bad for Wyatt, but also guilty about derailing the investigation. More so, he felt disappointed that he was being forced to give up the one time he thought he had a chance to make an impact. He watched Wyatt position his camera and start photographing people coming out of the house. He glanced at the house itself and couldn't believe his eyes.

No, he thought; it couldn't have been. *Could it?*

"That girl!" he shouted. "The one who just went back in the house!"

"Yeah, I saw her. So, what?"

"Let me see the picture!" Dwight demanded.

"Alright, relax," Wyatt told him. He pushed a couple of buttons on the back of the digital camera and handed it to Dwight.

"That's my niece…" Dwight said in disbelief. "I've been looking for her for two days."

"Fuck!" Wyatt said as he saw the volatility in Dwight's eyes. "Listen, man, does she have a phone we can call her on?"

"She won't answer," Dwight said. "I have to go get her."

"No, no, no!" Wyatt pled, grabbing Dwight by his shirt. "Listen to me. We cannot go in there. It will open up a shit storm in more ways than one!"

"She's all I have. She needs me," Dwight said.

He broke free of Wyatt's grasp and leaped from the car.

"Son of a bitch…" Wyatt said, chambering a round into his sidearm before following Dwight.

"MAEGAN!" Dwight yelled as he approached the house. He wasn't in uniform, but he wore a CT State Police T-shirt, and had a gun holstered on his hip.

"Five-Oh!" yelled numerous bangers, alerting others to the presence of law enforcement.

"MAEGAN!" Dwight yelled again as he crossed onto the front lawn.

That was when Dexter came down the front steps snarling, lunging for Dwight, just out of reach of his chain.

"What the fuck is this?!" Andrew yelled, emerging from the front door. "Piggy-piggy, go home!"

"Got a fucking warrant?" Michael asked, joining his brother on the porch.

Dexter lunged again as Dwight tried to move forward, his arms spread wide to show peaceful intent.

"I just want my niece, and I will leave you guys alone," Dwight said.

Wyatt came up behind Dwight and aimed his gun at the bull.

"Call your dog back now, or I put it down!" Wyatt ordered.

Andrew took a quick assessment of Wyatt and decided not to call his bluff.

"Dexter!" Andrew called. "Heel!"

The dog immediately stopped lunging at the officers and returned to Andrew's side.

"My niece," Dwight repeated.

"Let the man take his family from here, and we got no further business," Wyatt said, his gun still drawn.

"What if we say no?" Andrew asked.

209

"Bitch came here on her own, yo," Michael boasted. "What you think, we got her hostage? I've been treating her real well, don't you worry," he laughed, grabbing his crotch and thrusting his waist.

"Either we walk out of here with her, or I start tossing your place right now," Wyatt threatened.

"Bullshit! Get a warrant," Andrew shot back.

"I don't need one. Probable cause to believe all this foot traffic is a result of drug activity in this house. That and suspicion you're holding a girl against her will is all I need to start slapping cuffs on wrists and turning your place inside-out."

Andrew laughed and sat down on the porch rail to light a smoke.

"See me blinking?" he asked the cops.

"I know what you're thinking," Wyatt said, climbing the stairs and approaching the brothers. "You'll walk. You've got friends, I know… Thing is, I'm not your friend, and I don't play well with others. I'm a real problem for you because I will tear this whole place down and not give one damn who it pisses off or what the consequences are."

"She inside," Andrew said with a wave of his hand. "Go take the cunt."

"What the fuck?" Michael asked in protest.

"Bitch ain't worth this much trouble," Andrew said sharply. "Get her the fuck out of here."

With that, Dwight barged into the house to find his niece.

"Maegan?" he called as he went room to room.

He opened the back bedroom and found her. She was lying, passed out on a mattress with no sheets, in her underwear. The heroin and the needle she had just used was on the table beside her.

"Hey," he said touching her forehead.

Something was wrong. Dwight put his head close to her face—she was barely breathing. He checked her pulse—it was weak. He shook her, but she didn't respond.

"Christ, no!" he cried, lifting her limp body into his arms. "Come on, Maegan!"

He carried her through the house.

"Help!" he shouted as he burst through the door. *"Wyatt, help!"*

"Jesus Christ! Get her to the car! C'mon!" Wyatt yelled.

The two men ran to Wyatt's car. Michael and Andrew looked on from the porch.

"I told you," Andrew said with a laugh. "That shit is fucking fire!"

Michael was frozen in shock.

Wyatt had the car started and was flying down the road moments after they got in.

"She's got a pulse, but it's weak!" Dwight yelled from the back seat.

"Just hold on, buddy," Wyatt urged. He picked up his police radio and notified Winsted Hospital that they were en route with an overdose. Then he flipped on the sirens.

Dwight cradled Maegan in his arms, brushing her hair back with his fingers.

"Just stay with us, sweetie," he said. The ringing in his head was coming back. "Just stay with us."

DICKEY TOSSED THE TENNIS BALL high into the air. It came down, hit the ground, and bounced, sending the still unnamed puppy running and pouncing after it. Stacey and Marie laughed and cheered as the puppy finally captured the ball.

"Well, what are we going to name him, Daddy?" asked Marie.

"What do you girls think would be a good name?" Dickey asked, taking a seat on the bench beside the fountain that marked the entrance to Torrington Hospital. Maegan had been transferred there because Winsted Hospital did not have the space or resources to give her adequate care.

"Jason?" Stacey asked.

"No, we can't do that, silly," Dickey explained. "Then everyone would be confused all the time."

"That would be silly!" Marie laughed.

"What if we named him Thor?" Dickey asked.

"Nooo!" both girls groaned.

"I want to name him Courage," Marie said.

"Courage?" Dickey asked. "Why Courage?"

"Because you said the dog was to help you when you feel scared."

The dog chewed on Dickey's foot playfully and growled, its tail wagging in the air.

"Well, this guy isn't scared to chew on a Marine's foot. I think that name might just be perfect."

Marie and Stacey smiled. The newest member of the family was named Courage.

Inside the hospital, Jason stared through the hallway window into Maegan's room, watching the machines keep her alive. His shirt was wet from wiping away tears.

A hand on his shoulder took him by surprise.

"Hey."

Jason turned to see Dwight.

"Thanks for calling me," Jason said, turning his gaze back to Maegan.

"I'm sorry about today," Dwight said.

"Yeah," Jason replied, rubbing his bruised and swollen cheek.

"I haven't been myself lately, especially with worrying about her," Dwight explained. "If you want to press charges against me, it is within your rights."

"Nah, man, it's cool," Jason said. "You got her here. She's alive now and fighting to hold on because of you. If anything, I owe you my gratitude."

"Why don't you go home and get some rest. I will tell the nurses to call you if anything changes," Dwight told Jason.

Jason wanted to protest, to stay by Maegan's side, but he really needed the sleep. He had barely had any the past two nights. He thanked Dwight and headed outside to find Dickey and the girls.

Dwight stayed, looking through the glass at his niece, his anger brewing silently under the surface. The ringing had subsided again, but his headache remained. He grabbed a bottle of aspirin from his pocket, chewed a few, and rubbed his temples.

Wyatt returned from a conversation with several hospital staff.

"Hey man," he said. "We got overdoses flooding the whole area the past few days. Seven bodies and three survivors including Maegan. There's a real nasty batch of heroin on the streets. It's got too much fentanyl in it. Real dangerous shit."

"Is it them? The Trivotys and Augustine, is it them putting it on the street?" Dwight asked, his anger boiling over.

"Most likely, yes," Wyatt told him.

"Someone has to do something. They have to be shut down."

Wyatt pulled Dwight into his niece's room and shut the door.

"How many days do you have?"

"I don't know. Honestly, I could drop dead any time."

"You're joking," Wyatt said.

"No, I'm afraid not," Dwight replied. "Chances are I won't. I'll probably die on the operating table instead," he noted.

"How many days can you give me?" Wyatt asked.

"A couple… Maybe."

"Damn it, these guys have to pay," Wyatt said, looking at Maegan breathing through tubes.

"What can we do?"

"In two days? Nothing. And the state will freeze me out," Wyatt said, shaking his head in disgust.

213

"Somebody ought to do something," Dwight muttered.

"You talking like I think you're talking?" Wyatt asked under his breath.

"Just saying, they're scum. I wouldn't cry if something happened to them—if they couldn't hurt anyone anymore."

"Listen," Wyatt said softly. "I'm with you on wanting these guys to hurt. And if we have to get creative to do it, I'm not opposed. I've never been opposed to getting bad people off the street, but we don't talk about it here. And first, we make sure there's no other way."

Dwight nodded, his headache still making it hard to focus.

"Let me dig into all those photos and plate numbers—everything we got from watching the house, and see if there isn't an angle we can use. Are you with me as long as you can be?" Wyatt asked.

Dwight looked at his niece and sighed.

"I'm in it till the end, man."

WHEN DWIGHT RETURNED HOME, he found his nephew Danny smoking a cigarette on the porch. The poor kid had been through so much, and yet none of it seemed to surprise him.

"Fucking losers do drugs," was all he had to say about any of it when Dwight asked.

Danny had his own issues, though. Dwight knew he was a drinker.

"I don't want to have to lock up my booze, but I will," Dwight had told him his first night in the house.

Dwight was pretty sure he had stolen a couple of beers from the fridge but decided to choose his battles. The kid needed a friend right now; someone who cared.

He didn't acknowledge Dwight as he and Max climbed the front steps.

"Sister's stable for now, but she needs the machine to keep her breathing," Dwight told him as he let Max into the house.

"Dumb bitch," Danny said with a cynical yet wounded laugh.

"Hey, now," Dwight replied, taking a seat beside him. "I know you're angry, and that's your right, but that's your sister. You know, she's not perfect, but she's trying, just like we all are."

"She's just like my mother. The needle is all that matters. Family doesn't matter. I don't matter," he said.

For Dwight, it was like looking into a mirror through time. There he was, his pain turning to anger and resentment toward his sister. In Danny, he recognized the seeds of the feelings that would ultimately lead to his disowning her. That was if Maegan even lived as long as April had.

"I know what you're feeling. My sister—your mother… You know she and I didn't get along too well," he told his nephew. "Can I tell you something I haven't told anyone?" he asked.

Danny finally looked up.

"What?" he asked.

"When your mother died," Dwight began. "I didn't feel much of anything. No regret. No sorrow. If anything there was a sense of relief. Can you believe that? Relief. You get tired of worrying. Tired of seeing it their ups and downs. You find yourself almost hoping the inevitable would happen so that you could stop dreading it. Then you start to numb yourself to the idea. Before you know it, you hate them for making you feel that way. You hate them for choosing a life that will sooner or later take them from you... And in that way, they're already gone."

The words resonated with Danny. He didn't want to hate his sister. As Dwight spoke, he could no longer hold back his tears.

"Don't let your heart turn cold," Dwight said, holding back tears of his own. "Don't turn away from her. She needs you. Her story doesn't have to end like your mother's. It wasn't inevitable. I see that now."

Danny took out his smokes and lit another. Dwight gestured for one and joined him.

"Didn't know you smoked," Danny said.

"Recently took it up again," Dwight said with a sigh. "Your brother drop you off?"

"Yeah," Danny replied.

"Did you tell him what we talked about?"

"Yeah, he agrees," said Danny. "I should stay here for a while."

"Good," Dwight said. Soon he would have to tell him about the tumor and the surgery, but not today. The kid had already been through enough.

"Are you going back?" Danny asked as Dwight rose to leave. "To the hospital?"

"Yeah, I just have some things to take care of. I'm heading back there tonight if you want to come."

"That would be cool," Danny replied.

PATRICK LEAHY PRESSED DOWN on the French press, slowly straining coffee from the grounds.

"You take yours black, correct?" Leahy asked.

"That's right," Greg Hostetler grumbled.

Leahy poured two cups and brought them to the kitchen table where Hostetler sat.

"Always the gracious host," Hostetler said with a nod as he took the cup. "What's the latest?"

"Well, we cleaned up the mess in Sheffield," Leahy reported. "Boys up there owed me a solid."

"I still don't see why we're not hanging Sandusfield out to dry on those cops he killed."

"Because that would bring every law enforcement agency in the country into this."

"And then we would find him easily."

"Then we lose control. Feds see how badly fucked everything is here; we'll be the ones hanging out to dry."

"Well, our associates down south aren't too happy," Hostetler informed the captain. "How much do you think Randy knows?"

216

"Too much," Leahy sternly replied.

"They see this as your problem."

"C'mon, Hos! That's bullshit!" Leahy protested.

"You're supposed to keep a lid on these things. That's what they pay you for. Make sure everything runs smoothly."

"It's the Toros. They're making it impossible to maintain order."

"They're connected to our friends down south and our friends in Long Island. It's important that channel remains open for a little bit longer. Especially now that the weed pipeline is broken."

"We'll find someone else, that'll be easy. One of Randy's people. Plug them right in."

"First, you need to make sure he's not going to come back on us in any way."

"I will," Leahy replied. "We found the police SUV he stole in a ditch in Pleasant Valley, and a woman who lives nearby there just reported her stolen car. We're close."

MICHAEL SNORTED A LARGE LINE of cocaine and let out a savage yell as he began beating on his brother's punching bag.

"What's wrong, pussy?" Andrew teased. "You all twisted about that cunt still?"

"Fuck you. Fuck off," Michael retorted between shots. "Fucking hospital won't even let me see her, but that Terry fucker gets to?"

"Still letting that fucking scrub make you a bitch?"

"I oughta kill the fucking kid," Michael fumed.

"Then do it," Andrew taunted. "Go ahead and fucking do it. Don't just run your fucking mouth."

"You told me not to," Michael replied in confusion.

"Not worth the heat, bro. Still, it's better than listening to you run your mouth and not do anything," Andrew laughed, taking down a line of blow himself. "Eddie and the crew be here soon. Tighten up."

Andrew affectionately slapped Michael on the shoulders and went inside. Michael growled and began beating the bag again.

THE FUNERAL HOMES WERE GETTING plenty of business thanks to the scourge of opioids devastating the state.

Jason took a swig of whiskey from a metal flask as he sat teary-eyed outside the Mason-Monroe Funeral Home in Torrington. Maegan's mother's wake had recently been held at that very place. Now it was hosting calling hours for the family and friends of Jason's cousin Tim, who was found behind a dumpster on the north end of town; his death ruled an overdose of heroin laced with fentanyl.

He knew his extended family wouldn't receive him well and he was right. Most thought of him as a loser drug dealer. Many felt he must somehow be to blame.

Another long swig to make that numbness wash over him.

He wasn't to blame. Scum like Trivoty were.

He lit a joint and took yet another swig. Never in his life could he say he actually hated someone, but he *hated* Michael Trivoty. He stole Maegan away, led her back to heroin, and put her in the hospital. *It was his fault she was there!*

As if that weren't enough, Jason had just found out from Travis that it was Trivoty who started them on heroin. *Of course, it was. The filthy guttersnipe. The cancer.*

Jason remembered what Dickey said: there's a line. Someone had to keep that line, even if that meant crossing it yourself. He took a moment and contemplated what he was about to do.

Travis was standing outside the funeral home smoking.

"Travis!" Jason yelled from the car.

"What's up, man?" Travis asked when he got to the car.

"You can get a hold of Trivoty, right?"

"Michael? Yeah, man, of course. I owe him a little scratch right now, though," Travis confessed.

"How much?" asked Jason.

"Eighty…. A hundred."

"I'll give you two-hundred right now, but you gotta do me a favor," Jason said.

"Okay, man, anything."

A dope fiend is the easiest person to buy.

"Call Trivoty, tell him to meet you behind the Rock Creek dam at eleven PM tonight. Tell him you have his money and need more dope."

"Alright, then what do we do? Go shoot the dope somewhere?"

"No, dude, I am not trying to cop heroin," Jason explained. "You can get your heroin anywhere, just not from Trivoty; not tonight. Just get him to the dam and don't worry about the rest," Jason said.

"What are you gonna do?" Travis asked.

"Don't worry about it. Do you want the money or not?"

"Yeah, but how will I pay Trivoty what I owe him?"

"You won't have to," Jason replied with a smile. "You get to keep the whole two-hundred."

Travis nodded slowly then smiled.

"Oh, shit, it's like that, huh?" Travis asked.

"You want the money or not?" Jason asked, tiring of the sight of him.

"Yeah, man. I'll call right now."

DWIGHT PULLED HIS CRUISER up to the Canaan barracks and headed inside, leaving Max in the car.

"Captain Leahy," Dwight said. "I'm glad I caught you."

Leahy nodded and shook Dwight's hand.

"How are you, Trooper? How's quiet Colebrook?"

"Not so quiet," Dwight replied. "Captain, I keep following up and get no response regarding the lab work for Jennifer Martinez."

"Who?" the captain said, squinting with disdain.

"The Jane Doe from the reservoir, sir," Dwight said, noticeably perturbed by the captain's disinterest.

"Oh, yes. DNA came back to some banger."

"We looking for him?"

"No, Trooper. The banger is tied to a gang operating out of Winsted. They're part of a larger RICO investigation being carried out by the feds. We can't move on them because it will compromise the larger case the feds are building."

"Sir, my niece overdosed today."

Leahy stopped and sincerely placed his hand on Dwight's shoulder.

"I'm so sorry, Evans."

"She's one of many in a rash of ODs sweeping this area. Bad dope and lots of it and it is all coming out of that house in Winsted. From this guy's crew. The same people who put this girl in the reservoir!" Dwight exclaimed. "Fuck the feds, Captain. We gotta take these guys down! Someone has to do something!"

Leahy sighed and shook his head.

"I wish we could, Evans. I wish we could. The feds are calling the shots on this one. I know it's hard. I know you want to take these guys down. They're lowlife scum. If it makes you feel any better, just imagine the kind of vile, dangerous people they must work for. That's who I would be worried about. And the feds are trying to deal with that."

"So, we just sit here in the woods and mop up the blood and deal with the deadly drugs on our street."

"We can't move on the house or the gang. I'm sorry," Leahy said.

Dwight shook his head and sighed.

"I'm going to need some time off," Dwight said.

"For your niece? Of course," Leahy answered.

"No, I have to have surgery. I just found out I have a brain tumor."

"Jesus Christ."

"It looks good. Should be fine. But… uh… I have to get the fucker cut out of me. Probably going to be laid up for a few weeks."

"Christ, well, good luck. Take all the time you need. Just be sure to contact your PBA rep and file all the forms the bureaucrats require," Leahy said.

Back in his cruiser, about to drive home, Dwight took a deep breath and called his doctor.

"Hi, this is Dwight Evans. I want to go ahead and schedule that surgery as soon as possible. If someone can call me back at your next convenience, I would appreciate it," he said in the message.

He hung up and drove off, his music blasting, the wind whipping through his hair. Just a man and his dog headed down the road.

"YOU'RE NOT LOOKING SO HOT, BRO," Dickey said.

"It's been a rough week," Jason agreed. He thought of the meeting he had set for Michael that night and sighed. *Who was he kidding? He wasn't going to go through with it.*

The summer sunset still hung low behind the trees as the two sat on Dickey's back porch.

"Light that joint up and we'll try to forget our problems," Dickey said with a slight chuckle.

Inside Courage suddenly began to bark, which, as a puppy, was still very much a yelp. Then there was a knock at the front door.

"Who the hell could this be now?" Dickey snapped. "They're going to wake the girls up!"

"I'll go check on them, you get the door," Jason suggested.

The two went inside, and Jason headed up the stairs for the girls' room while Dickey tried to calm the puppy.

Jason opened the girls' door softly.

"What's happening?" Marie asked?

"Yeah, what's going on?" Stacey chimed in.

Jason turned their light on and closed the door behind him to keep the noise out.

"Just some visitor," Jason told them with a smile.

"Who is it, though?" Marie asked.

"It's a friend of mine and your father's. That's all. Now, why aren't you sleeping?"

"Hard when the stupid dog starts yapping and visitors knock on the door," Marie sassed.

"Alright, alright, get comfy," Jason urged. "I'm going to read you a story then you're going back to sleep."

They were both pleased with the suggestion.

Jason came downstairs about twenty minutes later to find a very somber Dickey.

"It's George," Dickey said, sipping a beer, his face grim. "Someone tied him to a tree and executed him."

"What?" Jason was in disbelief.

Dickey explained what the police had just told him.

"I guess Augustine caught up with him, or someone else," Dickey concluded.

"These people are cancer, all of them: the Trivotys, Augustine… "

"Yeah, they are. I guess if I'm honest, George was too."

"I'm tired of seeing people hurt, and nothing gets done," Jason said blankly.

"In the end, George got exactly what he chose," Dickey replied. "He got himself mixed up in something, I'm sure of it. He was no innocent victim. And your girl, as much as I feel for her… she made her choices, too."

Dickey rose from the couch to dispose of his empty can and grabbed another beer. Jason followed him to the kitchen.

"So, the people they hurt basically asked for it. You're saying they deserved it. If so, that's doubly true for scum like Augustine or Michael Trivoty. Don't they deserve to die?"

"Sure," Dickey answered immediately.

"Then someone should just fucking do the world a favor and kill them," Jason added. "Just cut their throats or shoot them like rabid dogs."

"I'm sure sooner or later, someone will," Dickey mused. He placed his hand on Jason's shoulder and handed him a beer.

"Come on out back," he said. "I need a smoke."

One smoke turned to several; cigarettes and weed chased by cans of cheap American beer. They drank and smoked till they were numb, Dickey recalling stories of George with fondness.

"I mean, he was always a fuck up. Even as a kid. But at least he had good intentions. I don't know what happened to that George," Dickey recalled with regret.

"What's it like to kill somebody?" Jason blurted out suddenly.

"The fuck you talking about? Shut up." Dickey guffawed.

"I mean, how does it feel? I'm serious. This guy tied George to a tree and shot him in the head. I just can't stop thinking, *what's it take to do something like that?* And what does it feel like after?"

"You're drunk," Dickey replied.

"Is it hard?"

"Doing it isn't so hard. You would be surprised, actually. Once you set your mind to it. The trick is to stop thinking. To let go," Dickey told him, lighting yet another joint. "Let that beast come out of you and take it off the leash. It only takes a moment, really. A little pull. Three pounds of force or less on the trigger."

"That guy you executed. He deserved it. Did that make it easier?"

"I don't know. Like I told you before, it was a light switch. I made a decision on some level, I guess, and then the rest was just automatic.

223

Training maybe. You can't second guess yourself on the battlefield, so you learn to turn off that part of your brain that says, 'hey, is this the *right* thing to do?' When you need to, you have to be able to make the decision to kill and not hesitate."

"You can't allow yourself to think about it…" Jason reiterated.

"Pretty much," Dickey said. "Of course, that's on the battlefield. Then we come back here, and we have to turn off those killer instincts. A lot of guys get in trouble with that."

"How did you feel after?"

"You live with it," Dickey said quietly. "It's not easy, but you live with it."

"I thought about killing someone," Jason confessed.

"Yeah, I'm sure everyone does," Dickey said dismissively.

"No, I really thought about it. I even planned it out," Jason told him.

"Come on." Dickey laughed. "You're puttin' me on."

"I had my cousin's friend set up a meet with Trivoty tonight. I was going to go ahead of time and surprise him. Up at the dam."

"And?" Dickey asked.

"And I was going to kill the fucking bastard!"

"How?"

"I don't know. I was going to bring a baseball ball or an ax."

"Holy shit!" Dickey laughed. "No way. Nope. Sorry. You don't have it in you, kid," he teased. "There's no way you would be able to do it."

"Why not?!" Jason asked, rising to his feet in anger. "I'm just as much of a man as you, Dickey. I can handle my own shit!"

"I'm sorry, buddy," Dickey said in a conciliatory tone. "Sit down," he urged. "Listen, when I said that, it's not a bad thing. You're a *good* person. I know it. You know right from wrong. You would not take someone's life unless you had to."

"You did," Jason replied.

"I was a soldier," said Dickey. "It's not the same."

"Are you going to tell me that killing the guy that killed George wouldn't be justified? That whoever did it wouldn't be a hero?"

"Alright, yeah. Part of me wants to see that. Hell, part of me wants to *do* that. But this is a society of laws…"

"The law isn't doing shit, just look around," Jason interrupted. "You said it before, man. Some people deserve to die."

"That may be, Jason. But that doesn't mean we can just start killing people, and it doesn't mean you're a killer. You're not. Push ever came to shove, I don't think you would be able to do it."

"Maybe you're right," Jason conceded. "I'm just drunk," he said.

"Man, it's been a hell of a week. I don't blame you for thinking about killing people," Dickey said between coughs of smoke. "You want to hit this joint?" he asked.

"Yeah man, I just have to piss," said Jason. "Too many beers."

Jason went inside, and Dickey puffed on the joint while he waited. He gazed up at the stars and thought about his brother. He wouldn't admit it to anyone, but he was going to miss the hell out of him. Despite his best efforts, he found himself wishing he had done more to try and help him.

After some time, Dickey reached the end of the joint, looked around, and became confused. *Where was Jason? Was he taking a shit? Perhaps the girls had been up, and he was putting them back to bed.*

Dickey went into the house and was bewildered to not find Jason there. It was unlike him to leave without saying goodbye. *Had he offended him?*

He thought about their conversation before Jason left and became slightly concerned. Jason was drunk and had a head full of bad ideas. Dickey rushed up the stairs to his bedroom. He put on his boots, gathered his things, and as prepared to leave. Before he did, he called his in-laws.

"Hello, Belle? Sorry to bother you. This is an emergency. I need you to come over to the house in case the girls wake up. I have to leave. I will explain later, I promise. Yes, I'm fine. Thank you, so much."

Dickey hung up the phone, threw on his John Deere hat and headed for the door. As he was about to turn off his bedroom light, he paused. Jason was potentially headed to confront dangerous criminals—he'd better bring a gun just in case he had to diffuse the situation.

He opened his dresser drawer to retrieve his .38 and sighed.

"Jason, you stupid son of a bitch," he muttered.

The gun was gone. Now Jason's intent was clear. Dickey rushed to his closet and dug out his .44 revolver before running down the stairs and out the door.

ANDREW TRIVOTY HANDED his brother his cell phone from the counter.

"One of your fiends calling," Andrew said.

"Yo, we're not meeting till later, right?" Michael asked into the phone. "Oh, is that so?" he said a few moments later. "That little fuckin' bitch! You did the right thing, Holmes. You come by; I will set you right. Debt forgiven. Yeah, come by tomorrow night."

"What's all that?" Andrew asked his brother.

"That Terry bitch was trying to set me up tonight. That kid Travis just dimed him out," Michael said, shaking his head.

"Set you up to do what? Andrew laughed. "Weak ass mofo."

"I don't know, but I'm going to go find out," Michael said, rubbing his fist with anticipation.

"Why don't you wait? Crew will be here later on. Bring some back-up," Andrew advised before blowing a line of heroin.

"Nah, man," Michael argued. "He's up there waiting for me. I'm not going to miss this chance. If he wants it like this, I'm not backing down."

"Don't be stupid. Don't you fucking kill him or anything. We don't need that heat right now," Andrew said sternly.

"I'm just going to beat his ass and scare him a little," Michael assured him as he tucked his 9mm into his waistband.

MAX BARKED AND HOWLED at the front door. Dwight pushed past him and looked out the window.

"It's alright, buddy. Calm down," he told Max. The dog stopped barking but remained alert.

Dwight opened the door and turned on his porch light.

"What's going on? What are you doing here? Why didn't you call? My nephew is sleeping upstairs."

"A million questions," Wyatt replied cynically. *"Don't you think I have a reason?"* he asked under his breath as he pushed passed Dwight through the door. "We gotta talk."

"What's going on?" Dwight asked.

"First, Winsted PD just found our buddy George Calloway tied to a tree down by the lake, half his skull blown off."

"Oh, shit!" Dwight exclaimed. "Did we see his murderer?"

"That's where things get sketchy," Wyatt said.

Dwight could see he was unnerved.

"I ran the plate you gave me," Wyatt continued. "Came back as a former cop named Randal Sandusfield. I don't know how he fits into all this, but I'm beginning to think pulling his file was a big mistake."

"Why do you say that?"

"First, my captain asked me about it. Then I came home tonight, and someone had been in my apartment."

"Jesus, are you sure?"

"I have my ways of knowing," Wyatt asserted. "Someone had been there. I have to assume it could be bugged."

"Wait, what?!" Dwight asked in a muted yell. "Hold on a minute. What is it you think is going on here?"

"I don't know, but we've stumbled into the middle of something we don't understand," Wyatt said.

"So, who would be bugging your place?"

227

"Crooked cops? I don't know. I think I was being followed on my way here, but I managed to shake them."

Dwight moved to the window and peered outside with concern.

"What have you gotten me into?" Dwight asked.

"Gets worse," Wyatt said, his hand loosely over his mouth. "Two of your boys, Canaan Troopers, are missing. Gowan and Delnero."

"Missing?" Dwight asked. He knew both of them, although not well. They were the kind of cops who got off on being dicks to people.

"I don't know what's going on, but keep your head down and your eyes open," Wyatt advised. "Get your gun. We're taking a ride."

"Where?"

"Sheffield, Massachusetts," Wyatt replied, already heading out the door. "I'll drive, you've had more to drink than me."

"Shit…" Dwight muttered under his breath. He grabbed his gun and wallet, said goodbye to Max, and quietly headed out the door, as to not wake Danny.

THE GREEN SUBARU PULLED UP to the Rock Creek dam at ten past ten. Jason took a deep breath to try and steady his nerves, then checked to make sure Dickey's gun was ready to fire—safety off, a round in the chamber. He got out of his car and went to go hide up in the woods and wait for Michael.

He climbed the trail that led up the dam, unsuspecting of what was about to befall him. Suddenly, Michael leapt out from behind a rock where he'd been hiding, and pistol whipped Jason in the back of the head.

Jason dropped to the ground, his face scraping the pavement. He tried to push himself up, but Michael kicked him hard in the gut. Unable to catch his breath, he writhed on the ground, and Michael kicked him several more times in the abdomen.

"What's up, bitch!?" Michael taunted between blows. "Did you think you were going to surprise me?!"

Jason rolled over onto his back, and the .38 fell out of his pants.

228

"What the fuck?" Michael was astounded. "You gonna fuckin' shoot me?!"

He brought his heel down hard across Jason's face, sending him tumbling.

"You gonna shoot me, huh?!" Michael yelled, aiming his gun at Jason.

Chapter 9

The Fall

Michael was about to fire when suddenly, something hit him with the force of a truck and knocked him clear off his feet. He hit the ground hard, his gun tumbling into the darkness.

Dickey stood over him like a predator lording over its kill.

"This is done," Dickey told him sternly. "No more."

Michael was stunned by the blow, but he managed to get up and dust himself off. Dickey helped Jason to his feet, and retrieved his .38.

"Let's go," he said to Jason.

The two men were walking away when Michael began to taunt them. Dickey turned and headed back, brushing Jason's hand off his shoulder.

"Yo! You're lucky your boy came and bailed you out, bitch!" Michael said, looking for his 9mm in the grass. He found it and tucked it into the back of his pants. "Next time won't be so lucky. Just me and you next time, homes," he said to Jason.

"This ends here. It's done. There ain't going to be a next time," Dickey warned Michael.

"Nah, fuck that!" Michael yelled back. "You don't get to decide. Me and your boy got business, and now you and me got business too. Someday soon I will be seeing you both, and then we'll see who's the big dog, mother fuckers!"

Dickey shook his head and slowly started towards Michael.

"I understand. Your pride is wounded. I am telling you now, it is in your best interest to let that go. Walk away and don't ever bother with any of this or my friend again."

"Shit," Michael laughed. "Wait, I know you. Aren't you George's brother?"

Dickey just glared.

"You are. Man, George is ice cold, man. Me and him robbed your supplier, shithead!" he yelled at Jason. "And Georgie boy, he fucking iced a kid," Michael said with a laugh. "Shot him dead."

"Shut your fucking face," Dickey snapped.

"Nah, fuck you. I'm gonna kill you, your brother, your friend and anyone else who happens to be in the way. I swear to God, you better be ready. Because I will come at you when you least expect it and I will put a bullet in your goddamn head. Then I will go down to the hospital, and I will wait for Maegan to wake up so I can take her home and make her suck heroin off my cock! Because I am Michael-fucking-Trivoty and I will do whatever the fuck I want and ain't you or any other mother fucker is going to stop me!"

Michael was close enough that Dickey could feel spit flying in his face as he shouted. Suddenly, there was a flash and a loud bang, and everything seemed to stand still.

Jason blinked twice in disbelief.

"No!!" Jason yelled, running to Dickey. "What did you do?"

"Exactly what you wanted to," Dickey said.

Trivoty lied on his back, blood spilling out onto the grass around him, a .44 caliber-sized hole in the center of his chest. He choked on blood and tried desperately to find his breath. Without flinching, Dickey raised his revolver and fired another round into his skull. There was no more movement, no more struggle.

Michael Trivoty was dead.

"Goddammit! Dickey!" Jason pled. "What the fuck do we do?!"

Dickey stood over Trivoty's body, contemplating what he'd just done. He had never intended on shooting the man, but when that scum threatened Jason and his girls, his rage broke loose in the briefest flash of fatal violence. He hadn't stopped to consider his actions or their consequences. He had just let go. *The world would be better off without Michael Trivoty.*

Now that the adrenaline and the alcohol were wearing off, the reality started to settle in. Dickey felt his hands start to tremble.

"We have to ditch his body!" Jason said, kneeling down to grab Trivoty.

"Stop!" Dickey snapped, grabbing Jason and pulling him back.

"We can't just leave him here…"

"Yes, we can, and that's just what we're going to do," Dickey said. "Let's get out of here."

"Dickey, we can't… Someone is going to find him!"

"They will either way. The gun I shot him with him isn't registered. We go moving that body; we're just going to get his blood and DNA all over us," he explained. "Leave him and everything the way it is. Let's get out of here. Meet me at my place."

"Alright," Jason said, noticeably shaken.

"Jason," Dickey said, placing his hand on Jason's shoulder. "We gotta go, brother."

Jason stared at Michael's face. It was frozen in horror.

"We gotta go, man! C'mon!" Dickey repeated.

Jason nodded, and the two walked quickly to the vehicles.

"You good to drive?" Dickey asked.

"Yeah," Jason replied sadly.

Dickey gave him a sympathetic look and nodded before pulling away in his truck. Jason followed moments later.

"I DON'T THINK WE'RE GOING TO FIND THIS PLACE," Dwight said hesitantly.

"Guy at the gas station said it was down a dirt road at the end of Hayes Road. Where the hell is it? This is the end of Hayes Road," Dwight exclaimed.

The two had been driving around for some time. After the GPS failed, Wyatt had taken to asking gas stations and restaurants in the local area if they had heard of a street called New Point Way—Randy Sandusfield's registered address. Finally, after several stops, Wyatt found a gas station that had delivered fuel to two houses on that road.

"It's hard to find," the station attendant had told them.

After repeated passes up and down Hayes Road, they were ready to give up.

"Wait," Dwight said. "What about the other end of Hayes Road?" he asked.

Wyatt turned the car around; the headlights pointed at the intersection where the sign for Hayes Road stood.

"It's not a very long road," Wyatt noted. "That's the end right there."

"What if there's another part?" Dwight asked.

Old Connecticut and Massachusetts roads were famous for being crooked, misaligned, and even broken into pieces.

Wyatt dug a map out of his glove box and opened it up. A moment later he tapped his finger on it and laughed, "There is another piece of it. Right around the corner. Good work!"

Soon they had found the dirt road and were making their way over rocky and muddy, washed-out terrain.

"There's houses down here?" Wyatt asked in disbelief.

"I think I see a light down there," Dwight pointed out.

"We've got no idea what we're driving into. Stay alert," Wyatt said, pulling out his sidearm and laying it in his lap.

Dwight pulled his .45 and tucked it under his leg.

Several abandoned, half-built houses littered the road.

"Think they get 4G out here?" Wyatt joked.

A single light shone from the end of the road—Randy's porch light. Wyatt parked the car in front of the house. He and Dwight both emerged from the car with guns drawn and flashlights in hand. Their beams of light scanned the yard and porch.

"Hold it right there!" a voice called down from the porch.

Wyatt and Dwight swung the lights and guns toward the voice. An officer held his hand up to shield his eyes.

"Easy, fellas," he said. "Put down the weapons."

"Connecticut State Police," Dwight replied.

"Deputy Biggs, Sheffield sheriff's office. I told your boys already, we'll let you know if he comes back. You coming out here, you could blow my position."

"Well," Dwight said, slighting shrugging his shoulders to Wyatt. "Captain told me to come make sure you guys still had the place covered. Guess he thought you guys might try to take off early."

"Leahy? Tell him to kiss my ass," the deputy said. "Fucking figures. Yeah, I'm still here. Now get the fuck out of here. If he comes back, he'll see you from a mile away."

Wyatt and Dwight left, curious about what they had learned.

"So, somebody wants Sandusfield, and your boss is helping. Funny thing, seeing how we're in Massachusetts right now."

"It's a gray area near the border. I can see us lending a hand. Maybe it's federal."

"Then why haven't you heard of it?" Wyatt asked, steering around holes in the road.

"I'm a resident trooper for Colebrook. It doesn't concern me," Dwight replied. He knew what Wyatt was insinuating, but he wasn't sold. "Not everyone is in on this conspiracy you're building."

"Yeah, right," Wyatt replied. "Somehow this all ties in with our heroin pipeline and those missing cops. Deputy Dipshit back there is probably on the take. And your boss is neck deep in it."

Dwight sighed. He didn't want to believe what Wyatt was saying. His head hurt, and the ringing was back, faintly echoing in the back of his skull.

"I need to rest," Dwight said after a pause.

GARY AUGUSTINE EMBRACED ANDREW and pounded fists with Eddie when he came through the door.

"It's good to be home!" Gary said. "I made some great deals that will make us all a lot of money," he told Andrew.

"My man!" Andrew cheered. "That's what I like to hear."

"Starting next week, we will be getting stronger, cheaper dope, and we are also going to start moving crystal," Gary informed the crew.

"Crystal? Crank?" Andrew asked. "There's no market for that here."

"There will be," Gary replied. "That's where we come in. It's a white trash drug, and there is plenty of white trash around."

"That's true," Eddie laughed. "This place is a shit hole."

"Amen," Gary retorted. "May it never change."

He helped himself to a beer from the fridge and said hello to the rest of the crew: Elton and Little Roy, both of whom Andrew knew from prison, Caesar, and Eddie's cousin from Atlanta, Jagger.

"The stock market might be doing great, but places like this are still dead," Gary laughed. "Just drive downtown and look at it. The economy is never coming back here. That means broken dreams and desperate people."

"Job security," Andrew added with a laugh.

"Where's little Michael at?" Gary asked.

"He had some business to attend to," said Andrew. "He'll be back soon."

"Good. I got something for him. A reward for this score he helped me pull."

"You keep saying," Andrew said, proud of his little brother. "Tell me what went down."

"Georgie put us onto something. Weed farm up in Sheffield. Pay-out was big," Gary told him. "Got some cash and some chronic for the little man. You would've been proud," he added. "He took charge. Did what had to be done."

"Word?"

"Oh, yeah. He's a real G now. Ice cold."

Andrew nodded approvingly.

WYATT PULLED THE CAR UP TO DWIGHT'S HOUSE and sighed. After a long day trying to make sense of what they were involved in, things seemed even more unclear.

"We still don't know what we're into," Wyatt admitted.

"No, but I have a feeling we're in deeper by the minute," Dwight retorted.

"I've got to bring my partner in on this," Wyatt said. "I've kept him out of this because he's a by-the-book type, but we need help figuring out exactly what is going on here."

"Or we could just back off," Dwight suggested. "This is too big for us. We have no idea what is going on or who's involved."

"No, we just got a bunch of bodies, a pipeline pumping poison onto our streets, murderers being protected by the feds, and dirty cops. We're the only ones who are going to do something about it because we're the ones stuck mopping up the shit."

Wyatt's cell phone rang.

"Mayhew," he answered, motioning for Dwight to wait. "Okay. Any ID on the vic? No, shit. Yeah, I'll be there as soon as I can."

Wyatt hung up the phone and dropped it into his shirt pocket.

"What's happened now?" asked Dwight.

"We got a body in the woods by Rock Creek Dam. Only about five-hundred feet from the Torrington line, so they're calling us in to help," Wyatt explained.

"Okay, well, good luck with that," said Dwight, opening the passenger door to leave.

"Victim is Michael Trivoty. Shot execution style."

Dwight shut the door.

"Let's go," he said.

"I've got a better idea," Wyatt replied, dropping the car into drive and pulling a U-turn.

ANDREW TRIVOTY HAD A NICE BUZZ GOING and was enjoying a winning streak at poker when a loud knock interrupted his hand.

"Goddammit!" he exclaimed, throwing his cards down on the table.

Dexter barked and snarled toward the door from the kitchen.

"Caesar, hold Dexter," Andrew commanded.

He found his way to the door with a few extra steps than needed. When he opened the door, the two cops he recognized from the other day were there to greet him.

"Detectives," Andrew said. "Whatever it is you want, I suggest you get a warrant or suck my dick!"

"We're just here to give you some news, homie," Wyatt retorted. "See, we just found your brother shot to death by the Rock Creek Dam."

Andrew's face dropped.

"Sorry if this doesn't come across as sympathetic, but we got a pile of bodies adding up, and me and my partner here think it all ties back to you," Wyatt said.

Andrew let out a blood-curdling yell and punched his fist through the nearest wall.

Gary, Eddie, and the others came to the door to see what was happening.

"They got Michael, yo!" Andrew cried.

The crew grumbled and gasped. Gary became instantly concerned.

"How do you guys know George Calloway?"

Gary grew even more concerned.

"He comes around sometimes, why?" Andrew sniffled.

"He was found yesterday, been dead a few days at least. Tied to a tree and executed. We know George was coming here to score. He was seen here before he was killed," Wyatt said, carefully studying each person's reaction.

238

"I don't know shit, and I ain't got shit to say," Andrew snapped, regaining composure.

"What about Randy Sandusfield?" Wyatt asked.

"Never heard of him," Andrew answered.

"Then I suppose you don't know why he was following George when he came here to score?" Dwight asked.

"Like I said," Andrew answered sternly.

"You seem awfully nervous over there," Wyatt called out. "You, what's your name?"

"I wouldn't worry about that," Gary replied. "I guess I don't like pigs."

"You must be Augustine," Wyatt remarked. "Whitest, greasiest guy in the room," he said to Dwight.

"You say mean things like that, it's going to hurt my feelings," Gary said sarcastically.

"Well, we just thought we would make a house call and see if you guys had anything to confess to… Gang activity… Drug sales… Racketeering… Murder… Whatever else you felt like throwing in," Wyatt quipped.

"I'd watch out, homes," Andrew told him. "We got more friends than you think. You think you got power? Maybe, I call some of my friends— show you what real power is."

"Try it," Wyatt said blankly, his steely blue eyes glaring widely at Andrew.

Andrew shut the door and watched from the window as the officers left.

"Find me Jason Terry," Andrew ordered. "That's who Michael was meeting."

"This shit wasn't that little bitch," Gary interjected. "Randy Sandusfield, the man following George—that's the guy we robbed. Michael, Georgie, and me. Your brother capped the man's son, Andrew."

"So, he's trying to settle the score," Andrew said. "The guy you robbed, George put you onto him? He's Terry's supplier! They probably lured Michael out there and killed him together!"

"That Terry kid ain't shit," Gary argued. "He might have played a part, but it's Sandusfield we should all be worried about."

Augustine grabbed his smokes and phone from the table and headed for the door.

"I'm getting the fuck out of here, man," he said. "That guy is going to be gunning for me next. I'm not just going to sit around playing cards, waiting for it to happen."

"Where you going? It's safer here!" Andrew yelled.

"The very place he probably tracked George and Michael from? I'll be in Riverton, hunkering down. I'll get in touch with some of my friends and see what I can learn about what the police know."

"I'm going to find Terry, torture him, find out what he knows, then beat him to death with my bare hands," Andrew declared.

"Just stay put. Don't be an idiot," Gary scolded. "Cops are going to be watching you and this place closely. Heat is on right now. Don't make any moves until our friends can settle things down."

DICKEY SPLASHED COLD WATER on his face then took a good, hard look at himself in the bathroom mirror. It wasn't what he had just done that bothered him. Instead, it was the fact that he had acted so quickly, without thought. Just like when he'd kill that Marine in Iraq.

Just another fucked up thing to bury in the graveyard that was his mind.

"Alright, I washed all my clothes," Jason told him. "You alright?"

"Yeah, I'm fine," Dickey said. "You, on the other hand, look like you got your ass kicked. That's not good."

The two had been up all night, and as the sun began to rise, their buzzes became hangovers.

"I got my ass kicked by Trivoty and the booze," Jason winced, reaching past Dickey to grab the aspirin from the medicine cabinet.

A knock on the door brought weary looks from both men.

"We busted already?" Jason asked.

"Stay in the bathroom," Dickey advised. "Don't come out till I tell you."

Dickey recognized the local resident trooper who was stood at his front door with an intimidating looking bald man. He opened the door with a smile.

"Richard Calloway, Jr.?" Dwight asked. "I'm Trooper Evans with the Connecticut State Police, and this is Detective Mayhew. We have a couple of questions related to your brother's case."

"Alright, come on in. I already gave my statement to the Winsted PD."

"We know, this will only take a minute," Dwight replied.

Jason heard them enter the house from the bathroom off the hall and cursed under his breath.

"First, have you seen or talked to Jason Terry at all this evening?" Dwight asked.

Dickey seemed on edge.

"Well, he was here having some beers last night. Why?"

"Do you know a Michael Trivoty?" Wyatt asked.

"No, I can't say that I do," Dickey said. "Why? What is this about and what does it have to with George?"

Jason pressed closely to the bathroom door, straining to hear.

"Michael was an associate of your brother's. Now they're both dead. Both executed. We have reason to believe a man named Randy Sandusfield is involved," Wyatt informed him.

"And who is he?"

"A local weed grower from what we've been able to figure out," Wyatt replied.

"Seems Jason is connected to Sandusfield and with what happened to Maegan, has plenty of reason to hate Trivoty," Dwight said. "Michael was Maegan's ex. She was at his house when she overdosed."

"You think *he's* connected to all this? *Jason?!*" Dickey laughed. "That's absurd."

"I think he knows enough to connect the dots," said Dwight. "Or maybe you do."

"George was in some trouble recently," Dickey explained.

"What kind of trouble?" Wyatt asked.

"He didn't say. A guy came here looking for him. Gary Augustine. He threatened me and my girls. Told me he would burn down the house with us in it," Dickey said, shaking his head.

"Jesus," Dwight replied.

"So, the other day, George shows up, really upset. Says he took care of whatever the problem was. I don't know anything else, but seems to me he got into some shit. Maybe this Trivoty kid got into the same shit," Dickey suggested.

"That's what we're thinking," Dwight concurred. "But we still need to talk to Jason. You haven't seen him? His car is here," he noted.

"Like I said," Dickey replied. "We were drinking, so he got a ride."

"You know from who?" Wyatt asked.

"No, he didn't say," Dickey replied.

"When you talk to Jason, tell him we need him to come in and answer some questions immediately," Wyatt said.

"Make sure he calls me," Dwight said, handing Dickey his card. "Not the station."

"Okay, I will," Dickey nodded. "Now, if there's nothing else, I have to get my girls up soon."

"Thanks for your time," Dwight said. "We'll show ourselves out."

Once they had left and driven away, Dickey retrieved Jason from the bathroom.

"Holy shit!" Jason exclaimed. "We are so fucked."

"This might work out, actually," Dickey said. "They might put Michael's murder on whoever killed George."

"They're going to find me—I look like this. They're going to end up thinking I killed both these guys!" Jason moaned.

"What the hell does Randy have to do…" Dickey stopped himself mid-sentence as a lightbulb went off in his head. "Shit…"

"George and Trivoty went after Randy to settle his debt to Augustine!" Jason exclaimed.

"Exactly, and that means Randy killed George."

"Fuck!" Jason yelled. "I brought George to Randy's."

"So, he could be looking for you as well," Dickey realized.

"Michael also knew I was coming," Jason sighed. "I forgot until now. Travis must have given me up."

"That means Michael's crew likely knows he was going to confront you."

"So, any guesses who's going to get me first?" Jason asked. "The cops? Randy? Trivoty's thugs?"

"This is getting out of hand," Dickey sighed. "Maybe we need to just go confess," he said solemnly.

"What?!"

"Just tell them everything. Get you protection and help them get Augustine. He's the one who set all this in motion."

"No, Dickey," Jason shook his head firmly. "You were only there because of me, saving my ass. Your life is not going to end over this. I won't let you be ripped away from your girls. Not after everything they've been through."

"Then what do we do?" Dickey asked.

"I don't know."

"I need some sleep. Maybe then this will make sense," Dickey groaned. "But I have to wake the girls up."

"They can sleep a little longer," Jason urged. "We both need to get some rest. Mind if I crash on the couch?"

"Maybe you're right," Dickey conceded. "Yeah, go for it, man. I'm going to get a few hours and then we're going to figure this out," he said on his way up the stairs.

"Sure will, brother," Jason said.

Once Dickey was gone, Jason put his head in his hands and cried.

"SIR, I AM BEGGING YOU," Dwight pleaded. "These animals are just going to put more bodies in the morgue. Call the brass, tell them it's time to move. Get the feds onboard, whatever has to happen."

Leahy looked up over the frames of his glasses with indignation.

"Evans, I thought you were taking a vacation to fucking die or something," he snapped. "Now you're in here telling me you won't leave alone the matter I specifically told you to leave alone. It's out of our hands!"

"I was there yesterday, following up on the shooting death of the little brother. Jennifer Martinez's murder suspect, Edward Stanton, is there. The place is loaded with illegal weapons and heroin. Let's take it down, and the RICO investigation can use them to take down higher targets."

"They will move when they are ready!" Leahy barked. "You don't get to decide that."

"We just have to clean up the fucking mess," Dwight challenged.

"Leave it be, or you won't have a job to come back to if you survive your surgery," Leahy told him. "Now get out of here, I have things to do."

Dwight left the barracks, his head ringing, and his temper red hot. Wyatt was right; something was rotten at the Canaan State Police. He needed to go home and get some rest. Even Wyatt had finally retreated to do as much, but Dwight felt like he was running out of time.

Defeated and exhausted he finally returned home. Danny was watching TV on the couch with Max. Dwight barely acknowledged them on the way up to his room. He needed a few solid hours of sleep.

IT WAS AFTERNOON WHEN WYATT finally made it into the office. Once there, he got word the captain was looking for him. Before he went to find out why, he tracked down Garcia in the locker room.

"Look who it is," Garcia scoffed. "My absentee partner."

"I've been working a few things," said Wyatt. "Not exactly coloring in the lines. I didn't want to put you in a position…"

"So, instead you put me in this one," Garcia shot back. "Save it, man. Whatever you're into, I can't help you."

"I've got my eyes on the pipeline. Crooked cops and who knows who else involved. But I can't trust anyone. Only you."

"Look, man," Garcia said, his eyes becoming more sympathetic, "Just walk away from all this. There's no way it ends well."

Wyatt couldn't believe what he was hearing.

"It's like that?"

"I have a family to think about,' Garcia said, hurrying to change his clothes and leave. "That's what it's like."

"Alright, I got it," Wyatt said.

"Good," Garcia replied. "Captain's looking for you. Nice working with you."

Garcia's words left Wyatt a bit confused until he saw the captain.

"Random hours, snooping around outside your jurisdiction, and continuing to persist on investigations that are interfering with the feds," the captain listed his transgressions.

"Somebody has to do something! Is it not my job anymore to go after bad guys?" Wyatt protested.

"For the next few months, your job is going to be writing traffic tickets. I'm busting you down to patrol."

"You have got to be fucking kidding me!" Wyatt charged. "This is bullshit."

"Keep it up. I will have you working as a meter maid until you quit."

Wyatt left the station in a rage and drove straight to the liquor store. *What was the point?* He felt like a joke for even thinking he could make a difference.

Wyatt purchased a fifth of whiskey and headed home. Wasting no time, he tore off the cap and began to guzzle the booze as he drove.

THE DESK OFFICER AT THE CANAAN STATE Police barracks looked up wryly from his computer screen and sighed.

"Can I help you?" he asked.

He was an older man, nearing retirement age, and wore a permanent expression that said he was done with everybody's shit.

"My name is Jason Terry, and I am here to confess to a murder," Jason told the officer.

The officer looked the lanky, roughed-up man up and down and then took off his glasses. He was unfazed by Terry's admission, but displeased about the paperwork it would require.

"Of course you do," he replied begrudgingly. "McAuliffe!" he yelled into the back of the station. "You got a live one."

Detective McAuliffe approached the desk. "What's up?" he asked.

"This guy claims he killed someone," the desk officer replied, motioning to Jason.

"Michael Trivoty. I killed Michael Trivoty," Jason announced.

Everyone in the station turned to look at him.

"Alright, c'mon around back," McAuliffe instructed.

Jason obliged. McAuliffe took him into custody.

"HELLO?" DWIGHT GROANED into his cell phone, struggling to wake himself.

"Trooper Evans? This is Detective Carlyle, up at the barracks."

"Yeah, what's up?"

"My partner and I are working the Trivoty murder and providing support on the Calloway and Martinez murders."

"I know." Dwight's head hurt. He didn't have time for games.

"Listen," Carlyle began. "Jason Terry, your niece's boyfriend, is down here copping to murdering Michael Trivoty. I think we might be able to tie him to the others, too."

"That's impossible," Dwight muttered, still groggy.

"We had him as a person of interest, already," Carlyle went on. "He's connected to every one of our victims."

"Doesn't make sense," Dwight insisted.

"You have inside information on this case and his relationship with your niece. We're going to need you to come down and help us fill in the blanks," Carlyle told him.

Dwight hung up his phone, sat up, and rubbed his eyes. He had slept all day. Downstairs, he could he hear Danny watching television.

With considerable effort, he managed to shower, dress, and make coffee before he and Max headed out for the barracks.

Something didn't make sense. He knew Jason had a motive to go after Trivoty; he had seen the pain in his eyes as they watched Maegan breathing through tubes. Even still, Dwight didn't believe Jason had hurt anyone. Jason was a burnout; a non-aggressive, laidback, pushover. He didn't seem like someone who would even own a gun, let alone shoot someone.

No, it wasn't Jason whose brother had been killed as blowback for something involving Trivoty. It wasn't Jason who owned firearms and was trained to kill with them. It was Dickey Calloway.

DWIGHT KNOCKED ON THE INTERROGATION room door and waited.

Moments later, Carlyle and McAuliffe walked out and exchanged greetings. Dwight requested he be allowed to speak to the suspect for a moment before conferencing with the detectives. They agreed and allowed him to briefly review their case files before entering the box with Jason.

After a few minutes in the room with Jason, Dwight emerged shaking his head.

"He didn't do it," Dwight concluded.

"What the hell do you mean? He just fucking confessed!" McAuliffe protested, throwing his arms in the air.

"What did he say?" Carlyle asked.

"He claims he shot Trivoty with a .38," Dwight explained, opening the case file on McAuliffe's desk and pointing at it. "But Trivoty was shot with a .44."

"How could he get that wrong?" Carlyle asked McAuliffe.

"So, he doesn't know guns. Big deal," McAuliffe rebutted.

"Then he would say he didn't know. He didn't," Dwight said. "I like the Calloway brother."

"Dickey? We were going to go talk with him today, then Terry walked in," said Carlyle.

"I think Terry's covering for the him," Dwight said. "What about Randy Sandusfield?" he asked, heading for the door.

"Who?" McAuliffe asked.

"Seriously?" Dwight shot back. "You guys don't have him on your radar?"

"Who is he?" asked Carlyle.

Dwight had heard all he needed to.

"Where are you going? We still need your help!" McAuliffe called after him.

"I'm going to talk to Dickey Calloway," he answered without looking back.

GARY AUGUSTINE DROVE ALONG the Colebrook Dam heading to his apartment in Riverton, his new black Mustang shining in the sun.

When his phone rang, his car asked if he wanted to answer. He tapped a button on his steering wheel and the call came over his speakers.

"Captain Leahy, how are you?" Gary said, relieved.

"Trying to clean up the mess you caused."

"I had no idea that weed farm was connected to you," Gary said nervously.

"That's why you should have fucking checked with me," Leahy replied.

"Now this Sandusfield is out to kill us? Is that what's happening?"

"Yes, but that may not have been what happened to the Trivoty punk," Leahy informed him. "Kid named Jason Terry is down here. He's confessing to killing Trivoty—some kind of losers' love triangle gone wrong."

"I honestly didn't think he had it in him," Gary said with a slight laugh.

"Yeah, well, he's a problem. Knows too much about what is going on at the Trivoty house. And he's blabbing his mouth a mile a minute. He needs to be dealt with."

"Okay, how?"

"We'll move him to county lock-up in the morning. You can get to him there."

"Yeah, that won't be a problem," said Gary.

He would call Andrew and arrange for the Toros to shiv the bastard as soon as he arrived at county lockup. Jason Terry would be dead by noon tomorrow.

"And you'll take care of Sandusfield?" Gary asked.

"He'll be dead as soon as he pops his head up."

"I DIDN'T DO ANYTHING, MAN!" Travis cried. "I told Michael what he was doing! I warned him!!"

Andrew struck the boy in the gut as hard as he could, Eddie and Caesar holding him by each arm.

"You set up the meeting, homes!" Andrew fumed. "Now my little brother is dead. People have to pay. Don't you think someone should pay!?"

"Then make Jason pay! Not me!!" Travis pleaded.

"So, it was that Terry bitch who killed Michael?" Andrew asked, grabbing Travis by his hair and pulling.

"It had to be! He wanted to set him up, right?"

Andrew's phone rang from inside his jeans' pocket. He tried to answer, but he had shoddy service. They had lured Travis with the promise of free dope and then drove him to a dead end street near Winchester Lake.

"It's Augustine," Andrew told his boys. He walked down the road until he had a signal and answered.

"It was Terry!" Gary yelled through the choppy connection.

Andrew came back, butterfly knife in hand.

"You were right," he said to Travis. "It was that bitch ass, Jason Terry."

"Oh, thank God, you can let me go," Travis exclaimed. "I can go now. I won't say a word. And you can keep the heroin."

Andrew laughed, prompting Eddie and Caesar to laugh as well. Travis awkwardly joined in.

"I don't think so," Andrew said.

"What do you mean?" Travis said, panic taking hold of his voice.

Andrew came closer, and Travis tried to squirm away, but Caesar and Eddie held him tightly.

"No, no, please!" Travis pleaded as Andrew pulled the blade and stepped toward him.

His pleading was to no avail. Andrew plunged the blade forward and into Travis's abdomen. Once, twice, and then a third time with anger.

Caesar and Eddie let Travis fall to the ground. Travis grabbed his abdomen and writhed in pain, tears streaming from his eyes.

"Leave him," Andrew ordered. "We have to go home and make sure this Terry kid is welcomed to county properly tomorrow."

The three climbed into Eddie's car and drove away without looking back, leaving Travis bleeding out in the middle of the road.

Chapter Ten
Inferno

"…and the princess lived happily ever after," Dickey read to his girls, though they had both already fallen asleep.

He spent a few moments rubbing their backs and kissing them each softly on the head. His eyes began to tear up as he contemplated what their future would now be.

"I'm sorry," he whispered. "I think I've let you girls down. I didn't want to, but I did…"

The sun was still setting when he came downstairs. He reread Jason's letter and considered his options. None of them were particularly good.

He lit a joint, grabbed a bottle of vodka from under the sink, and went out to sit on his front porch for what could be his last time.

Dwight was already there, sitting comfortably in one of Dickey's chairs. He looked as if he had been there for some time.

"Comfortable?" Dickey asked, continuing to smoke his joint.

"I saw you going up with the girls when I came up," Dwight answered. "Figured I would let you put them to sleep. And I've just been sitting here thinking about all this bloodshed and death and all the pain that this town has suffered. I guess I don't know what to think anymore."

"It's ugly. Hard to face," Dickey replied, taking a seat beside Dwight and offering him the bottle. "Officer Evans, right?"

"Trooper," Dwight corrected him.

"You're Maegan's uncle. Jason told me. I'm sorry about what happened to her."

Dwight hesitated for a moment, then grabbed the bottle, held it to his lips, and took a large swig.

"So, you're a veteran, right?" Dwight asked.

"Yeah," Dickey replied, unsure of Dwight's motives. He knew he shouldn't be smoking weed in front of a cop, but somehow he didn't care.

"The girls' mother. She's gone?"

"Cancer," Dickey nodded.

"I'm awfully sorry about that," Dwight sighed. He had read the file, and he believed Dickey to be a good man. "Seems like the worst shit always happens to the best of us," he continued.

Dickey saw Dwight eyeballing the joint and offered it to him. Dwight hesitated and then took it.

"Oh, what the hell, I have a brain tumor," he explained. "I'm probably going to be dead in three days."

"Damn, I am sorry to hear that," Dickey said.

"We tell ourselves we'll always have more time..." Dwight muttered, staring off at the pine trees in Dickey's front yard.

Suddenly, Courage was scratching against the glass of the front door and yelping to come out.

"That's a cute puppy," Dwight remarked, attempting to hit the joint.

The smoke hurt his lungs and made him cough loudly. Dickey laughed as he let Courage out to pee.

"Thanks," said Dickey. "He's supposed to help me relax."

"Dogs are great," Dwight said, rising from his seat. "He ever meet another dog?"

"I don't know," Dickey answered. "Maybe in the kennel, I assume."

Max and Courage were instantly friends. For Dwight, it was good to see Max bouncing around and playing like a puppy again. The two dogs rolled around and chased each other about the front yard, while Dwight and Dickey talked for over an hour.

"That's when I couldn't do it anymore. I had to be home with my family," Dickey finished telling Dwight.

"Well, thank you for your service," Dwight said with a nod.

"Oh, please, don't give me that shit," Dickey laughed.

"I mean it. I appreciate it. I never stood up like that. I never put it on the line for something greater than me," Dwight admitted.

"You're a cop," Dickey replied. "You do serve a greater purpose."

"I'm a resident trooper who spent his whole life avoiding fights and avoiding the things that scared me."

"A lot of people do," Dickey replied.

Dwight nodded and called Max to his side.

"How does it feel to take a life?"

"Everyone wants to ask me that lately," said Dickey, tossing a tennis ball lightly toward Courage. "Honestly, the truth is it can't be explained. It doesn't feel good."

"I honestly don't know if I could," Dwight admitted. He stared up at the tall pines and honestly wondered if he could take a life. He had always thought he could, hypothetically speaking. Now, the bloodshed and violence he was witnessing had him second-guessing himself.

"Really?" Dickey asked candidly. "I think you'd be surprised what you're capable of."

"What makes you say that?"

"Over there, my life depended on my ability to take quick measure of a man. I'd ask myself, 'would that man pull a trigger?' More often than not, the answer was yes."

"Gotta admit, there is something I like about guys like you," Dwight continued. "You stand up to the animals in the world. You confront them head on. Even when there's consequences."

People like to ignore things," Dickey said. "That creates problems. They don't think these things will touch their lives. Guys like me and you," he said, nodding to Dwight's uniform. "We know you can't ignore what's happening in the world. If you ignore it—if you refuse to face it, it'll take everything from you. Sooner or later. Yeah, sometimes there's consequences, but they're easy to pay when you consider the cost of doing nothing."

"Perhaps, but you have to face those consequences. Someone else can't pay them for you."

Dickey laughed and nodded.

"I would never let Jason do that," Dickey replied. "I just wanted one more night at home with my daughters. Tomorrow I will turn myself in after I drop them off at their grandparents'."

Dwight nodded.

"I'm sorry," he said. "For what it's worth, I don't think you're a bad guy."

"Thanks," Dickey replied.

"Jason tell you he was going to do this?"

"He wrote a letter," Dickey said. "I'll get it for you."

Soon after, Dwight and Max left Dickey's, Jason's letter on the front seat.

It read:

Dear Dickey,

I can't let those girls pay for something I got you sucked into. I've gone to the police station to make it right. I'm going to tell them I stole your gun because I did. The rest is just a matter of twisting the truth.

You have always been a brother to me. I got your back on this one. I'll see you when I can. Take care of the girls, and please tell them I love them very much.

Your brother,

Jay

Dwight called Carlyle to give him an update.

"Listen, I was right. Dickey Calloway is coming in first thing in the morning to confess. Terry was trying to cover for him."

"Are you shitting me?" Carlyle asked.

"I have a letter here from Terry to Calloway saying exactly that."

"Alright. Bring the letter here; we'll confirm it and cut him loose."

"No, no. These bastards are going to be looking for blood. Just keep Terry there till the morning. He'll be safe there."

"What are you going to do?" asked Carlyle.

"I'm going to do whatever I can to try and put an end to this violence. I'm going to plead with the captain to move on Andrew Trivoty and his crew tomorrow."

"Good luck," Carlyle quipped. "We've been waiting for federal approval to move on that address to grab a murder suspect we know is there. Day after day, nothing comes. Cap won't move without it."

"Why am I not surprised?" Dwight asked.

He hung up his phone and lit a cigarette. He didn't want to smell like weed when he came home to Danny.

ANDREW AND HIS CREW became concerned when Dexter alerted them to a car pulling into the yard.

"Chill, it's just Augustine," Andrew informed the others as he peered out the window.

"It is going to be a fun night, gentlemen!" Gary proclaimed upon entering the house.

"What's up?" Andrew asked.

"Just got a tip from one of our birdies. Seems the cops are turning Terry loose in the morning."

"What?"

"He didn't do it. He was covering for Georgie's brother, Dickey Calloway."

"That motherfucker…"

"Yeah, and I already warned that motherfucker what would happen if he got in my way."

Andrew and Gary exchanged devilish smiles.

DANNY WAS SMOKING on the porch when Dwight found him.

"Thought you were getting a ride to see your sister?"

"Was gonna," Danny replied. "Didn't feel like it, I guess."

Dwight grabbed Danny's pack of smokes and took one for himself.

"Listen, Danny, somethings come up," he tried to explain. "I have a brain tumor. I have to have surgery in two days to remove it."

"Shit, are you going to be okay?"

"I am, but I am going to be staying there for a bit to get better. So, I've arranged for you to go stay with grandma and grandpa down in Kentucky for a bit."

"Kentucky?! I don't want to live in fucking Hicksville, Uncle Dwight."

"Doesn't have to be permanent."

"When you get better, I can come live here?"

"Yeah," Dwight said hesitantly. "Yeah, of course."

"With Maegan?"

"That's right. We can all live together."

"Are you scared?"

Dwight sighed and contemplated his answer to that question.

"Yeah, I'm scared," he admitted. "But I guess I'd rather face that fear than run from it. You can't spend your life running from fear. Fear's a funny thing. Makes you freeze when you should move and makes you jump when you should be still."

"I'm afraid my sister is going to die."

"And that's why you didn't go see her today," Dwight nodded.

"When am I going to Kentucky?"

"Tomorrow. Your flight leaves at one-thirty. I have a car picking you up at noon."

"I won't be able to see Maegan."

"That's the thing. When we fail to act, time marches on. We miss opportunities."

"Who's going to take care of Max?" Danny asked.

"I have a friend who I think could use the company," said Dwight. He finished his smoke and pressed his fingers against the bridge of his nose.

The pain was getting worse, but the Dilaudid clouded his mind too much. He was chewing ibuprofen, naproxen, and Tylenol all day to dull the edge.

Two more days.

The doctor had pushed for sooner, but Dwight had insisted that he needed time to prepare his affairs. If there was a good chance he was going to die on that table, he was going to make damn sure things were in order. To that end, he had an appointment with his lawyer the next morning. He said goodnight to his nephew, let Max out to pee, and then went to bed.

Tomorrow was going to be a big day. He was going to prepare to die.

THE ENGINE OF DWIGHT'S CRUISER REVVED LOUDLY, its flashing red and blue lights reflecting in the tree cover, illuminating the dark road ahead. His heart raced as he punched the accelerator and negotiated the turns. His siren pierced the serenity of the country night, waking residents and lighting up homes. A whaling cry of emergency alerting all that something was once again wrong in their town.

No, no, no!

He was barely dressed, wearing sweatpants and a stained undershirt.

His speedometer crept up to 70mph on an unlit, windy country road. He could see the orange glow on the horizon and the smoke billowing over the tree line.

The call had woken him from a dead sleep; a fire reported by neighbors near the town line. Dwight had immediately recognized the address.

He sped down street after street till he arrived, the ringing in his head blurring into the sirens. He was the first responder on the scene. Neighbors looked on with concern, gathered in groups. He flipped his siren off and on to quickly move the crowd, then pulled directly over the lawn.

Flames roared from the windows of the lower floor and spread up the exterior walls. The house was quickly becoming fully engulfed.

There wasn't time to think; Dwight grabbed his flashlight and darted into the house.

Through the door, he was knocked back by the immense heat and thick black smoke. It smacked him in the face and immediately begin to constrict his lungs. He jumped back through the door and gasped for air. Tears streamed down his face as he repeatedly coughed, the ringing in his head growing louder than ever before. He shook his head, rose up, took three deep gulps of air, and crawled back into the house on his hands and knees.

Blinded by smoke, he heard the yelping of a puppy coming from the living room, muffled by the fire's roar. There he saw a dark lump on the floor and crawled to it.

It was Dickey. He had been shot several times through the back. Courage was nuzzled next to his body, trying to wake him and hide from the heat. Dwight shook Dickey. When he didn't respond, Dwight felt for a pulse. Nothing.

Dwight shook his head and grabbed Courage by the scruff of his neck. He crawled back to the front door and gently tossed Courage outside. Already a loyal friend, the dog tried to run back but was scooped up by spectators.

Dwight continued to crawl, the smoke getting lower and thicker as he made his way up the stairs to the second floor. He made his way past the first room, in which he saw a queen-sized bed.

The flames were creeping up the walls and through the floors from below. Smoke completely filled the hallway.

He crawled to the second room, pressed to the floor, took a deep breath, and stood up. He tried to open the door, but the heat had caused it to swell. Stepping back, he lunged against it with his shoulder, crashing it open. The room was less smoky, and Dwight could see Stacey and Marie huddled together in the corner crying.

The flames began to creep up through the room's exterior wall. The girls cried and held each other closely, Mr. Bear squeezed between them. Dwight knelt down and wrapped his arms around them. "I'm here to help

261

you! I'm a police officer!" he told the girls. They both nodded, relieved to see him, but still gripped in terror.

He tried to shine his flashlight toward the hallway, but the smoke was now too thick. He turned the flashlight off and discarded it. The hallway would soon be impassable.

"Where's the bathroom?!" he asked the girls.

"Across the hall!" Marie yelled.

Dwight nodded and held up one finger. "I'll be right back!"

He grabbed the bedspread off the nearest bed and bolted across the hallway through an open bathroom door. He found the tub faucet and quickly wet the bedspread then rushed back across the hall. Somewhere in the process, he burned both his legs and his right arm.

He wrapped the girls in the wet blanket and lifted them into his arms. "Hold on tight and hold your breath!" he shouted.

The girls did as they were told, and Marie took care to make sure Mr. Bear was secure. Dwight covered their heads with the blanket, took a breath, and bolted out of the bedroom and down the stairs through a wall of flames.

A stair gave way under his weight, nearly causing them to fall, but he recovered and jumped over the remaining three steps. He stumbled, but held onto those girls with all his might. Through the front door he emerged, his lungs burning, his hair singed, gasping for air. He collapsed onto the lawn, paramedics quickly taking the girls and then seeing to him.

Everyone was there now: firetrucks, ambulances, state police, and scores of locals watching the show. Dwight sat on the ground while medics tried to talk to him, watching the house burn with tears in his eyes. The cries of the girls and the yelping of the puppy echoing behind him. The ringing in his ears and the pain in his head leaving him unable to speak.

"YOUR ARM LOOKS PRETTY BAD," Danny said.

"It'll be fine," Dwight replied, sipping from his glass of whiskey. "Last thing I need to worry about today."

"Should you be drinking before surgery?"

"Danny," Dwight said sternly.

"Yeah?"

"Go get ready. Your ride will be here shortly."

The kid's right. Don't be a coward and give up now. Face the fear.

He went to the sink and poured the glass down the drain. He could still hear those girls crying. He thought of Dickey's smiling face, and of Courage and Max playing together. It was hard to admit, but Dwight had to acknowledge to himself that, although he might have been a murderer, Dickey was a good man. A man whom he liked considerably more than the monsters who killed him, burned his house, and left his little girls to die. Dwight couldn't help but feel glad that Dickey had at least killed one of them.

Danny left for the airport soon after and Dwight assured him they would see each other soon.

The ringing in his head had been persistent since the fire. He had not slept. He hadn't even changed.

These aren't men; they're monsters.

He tried to call Wyatt for the third time that day and again received no answer. It was afternoon, and he was late for his lawyer's appointment, so he grabbed his keys, called Max, and the two headed out.

Once there, he was curt and to the point.

"And you are leaving everything to your niece, Maegan Riley?" his lawyer confirmed.

"Yeah, whatever there is, give it to her," he said.

"And in the event she does not come out of her coma, your estate shall go to her brother, Daniel."

"Correct."

"And we have gone over the details of your DNR."

"If I can't breathe on my own, let me go," he nodded.

"Is there anything else?" the lawyer asked as Dwight signed his life away.

"Yeah, my dog."

"We… didn't cover the dog in the will."

"I know. If I die… for any reason. Can you check with a Detective Mayhew at the Torrington Police Department and ask if he'll take Max? If he can't, just see that he gets a good home? As a personal favor?"

The lawyer hesitated, then smiled, nodded, and shook Dwight's hand.

"I can do that. Best of luck on your surgery, Dwight."

"Thanks, Bill."

"Hey, Dwight. What do you mean, 'for any reason'? There's only one reason, right?"

Dwight raised his eyebrows and shrugged. "It's a dangerous world."

On the way home, he tried Wyatt again but received no answer. When he got home, he tried him twice more. Finally, he called the Torrington station house to ask for him.

"Please hold," a gruff voice told him.

A few minutes later, a man picked up the line.

"Who's this?" he asked.

"State Trooper Dwight Evans."

"Officer Mayhew is no longer with us. That's all I can say at this time."

"What do you mean? He was fired?"

There was silence on the other end.

"What happened?" Dwight asked.

"Officer Mayhew took his own life last night."

The voice sounded heavy with grief.

Dwight hung up the phone and held his hand over his mouth in shock. Had Wyatt been driven to such a place of desperation, or had someone gotten to him?

It doesn't matter now.

He opened his phone and dialed the number he had lifted off Michael Trivoty's phone.

"Who dis?" Andrew Trivoty asked.

"This is Maegan's uncle. The cop."

"Yeah, so what?"

"I'm going to speak slowly, so you understand everything I say because it's very important. You, your crew, and Augustine have until 8 o'clock to turn yourselves into law enforcement."

Andrew laughed heartily on the other end of the line.

"Hold on, dog. Lemme put you on a speaker," he cackled. "Okay, say that again, homie."

"You have until 8 PM to turn yourselves in and confess to your crimes."

"Or what?" Andrew scoffed.

"Or I am coming down there tonight."

"You gonna arrest us all?" Andrew asked snidely.

"I am not going to arrest you."

"Oh, it's like that?" Andrew asked, still laughing.

"Yeah, it's like that."

"You want to come down here and shoot it out, Wild West style, old man?"

"8 PM."

"We'll be waiting."

Dwight hung up the phone and looked at Max. "Don't look at me like that," he said to his partner. "I know."

AUGUSTINE GRABBED HIS KEYS and stuffed his bag of weed into his pants pocket.

"Nope," he told Andrew and his crew. "I don't give a fuck. This guy is clearly off the fucking rails. You guys want to have a shootout with a fucking state cop. No way. I am fucking out of here."

"Now you're scared?" Andrew asked.

"There are limits to what I can protect us on," Gary said. "We are quickly moving way past those limits. We all need to get the fuck out of here! Get Eddie out of town. The rest of you guys should come with me to Long Island. We'll get set up in some small town down there."

"I'm not running from some bitch lawman who's calling me out," Andrew said, slamming his fist on his kitchen table.

"That's right!" Caesar shouted, racking a round into his .45.

"He's probably not even coming," Eddie said, shaking his head. "He's just trying to scare us. He's a fucking cop. He can't just come down here and start shooting."

"And if he does," Andrew said. "We are going to feed his body to Dexter."

"You guys are fucking idiots," Gary said, shaking his head. "Just get the fuck out of here. I'm leaving now. I'm stopping at my place and grabbing some shit, then I am getting the fuck out of this godforsaken state. Get ready and come with me."

"We will call you once this bitch is dog chow," Andrew said.

"Do what you have to do. Just don't make a fucking scene about it."

Gary was out the door and in his Mustang heading home just moments later.

MOSSBERG 12-GUAGE WITH A PISTOL GRIP. Remington lever action Carbine. Police-issued, Remington 1911 pistol. Taurus 357 magnum revolver. 8" stainless steel hunting knife. One box of shotgun shells; standard buckshot. Box of Remington .35. Box of Remington .45 ACP. Six rounds of 357.

Dwight spread all the items out on his bed and held his gaze on them as he dressed. He thought about each gun, how it fired, how it loaded, determining which order was best to use them.

He fastened his bulletproof vest and looked at himself in the mirror. The vest had a badge embedded into it. He took the hunting knife and pried it out, set it down on his dresser, and left it there as he began to load his weapons.

He slung the rifle over his back. The .45 was holstered on his hip, the revolver tucked under his vest, and the hunting knife fastened to his ankle. The ammo was tucked into the pockets of his vest. He carried the shotgun.

He came downstairs and looked at Max.

"I'm not going to force you, but I'm going to ask you to come with me boy."

Max barked and sat up quickly.

"I got this for you a while back, just in case," Dwight told his partner as he dug through his car's trunk. He emerged with a bulletproof doggie vest. Max sat dutifully as Dwight secured it around his torso and legs.

"That's a good boy," he said affectionately, placing his head against his dog's and rubbing his neck. "Thanks for always being there for me, buddy."

With that, he opened the passenger door to the truck and Max leaped in. Dwight climbed in the driver side, lit a smoke, and started the engine.

GARY ARRIVED HOME NEARLY TWENTY minutes after he'd left Andrew's. He discarded his cigarette and hustled quickly up the stairs and into his apartment.

He quickly grabbed a suitcase from under his bed and began stuffing it with clothes, stacks of money, and baggies of pills. His nerves were making him shake, causing him to drop things. He wiped the sweat from his brow, brushed his greasy hair back behind his ear, and tried to make sure he didn't forget anything.

"Don't forget to pack a bathing suit," Randy said.

Gary had forgotten to shut the door. Randy stood casually in the doorway, his gun trained on Gary. Before Gary could say anything, he fired two shots into his chest. The shots sent him flying back, his body crashing through the coffee table.

Randy approached with his gun still trained and fired one more shot to the head for good measure.

That's for Mark.

He checked Augustine's pockets and pulled out his phone. Inside he found the number.

"Just as I suspected."

He read through the messages and smiled, then sent a message to the number: "*Got that new action going. You want your piece?*"

A few moments later he received a reply.

"*It's cute you ask. Like you have a choice,*" the message read.

"*Come get it then. My place. Winsted is too hot right now,*" Randy wrote in reply.

CAESAR HELD A SHOTGUN at his waist as he paced around the front yard, waiting. It was ten minutes after eight, and as usual, the street was quiet.

Inside, Andrew peered out the window, a pistol in his hand. Eddie and Jagger brandished Uzi hand-held machine guns behind him. Dexter was alert by his side. Elton and Little Roy were on the back porch, each armed with shotguns.

Dwight peered through the bushes from the neighboring yard and spied Elton and Little Roy joking around on the back porch.

With the asshole out front, that makes three outside. Probably at least three more inside.

He quietly made his way back to his truck and laid the shotgun across his lap. He dropped the gear shift into drive and slowly eased the truck down the road.

Caesar was growing doubtful anything would happen. He paced along the yard, watching the occasional car pass. If he had known what kind of truck Dwight drove, he would have likely seen it when Dwight drove by to scope things out. Blissfully unaware of what was about to happen, Caesar stood at the base of the yard's embankment and gazed down the road.

The sound of a truck engine coming from the other direction made him turn. Because of the slope on the embankment, Caesar didn't see it coming until it was already over the ridge. The truck caught air as it hurtled down the embankment to the yard. Caesar yelled, but was immediately struck by the truck at full speed.

His skull cracked against the grill as the truck ran him over. Dwight exited with his shotgun drawn, Max by his side. From under the car, Caesar groaned, and Dwight quickly discharged the shotgun inches from his face, blowing him apart like a watermelon.

Little Roy rounded the corner and fired. Some buckshot struck Dwight in the right arm. The glass shattered in the truck door. Dwight grimaced in pain then turned and fired, striking Little Roy in the gut.

Another blast of buckshot hit the hood of the truck, then a moment later another hit the windshield. Dwight crouched down low beside Max and racked his shotgun. He wasn't sure if the ringing in his ears was from the tumor, the gunshots, or both. It didn't much matter now.

He rose up and fired in the direction the shots were coming from then crouched back down and racked his gun. Elton had gone around to the other side of the house to flank Dwight.

Max barked as Elton came around the corner. Dwight turned and fired, and Elton dove back behind the house. Dwight pumped, and fired again. Then he discarded his shotgun and pulled his rifle off his back. He knelt down and aimed at the corner of the house. When Elton peered around the corner, Dwight squeezed the trigger. The bullet struck Elton in the forehead with precision, dropping him close to where Little Roy was bleeding out.

The sound of automatic fire made him retreat to the rear of the truck. Max followed closely on his heels. "Stay with me, boy," he instructed.

The Uzi fire tore into his truck and pierced its tires, raining down from the front porch.

Dwight rose up and fired a shot but missed. Jagger returned the volley with another burst of automatic fire. The bullets struck the truck in a barrage. Then the gun ran dry. Jagger tried to load another clip quickly, but Dwight had already risen up and quickly fired two rounds from his rifle. The first struck Jagger in the throat, the second in the chest.

More Uzi fire came from the front window of the house. One round struck Dwight square in the chest and knocked him to the ground. Max groaned with concern. Dwight rose up to his knees and coughed. His head hurt. The ringing in his ears felt like it was going to split his skull. More Uzi fire from the window.

Dwight laid flat on the ground and crawled under the truck. He trained his gun on the window and fired a couple of shots to suppress the shooter. He then crawled forward, rose up to his knees, and fired twice more. He drew his .45 from his holster and made his way for the front door.

Dexter emerged from the side of the house, his jowl dripping with drool, spraying foam with every bark. The bull bore down and bared its teeth, preparing to attack. Before Dwight could react, Max charged the dog.

The two locked jaws, snarled, growled, and fought, tumbling away into the darkness.

Dwight kicked the front door open and swept the living room. He came around the corner to the dining room and was struck hard with a bat. The blow knocked his gun from his hand, sending it somewhere into the dark room. The next one came down hard across his neck and shoulder, dropping him to the floor.

Eddie loomed over him, a giant ready to squash a bug. The bat struck him again, breaking his left wrist as he tried to shield his head from the blow. Dwight drew his hunting blade from his ankle holster with his right hand, rose up, and stabbed Eddie in the gut.

Eddie sneered and growled in pain, dropping the bat and grabbing Dwight by the neck with both hands. He smashed Dwight into a cabinet and then into a wall, choking him as hard as he could. Dwight pulled the blade out and stuck the monster again, but he was unfazed. Eddie let go of his grasp with one hand and grabbed the knife hilt away from Dwight. He pulled the blade from his torso and rammed it between Dwight's shoulder and his vest. Dwight screamed in pain as the blade sunk in. Eddie laughed, twisting the hilt.

Dwight desperately tried to reach into his vest. He could feel himself about to pass out. The ringing in his head became all he could hear, washing over him in a warm numbness. His fingertips felt the stock of the revolver under his vest. He pulled it out and just before he passed out he squeezed the trigger.

Eddie dropped Dwight and stumbled back, confused by what had happened. Blood poured from his chest and down his shirt. He tried to hold it in but could not. He fell to one knee as Dwight rose to his feet and shot him point-blank in the head. The giant was no more.

Dwight kicked the back door open and found Andrew there laughing with his hands in the air.

"Alright, player! Damn! You proved your point! I give up!" Andrew said, laughing. "Take me in! I don't even mind prison!"

271

Dwight could barely hear him over the ringing in his head. He walked up to him and looked him in the eye.

"I give up," Andrew repeated. He offered Dwight his hands to cuff.

Dwight looked at Andrew's hands, looked into his eyes again, raised his gun, and executed him with one shot to the head.

Aside from the ringing in his head, there was silence. Calmness. A sense of relief washed over him, though he still shook with adrenaline.

He walked around to the front porch and sat down with a groan. He lit a smoke. A few moments later, Max limped up to the porch, bloodied and dirty, and sat down beside him. He petted his dog and smoked.

"Jesus Christ." Detective Carlyle said as he walked down the driveway. "What the hell have you done?"

"I told you to hurry up," Dwight said with a slight laugh. The blood was filling his vest. He slowly took it off and grimaced. "I got shot... and stabbed," he replied.

Carlyle rushed over to his car and grabbed a first aid kit.

Sirens bellowed in the distance.

"Taking them long enough," Dwight remarked when Carlyle came back.

"Nobody wants to rush to a scene with active gunfire." Carlyle laughed.

He gave Dwight some gauze to hold against his wounds.

"Suppose this is quite the mess," Dwight said, lighting another smoke.

"Well, you came here per my request. I was late. The suspects saw you and opened fire. What choice did you have?"

"Yeah... What choice did I have?"

Dwight wasn't sure if it would fly. He was still surprised to be alive. Nothing else really mattered. He didn't know what the future held at all. Had rvived all this just to die on the operating table the next day? That is, if they would still operate on him at all. Nothing was certain. All he knew for sure was at that moment he was alive. Then he understood that was true of every person in every moment, only no one ever realized it. The future is a promise wrought with frailty, yet many waste their lives waiting for a day that may never come.

Whatever was going to happen, he was going to face it head-on. Nothing was certain, and yet, for the first time in his life, Dwight was alright with that. He felt more alive than he ever had.

He patted Max and checked his wounds. They would both live to fight another day.

LEAHY PARKED HIS CAR behind the Mustang and shook his head disapprovingly at Augustine's flashy new ride. "Fucking idiot," he said to himself.

Leahy made his way up the stairs to Augustine's apartment and drew his gun when he found the door ajar. He entered the apartment and found Augustine's body. The blood looked fresh. He carefully checked the apartment. Satisfied no one was there, he left, eager to get away from the scene.

He hopped in his car and quickly hightailed it out of there. A bit of the way down the road he turned right down a back road and reached for his phone. That's when the cord came over his head and around his neck.

Leahy grabbed at the cord and gasped for air. The car veered wildly. He saw Randy Sandusfield's face in his rearview mirror, leaning over the seat, pulling back a black electrical cord as hard as he could.

Leahy's eyes widened in terror. Randy smiled and pulled harder, bracing his knee against the back of the seat. The car veered off the road and crashed into a group of saplings. Leahy pulled his gun and fired aimlessly into the ceiling. Randy pulled harder, crushing the larynx. Moments later, Leahy was dead.

Randy casually emerged from the back seat, pulled Leahy's body from the car, and left it in the brush on the side of the road before driving away into the night.

JASON PRESSED MAEGAN'S HAND firmly against his cheek and sobbed. He felt like he had lost so much.

He knew he had reason to be upset with her, but he didn't care. She meant too much to him. Now that Dickey was gone, he felt alone. He just wanted her to wake up so he could tell her he still loved her. Maybe she wouldn't have him. He was alright with that. But she had to know he still loved her. After everything, he still loved her.

The night passed and the day brought news of a shootout in Winsted. Everyone in the hospital was talking about it. Jason didn't care what had happened. He couldn't stand to hear about any more violence. He just remained by Maegan's side.

That evening he dozed off, and when he awoke, he thought he was dreaming. Maegan was awake, smiling faintly at him.

"Hey," she managed to say. "I didn't expect to see you."

He grabbed her hand and kissed it.

"I'm so happy you're okay," he said.

The nurses had already been by while he slept; Maegan had a tray of food by her side.

"You want some?" she asked, offering him a pudding cup.

"I want to say no, but is that chocolate?" he asked with a laugh. "How long have I been out?"

"At least a couple hours."

"Sorry I was asleep when you woke up," he said.

"I was just happy you were here," she said, squeezing his hand lightly. "I'm sorry," she said beginning to sob. "I'm so sorry. I do love you, Jason. I do. I just didn't think I was worthy of love."

"I know," he said, grabbing her. "I know."

They held each other and cried, broken but consoled by the love they held for each other.

"I have a problem, Jason," she said. "I can't smoke pot, or drink, or anything. I need to be sober."

"I know," Jason told her. "I'm done smoking and dealing. I'm done with it all. I just want a normal life."

"I still want that with you, if you still want it with me… after everything I've done."

He kissed her gently on the lips and brushed his fingers through her hair.

"Yes."

THE LIGHT BLUE OF THE MORNING sky was just creeping over the eastern hills when Randy pulled Leahy's car into Springtown Hills in Lakeville, and parked in front of the third house on the left.

Set at the bottom of a steeply sloped backyard was a boathouse. Randy made his way down the hill and retrieved a key from under a paver stone. He opened the boathouse door and pulled back the cover on the speedboat. There were two large duffel bags in the back, and a letter he knew was from Albert.

He smiled. There were only two bags of money. Albert had taken his already and was no doubt sipping drinks on a sandy beach somewhere, letting that bald head of his cook in the sun. The thought made Randy happy. He supposed he would try to start a similar life, though he wasn't sure what the point was. Nonetheless, he would continue on this merry-go-round called life for as long as it saw fit to allow him.

He carried the bags of cash one-by-one to a Jeep Cherokee that was parked on the side of the house and loaded them into the back. He checked one of the bags and pulled out a driver's license and passport which read, 'Samuel Drake'. He retrieved the keys to the Cherokee from under the visor and started the vehicle.

Randy let the air blow through his hair, the sun rising behind him.

The open road welcomed him. Another passerby on the highway; just another toxin transiting through the nation's arteries. Past towns and cities washed in morning sunlight; places where nothing good seemed to happen anymore. Shuttered schools and rusted factory buildings. Baseball fields where children play, and dealers push. Quiet little hills. Peaceful mountain towns, perfectly hiding their disease and decay. Past mansions, subdivisions, and beautiful little parks, all laid out so carefully; places where people worked and lived, never giving much thought to the world that exists beside their own.

A world where men like Randy Sandusfield and Dickey Calloway could be decent men and yet still be killers. A world where men like that had to kill if they wanted to survive. A world where the line is not so clear and the men not so virtuous. A world where addicts can be victims or become predators to get by. A world where the *good guys* can hurt you more than the bad. A world where sometimes a happy ending is just living to struggle another day.

Epilogue

"Happy birthday!!" Maegan and Jason shouted with joy.

Stacey smiled and blew out her candles.

"You missed one!" Marie yelled excitedly.

Stacey took another breath and blew out the big number 6 candle. Maegan, Marie, and Jason all cheered.

"You're getting so big!" Marie told her encouragingly.

Jason and Maegan laughed and exchanged a kiss.

"Okay, let's cut this bad boy," Maegan joked as she began to cut the cake.

"Uncle Jason?" Marie asked.

"Yeah, baby, what's up?" he replied, placing his hand softly on her back.

"Can we play video games later?" she asked.

"When I get back from work later, you bet," he said, kissing her on the top of her head.

His job wasn't anything glamorous. He scrubbed pans and bused tables at a local pizza place in the evenings, and worked as a clerk at the local grocery store during the day. Maegan had taken a job waitressing at the same pizza place, and was taking business courses at the local community college. They each hated their jobs, however, with some random drug testing they were able to satisfy social service's requirements to adopt the girls. Dickey had requested Jason take care of them in his will.

"They need so much," Maegan had said in hesitance to the idea. "Can we provide it?"

"I'm all they have left," he had told her. "I'm going to do whatever I can to make sure they don't lose me, too."

Neither of them had had as much as a drink in the past eighteen months.

Jason walked outside to leave, his new family walked out with him to say goodbye.

"I'm sorry I have to work on your birthday," he told Stacey.

"That's alright," she said.

He hugged and kissed them both and looked off to the distance.

"Some weather blowing in?" Maegan asked.

"You never know…" Jason replied after a moment. "But I think it's going to miss us."

"Be careful," she told him. They kissed, and he smiled.

"Always."

"You'll be okay if it storms," Marie told him confidently. "Sometimes we have to go through the storm to get home."

He smiled and hugged her again. He remembered telling her that, what seemed like so long ago. He drove away, and Maegan brought the girls inside their house to finish their cake.

278

The girls ran ahead of her toward the kitchen, and she smiled. Their life was far from perfect. In many ways, it was very broken, but that didn't matter. For her, it was everything she had ever wanted.